Snowbird Gothic

www.neconebooks.com

Snowbird Gothic

by Richard Dansky

Necon Contemporary Horror #19

Cover by Richard Case

Originally Published by Necon E-Books

This Edition Published by Six Star Tree Publications

Table of Contents

"The Mad Eyes of the Heron King" originally appeared in Dark Faith, Apex Publishing, 2010

"And the Rain Fell Through Her Fingers" originally appeared at StorySouth, 2011

"Connecting Door" originally appeared at Pseudopod, 2007

"Unhaunted House" originally appeared at Storytellers Unplugged, 2006

"Small Cold Things" originally appeared at Wily Writers, 2009

"The Road Best Not Taken" originally appeared at amazon.com in 2005

"For the Autumn Queen, Where She Rests Among the Fallen" originally appeared at Storytellers Unplugged, 2007

"Come Quietly and No One Gets Hurt" originally appeared in Quietus, 2004

"Losing Altitude" originally appeared in Stranded, 2010

"The Deep End of the Shallow Water" orginally appeared at Storytellers Unplugged, 2008

"Suburban Sprawl" originally appeared at amazon.com in 2005

"Fat Man on an Airplane" originally appeared in Sinisteria: Horror for the Hellbound, 2005

"Good Advice" originally appeared at Pseudopod, 2006

"Missing Pages" originally appeared in Astounding Hero Tales, Hero Games, 2007

"There Is No Bird" originally appeared at Tainted Tea, 2011

"Shadows In Green" was originally published by Yard Dog Press, 2004

"Jeremy's Castle" originally appeared in Flush Fiction, Yard Dog Press, 2006

"Let The House Sing Me To Sleep" and "Minus One" appear here for the first time.

Introduction

The best thing — or the worst thing — about the stories you're about to read is that none of them contain twenty variants on "Arggh, he shot me," or "I'm going to go kill Sam Fisher." That's my day job, writing video games, and as much as I love it, it's a very different animal than writing fiction. Video game writing demands that you collaborate with the rest of the development team, matching your words to animations, asset lists, AI conditions and a million other things I'm not going to go into here. Suffice to say that it gets very intricate, very fast, and that as a game writer you are one small cog in a finely tuned, cyclopean mechanism. It's a supremely collaborative art in a way that little else out there is, and it provides challenges and — if things go well — triumphs that are unique.

But the thing it *doesn't* offer is the chance to run off and play in your own sandbox. That's what fiction's for, and that's why I write it. It's a place I can go where I can tell stories that don't run up against production pipelines and level designs, where I can go ahead and do anything because the only limits on assets are the ones between my ears.

(True story: on the first game I was lead designer on, I wanted to tie off the simmering romantic tension between two of the characters in the closing cinematic, and I was told by the lead engineer that our technology wouldn't allow for them to kiss. "Can I get an embrace?" I asked him? No. "A handshake?" No. "So what can I get?" And he looked at me and said, "I can give you a curt nod." We've come a long way since then, but it's still a question of degree.)

But that's good, because the sorts of stories I like to tell on my own are very different than the ones I tell at work. You're not going to find intrepid secret agents here, or counter-terrorist operatives. That's a world I enjoy working in — and one that's been very good to me over the years — but it's not mine. Mine's got haunted houses in it, and unhaunted ones. It's got unpleasant solutions to problems with the family pet and small children making bargains with powers beyond comprehension. It's got miracles at thirty thousand feet and death on the ground, and the despair of a single fallen leaf.

Or to put it another way, when I first started putting this together, my wife asked me "Why don't you just use the spooky stuff?" Because when I'm being me, it's the spooky stuff I'm good at.

Richard Dansky

So here you go and here it is, all the scary bits and bobs to come out of a life that's full of plane trips and professional nerdery and setting down roots in a place I never thought I'd be, filtered through a lens of late nights and off-kilter glances and that little nagging voice in the back of my head that constantly says, "But what if..."

What if that noise is something that it shouldn't be, instead of what I know it is? What if flying into a volcanic cloud's a little trickier than the news reports are giving it credit for being? What if that figure walking down the road isn't quite human after all? What if?

What if. It's a question I ask a lot. I hope you enjoy the answers.

— Richard Dansky
Durham, NC 2012

The Mad Eyes of the Heron King

There was a lake or something like one near Leonard's office, and it was to that lake that Leonard occasionally took himself after work. He did so in order to relax, to avoid thinking about work, and generally to sidestep the possibility of doing anything he might later regret.

But mostly, he did it to watch the herons.

Leonard liked watching them, finding something soothing in their manner. He admired the way they moved, standing still for untold minutes before suddenly striking, or advancing robotically back and forth on some secret avian agenda that only they would ever know.

And thus it was that when his work day was done, Leonard would come to the lake, and watch the herons, and do nothing else because nothing else needed doing. At least, not until the day the Heron King spoke to him.

He had been watching this most impressive specimen of avian elegance for a while, through the course of several hourlong visits during which he would simply sit down in the mud, pull his knees up to his chin, and observe with a faint but palpable air of envious longing. Once or twice he thought he had seen this particular heron, a magnificent specimen of the great blue variety look back at him, with head cocked and beak angled and eye agleam with something that stood in for curiosity. Leonard had dismissed all such thoughts out of hand, of course. Herons, even great blues, were not curious creatures. They were placid, and they were predatory, and they soared above the still waters while giving their great calls of *gronk, gronk, gronk* that would not have sounded amiss in the epoch of the dinosaurs.

On the fourth visit of that week, however, or perhaps it was the fifth, the great blue heron abruptly changed its course when Leonard settled in, squelchily, for his customary period of observation and contemplation. Hardly had Leonard seated himself in his accustomed place in the grass, which, in truth, had become matted and pressed down under the repeated and weighty attentions of Leonard's posterior before the heron, with great lanky strides, crossed the water to stand directly before him.

Leonard looked at the heron, a faint frisson of fear wafting deliciously through him. He had felt fear before, had felt it all day as a matter of fact. That had been small man's fear, though, the fear of humiliation and of being yelled at, the fear of losing a job one hated but needed and the fear of being trapped in it forever. This was different, tantalizingly so. Even in the most civilized of deskbound men, the most thoroughly domesticated pusher of paper and pencils and long-tailed electronic mice, there remains the atavistic remnants of the hunter his forefather once was. It was this long-buried fragment that Leonard felt now, the fear of the lone man facing a wild creature whose habits and perils were unknown.

Carefully, Leonard counseled himself in the tactics he felt most conducive to an unscathed escape. He would make no sudden moves. He would not show fear. He would not make eye contact. He would —

"Have you come," the heron said, "to pay homage, to make obeisance, to show the proper respect that is my due?" And it cocked its head to the side and stared at him through eyes that, even in the lowering twilight, he could see were golden and flecked with deepest black.

"Err," Leonard heard himself saying, and then, "Umm." He opened his mouth, closed it, and shuddered once, violently.

"Bah," said the heron, and waggled its head in disapproval. "Stupid, speechless, dumb. Unworthy of our time, and thus guilty of a crime against our person."

Suddenly, and without warning, the slender head came down and the stiletto beak stabbed forward, and Leonard found himself thinking most sincerely that he was about to die a most ridiculous and unbelievable death. Then, at the last second, the trajectory of the lunge changed, the beak lowered, and there was a sickening crunch as the heron instead impaled a moderate-sized frog of immodest ambition that had hopped up to a position near Leonard's feet. Then, the heron lifted its head until its beak pointed directly toward the zenith, shook itself in quick fashion, and wolfed the remnants of the unfortunate amphibian down. It made a lump in the heron's neck as it slid slowly down the bird's gullet, until it disappeared from view and the predator once again lowered its gaze to meet Leonard's.

"Next time, show respect, present yourself, be not a fool," it said. Without a further word, it turned on its heel and stalked back across the submerged mudflats with imperial disdain.

Watching the retrograde advance of his erstwhile conversational partner, Leonard did not think, "I could have died." Nor did he think, "I must be dreaming," or "That's impossible," or even "It talked."

Rather, he held one thought and one thought only to his feverish mind, and held it close with a secret glee: "It talked to me."

* * *

For several days, Leonard did not return to the lake. Every day, he would walk out the front door of the office building where he worked, stride down the sidewalk to where his car sat in the immaculately paved lot, and then, hesitate and turn and get behind the wheel. He did not walk past, did not stride further toward the pond and the marvelous creature that dwelt within it. Instead, he heaved himself into his car and drove himself home, taking care to travel by an alternate route that would not provide temptation.

It was, he admitted to himself, an act of fear. The memory of the Heron King speaking to him was one he treasured. He turned it over in his mind at night, searching it for meaning. He found himself pondering it during the day, when the numbers that lined up in serried ranks on the spreadsheets before him should have occupied his entire attention. But mostly he found himself terrified that it had all been a hallucination, a fever dream of wonder that a return visit to the lake would strip bare. He dreaded the possibility of returning to the lake, of seeing the majestic heron and hearing it intone nothing but that familiar *gronk*. In short, he did not wish to put his memory to the test, for fear that it be found wanting, and illusory, and less than true.

But the lure of the lake was strong, and the thought of another conversation with the Heron King was strong as well, and not too many nights had passed before Leonard stopped at the place where his car was parked and then, after an endless, agonizing hesitation with his foot suspended in mid-step, kept moving.

* * *

The sun had commenced scraping the tops of the trees when he reached the lakeside, and the fat red light washed low over everything. Leonard's eyes strained against the unnerving light as he strove to pick out the wading birds from the red-reflected waters in hopes of spotting the Heron King. At first he could see nothing except a blinding glare off the still surface of the lake, but then gradually and by increments, his eyes adjusted. There was one shape, standing motionless amongst cattails at the water's edge. There, further on, was a slight and slender bird, picking its way through the shallows. There, in the distance was a delicate and predatory creature standing on one leg, its beak stabbing down suddenly to pierce the waters.

And there, gliding slowly across the face of the waters, blue-grey wings turned black by the sun's red light, was the Heron King.

He circled the lake once, silently. Leonard crouched down, feeling as if he ought to make some gesture of recognition that he was in the presence of royalty and yet paralyzed between a bow and a kneel and a simple stance to show respect. The bird made no sound as it flew, nor did it speak, nor did it give any sign that it recognized Leonard and acknowledged his presence here. Leonard watched it fly and his heart sank, and he imagined he could already hear the sound of the edifice of his imagination crumbling. He had imagined it after all, had dreamed or wished the conversation, and the one special thing that had happened in his life had not, in fact, happened at all.

And then the heron turned, wheeling toward him in a great silent arc. He watched in wonder as it glided toward him, its legs skimming the surface of the water before finally settling to rest a scant five feet away.

"You have returned, rethought, reconsidered," it said to him without preamble. "We would know why."

Leonard licked his lips, which were dry and chapped despite the humid summer heat. He knew that these words would be perhaps the most important ones he would utter. He knew that, despite the fact that his heart was doing leaps of joy in his hollow cave of chest, what he said now could not be light-hearted, or flippant, or ill-considered.

He was, after all, in the presence of royalty.

"Your majesty," he began, and flicked a glance at those impassive, golden eyes before continuing. They remained golden and utterly impassive, and gave no clue as to what the Heron King might be thinking. "I wished to make an apology for my previous rudeness, and to see if it might please you to converse with me further." It was a tidy speech, and one that he had spent much time writing and re-writing in various templates and formats in those too-lucid moments when he thought that his encounter had not been a dream.

"Ah," said the Heron King. "We will think on your words, ponder, consider. You will return and know our decision." Two stilt-legged steps backwards he took, and then leapt into the air with an ear-splitting call of *gronk* that left little uncertainty that the interview was indeed over, at least for the nonce.

Leonard watched him go, and his fingers scraped up a little mud from the lakeside. Without taking his eyes from the retreating silhouette of the magnificent bird in flight, he rolled it into a tiny ball, and then placed it in his pocket, a tangible memento of the moment that had just passed. No more would he doubt. No more would he question. He would remember, and in due time he would return, and in the meantime a tiny ball of clay and mud would serve to sustain him.

He slipped the ball into his pocket, lifted himself to his feet, and then walked away.

* * *

"You see them, do you not?" asked the Heron King, gesturing in the direction of the other wading birds stalking the shallows of the lake. One by one his beak pointed them out, near or far or hidden by reeds and cattails, and as he identified each he bobbed his head and quirked his neck, as if to see if Leonard were paying attention.

He had been waiting for Leonard when Leonard returned, and had wasted no time in pleasantries or preambles before speaking.

Leonard, privately, was quite thrilled, and hung on the Heron King's every word.

"I do," he said. "Are they your subjects?"

The Heron King wheeled to face him, eyes blinking twice in incredulous confusion. "Subjects? Servitors, lessors, vassals? You are more of a fool than you look."

"But...but..." Leonard scrambled back a foot or two, muddying the palms of his hands. "But if you are the Heron King, and they're herons, you're their kind, right?"

A violent shake of the head was his first response, followed by an angry, bellowed *gronk*.

"You are hopeless, stupid, ignorant of our ways! How dare you insult my brothers by calling them lesser? The heron raised itself up to its full height and spread its wings, the great arc of which cast a shadow over Leonard where he sat. "How can one such as I be less than a king?"

"But if you're the king — "

"Silence! We are all the Heron King! Each of us born ineffably noble, royal, of ancient and proper lineage!"

"Oh," Leonard said. His mouth hung open. "So you're all kings?"

"King," the Heron King corrected him. "Each of us is in fact and deed and word, in right and privilege and in honor, the Heron King."

"How can that be?"

The Heron King stamped one muddy foot onto the grass. "Where I stand, I am absolute ruler, king and unquestioned. Where he stands," and its head whipped around suddenly so that its beak could point out another, particularly impressive specimen of mature heron. This one stood, one leg in the air at the edge of a clump of rushes, and even from halfway across the lake Leonard could feel the jagged weight of its stare. "Where he stands, he is king and monarch, unquestioned sovereign. At any time any of us lay absolute right and proper claim to the ground beneath us." It turned back to look at Leonard, its head canted at a forty-five degree angle. "If the particulars of that land change, it is nothing to us. Our rule remains."

Solemnly, Leonard nodded. "But what happens if two of you are together? I mean, which one is king?"

"We are all king," the Heron King said, and his voice was soft and dangerous. "And we are all jealous, as is our right, our duty, our honor, of our role as king. You would do well to remember that."

"I will," said Leonard, thinking that under no circumstances would he ever try to bring two herons together. His mind briefly put forward some awkward possibilities dealing with mating, but he quickly tamped the thoughts down, to focus on the here and now. "I speak to you because you are nothing, worthless, base-born. You are not a king. As such, you may be in our presence without fear or worry."

And with that, the Heron King turned and walked away, pausing only to give an admonition over his bony shoulder that Leonard should return another day.

* * *

Return Leonard did, again and again. He learned much of the ways of the Heron King, who seemed almost appreciative of the opportunity to unburden himself to another thinking being. Leonard even flattered himself to think that the Heron King liked him, enjoyed his company and his presence, and thus had told him more than was strictly necessary.

And so he had learned that no creatures of the lake dared strike at the Heron King, for fear of upsetting the divine, righteous, and proper order of things. Neither snake nor turtle nor great toothy fish would tempt fate or the heavens by daring to bite at a single heron's foot placed in muddy water. Alligators might, but alligators were uncouth beasts unworthy of discussion, and besides, their foul presence did not sully this lake.

At work, some noticed that Leonard was…different. He was no longer the last one out of the office every night, for one thing. Indeed, he was rarely seen in the office after sunset, and gossip ran wild that he had at last found a lover, or a hobby, or at least a favorite restaurant with early dinner specials.

They noticed, too, that his behavior had changed. His speech, for one thing, was now more formal, and he was fond of stating things in triplicate for effect. His posture had also changed, his usual shuffle giving way to a long-legged tiptoe that could only be described as stalking down the carpeted hallways and tiled floors of his place of employment. As for his eyes, few now cared to meet them, as they seemed too bright, too fierce, and all together too unblinking to be quite comforting. Or perhaps it was the way he held his head now, always cocked at a slight angle when he thought no one was watching.

But since they had never said anything to Leonard before, they did not say anything to him now. Besides, it was not as if he were any less efficient, or useful, or productive. He was simply odd in a different way, and to most of them, that made as much difference in their daily lives as would the vast bulk of the planet Jupiter suddenly turning purple.

Leonard, for his part, did not particularly care what they thought of him at work. Instead, he did his work and daydreamed of the evenings when the secrets of the Heron King would be imparted to him. He thought of hours spent sitting on the cool grass, and imagined what it would be like to do as the Heron King did, to stalk across muddy bottoms in bare feet and feel no fear.

Once he even slipped his shoes off at work, but only for a moment, and without anyone noticing. Then he put them back on, and carried with himself a secret smile the rest of the day.

It was not that day, nor the day after, nor even the day after that, but some time as much as two weeks later when Leonard arrived at the lake to find that the Heron King was not waiting for him. This was in and of itself unusual, in that not since their second conversation had there been a time when Leonard had not reached their appointed rendezvous second. Anxious, he walked down to the water's edge. The sun, he noticed, was lower in the sky than it had been even one week before. Summer was going, and with it the long evenings of discussion that he treasured so dearly. Soon enough it would be fall, with its leafsmoke smell and early nightfall, and the migration of the herons southward.

Soon enough, he realized, it would be over. Perhaps the Heron King would return in the spring, perhaps not, but one way or another this magical summer of clandestine wisdom and blue-feathered magic was winding down.

There were, he noticed, no herons near him. A few, unfamiliar shapes in silhouette, were visible in the distance, but nowhere did he see the Heron King, nor any other shape that he recognized.

The thought chilled him. The Heron King was not here. Perhaps he had forgotten. Perhaps he had grown bored with Leonard, and would not be returning. Perhaps there had been — and he shuddered at the very notion — an accident of some sort, and the Heron King was wounded or struck down, assassinated by a hunter or a passing car.

It was all terribly confusing, and so he sat himself down on the lakeshore to think. The water lapped against the mixed bank of sand and grass and mud, mere inches from his loafer-encased toes. The sound was soothing, wave upon tiny wave, and it gave him an idea.

The Heron King was not here, after all. Nor were any of the other herons nearby. Surely, Leonard told himself, this was a golden opportunity, a chance to walk as the Heron King did. It was his moment, his turn to feel the muddy bottom between his toes and understand all the things he had been told.

After all, the Heron King had left him here alone.

Quickly, he shucked off his shoes. His socks he slipped out of and rolled up neatly, each tucked into one loafer for later use. His pants, slacks he'd bought some six years prior and husbanded fiercely, he rolled up to nearly his bony knees. Barefoot, shivering with excitement and the first touch of cold water against the tips of his toes, he stood on the brink transformation. One last look around for the Heron King, whose regal figure he did not see, and Leonard set one tremulous foot in the water.

It was, as he'd previously discerned, cold. The mud of the bottom gave slightly under the pressure of his weight, but maintained a spongy strength that kept him from sinking. A tickle at his ankle told of a passing brush with a small fish. He looked down, and could see the wavering outline of his pale flesh, the edges blurred by mud and silt stirred up by his footfall.

Nothing else happened.

After a minute, he put his other foot in the water.

Again, nothing happened, and that was indescribable joy. Minnows darted through the water around him. Grass waved in the slow shallow current, beckoning him to step into deeper water. A dim shape in the near distance could only be a turtle, paddling in best ungainly fashion. And there he was, in the middle of it. Observing it, feeling it, ever so much a part of it. At last, he understood what the Heron King had told him, comprehended the sheer ineffable power of it all. As if of their own accord, his feet rose and fell, and he moved away from the shoreline. Mud between his toes, water licking at the now-sagging cuffs of his pant legs, a trail of silt billowing behind him, Leonard laughed. Truly, he understood now. He could share in what the Heron King had told him, could give back his comprehension as a gift equal to the knowledge he had been bequeathed. At long last, he could show his respect properly, his thanks definitively, his delight emphatically. He threw up his arms, in imitation of the raised wings of the one who had led him to this place, and let out a shout of pure joy. Echoes followed it, startled frogs splashing into the water and surprised birds leaping from the trees.

And behind him, a solitary, quiet susurrus, the pressure of air against the nape of his neck, the hint of a wave washing against his muddy calves.

"Your Majesty." Leonard knew what that portended, could barely wait to greet his blue-feathered magister. Trembling with excitement — how the Heron King would be pleased to see he understood — he turned and bowed, then lifted his eyes to meet the royal gaze.

For indeed, the Heron King was staring at him, intently and unblinkingly. Those golden eyes that had seemed so strange at their first meeting were stranger still now, flecked with black and hazel and slivers of bloody red. Through them the Heron King regarded Leonard, his head once canted at an angle both quizzical and alarming.

"Your Majesty?" Leonard asked, or at least intended to. For no sooner had he opened his mouth to speak than the Heron King stepped forward, and drove his great stiletto of a beak into the soft hollow of Leonard's throat.

Leonard's eyes widened in shock, and in horror and pain. The hands that had so recently been upthrust in imitation of wings clutched at his punctured flesh, the blood leaking through the gaps between his fingers. "I don't...understand," he started, and then collapsed to his knees. He looked up in supplication, and in return the Heron King placed one clawed foot flush against the center of his chest.

"You _do_ understand," the Heron King said, and pushed.

"Oh," said Leonard, and went over backwards so that the waters might close over him.

"Impostors, traitors, fools," the Heron King said, "We do not suffer them gladly". His royal judgment thus having been rendered, he turned and walked away, having spotted a fish perhaps, or a particularly succulent amphibian in the nearby shallows.

And the Rain Fell Through Her Fingers

"I miss you," she told me, and the phone crackled static into my ear.

"I miss you too," Really, it was all I could say. "Is the hotel room nice, at least?"

"There's no cable. For two hundred bucks a night, you'd think there would be cable." She laughed. I laughed with her.

The laughter died, and silence sat between us for a moment. "How long are you in Boston?"

"Three more days. The course wraps up Thursday afternoon and if we wrap up early, I can fly out that night." There was a note of grim satisfaction in her voice. I felt sorry for her students.

"And two weeks after that, I see you."

"Two weeks.

There was another pause.

"I miss you."

* * *

I hung up the phone, frustrated. It had been another two hour conversation with no resolution, laying utter waste to the evening. "I miss you" was what it always came back to, "I miss you" and that was all. Not "I miss you enough to do something about it." Not even "I miss you so much I can't do this anymore" — not that I wanted to hear anything along those lines, either. Just "I miss you", a placeholder that let us vamp from phone call to phone call to phone call, and on through the night.

On average, we had about five of these conversations per week. The question of "what next" always sat there in the middle, too big for us to ignore or handle. Occasionally we'd get close — there'd be an "If my headhunter finds me something in Raleigh..." or "My project wraps up in October and I can think about something new then" — but that was always where it ended, with maybes and delays and nothing more.

The clock on the stove told me that it was 10:30, and any thoughts of getting real work done that evening were pure fantasy. Through the blinds, I could see that the evening's clouds hadn't been making idle threats of rain. It was coming down now, hard and steady and dull. Irrationally, I prayed for a bolt of lightning, a roll of thunder — anything to break up the flat sound of water pouring off a poorly built patio. Instead, all I got was the sound of more rain.

Suddenly the apartment seemed tiny and stifling. I took a deep breath of hot air, let it out slowly, and grabbed my keys off the kitchen table. In the corner, the white glow from the computer monitor tried to lure me back for another hour's pointless labor. Even catching a glimpse of it made my eyes ache.

"The hell with it." Going outside to get rained on suddenly seemed much more appealing than staying inside and caged. I let myself out the front door and into the night.

The night air was cool and wet, and each breath tasted sweet, heavy with the taste of rain. A low roll of thunder grumbled to itself off in the distance, a late arrival on the scene, and I briefly entertained the notion of going back in to turn off the computer.

"No," I told myself, and banished the notion of responsible computer ownership from my mind. Let the damn thing fry, if it came to that; if I went back to shut it off, I wouldn't be able to tear myself away for the rest of the evening. And right now I wanted, no, I needed to be away from it, to be away from the apartment and all the clutter I had stuffed it with and most of all the damned phone, which kept reminding me of how damned temporary everything that I was doing really was.

A walk wasn't an answer. But, it would do for relief, at least for a little while.

And so I walked around one building, and then another, and then suddenly I was at the front of the apartment complex, with the steady hiss of tires in the air to tell me how close I was to the main road.

That's where the girl was sitting, directly underneath one of the streetlamps, and I couldn't take my eyes off her.

She looked twenty, or maybe twenty-two. Her hair was long and black, and water had matted it to her face. A long grey skirt was plastered to her legs, the hemline just above her shoes, and she had a white blouse that had done a masterful job of not turning see-through in the rain. She looked up at me, her eyes catching mine, and the corners of her mouth quirked up in a look that said, "I see you looking at me, and it's all right".

And as she smiled at me from across the sort-of road, I saw that the raindrops were falling right through her.

"Hi," she said. I blinked, and rubbed my eyes. Maybe it was a trick of the light. Maybe I was tired and seeing things. Maybe...

A leaf blew through her face. She blinked, as if she'd felt it, and then tried again.

"Hi," she said.

"Hi." It seemed the right thing to say.

"Nice night for a walk."

I looked left, and then right. "Kind of crappy, really. I wouldn't be out here if I actually liked my apartment."

"Ah. Bad layout?"

"More like bad karma." I blinked. "Ah, hell, that was out of line. I don't usually throw a pity party in front of a total stranger. Can I start over?"

"It's okay, really." She stood up, slowly. I think she was trying not to alarm me by accidentally falling through the lamppost, or the sidewalk, or the shrubbery behind her.

I took a step back. "Is it? Because — and you can tell me if I'm wrong here — I think I've just seen a ghost."

She opened her mouth, said nothing, closed it again. Her smile faded, and she looked down at her shoes. Suddenly, I felt like an idiot.

"Look, I'm sorry." I could feel my face heating up with embarrassment. "That was a stupid thing to say. It's just in the light, it looked like, well, I thought I saw — "

She cut me off, her eyes still focused on her feet. "No, you're right. Most people don't notice." She wrapped her arms around herself and swayed a little.

A car drove down the asphalt between us, too fast for the road it was on. Its tires kicked up veils of water. I got soaked. The ghost just stood there, shivering now. "Asshole," she said without rancor, and turned back to me. "I talked to him last week. He tried to pick me up."

"I'm not surprised, actually. You certainly are attractive, for someone who is...I mean..." I caught myself. "This is sounding a lot worse than it actually is, I swear."

She threw back her head and laughed. "No, no, please don't apologize. Really, I should thank you."

"For what?"

"For talking to me like a person, even after finding out."

I bit back the first few replies that came to mind. "It seemed like the thing to do," is what finally, lamely passed muster.

She kept her grin. "Believe me, it means a lot." For a moment she paused, and looked worried. "You can still run off and scream if you want."

I shrugged. "Why would I?"

Neither of us said anything for a moment. All I could think of was junior high dances, the boys trying to work up the nerve to talk to the girls and the girls too nervous to answer.

"So."

"So." I waited for her to say something with a few nouns and verbs in it, and when she didn't, I stumbled onward. "Can I ask you a question?"

She gazed at me, wide-eyed with mock surprise. "What happened to me? Why am I here? Have I seen Elvis?"

Somehow, my lips had managed to go dry in the middle of the downpour. "No, actually. What I really want to know is — look, I know this is kind of weird, but — what's your name?"

The ghost blinked. "My name. All that song and dance, and the only thing you want to know is my name?"

I blinked back at her. "Well, not the only thing, but it's a good place to start. But if it's not something you want to tell me..."

"Oh, relax. That's not it at all." She pursed her lips. "Usually people want to how you died. No one's ever asked my name before."

"I'm a rebel," I said.

She smiled sadly. "No, no you're not." She paused for a minute, then crossed a rubicon. "My name is Anna."

"Brian."

"Nice to meet you, Brian. Do you want to know the rest of it?"

I made a noncommittal gesture and sat myself down on the curb. Cold water immediately soaked through the seat of my jeans. "If you want to tell. I figured that sort of thing was too personal to ask about. I mean, I know I won't want to talk about it when I...oh, crap, I'm doing it again. Let me start over." She snickered, and I hurried on.

"I'm just surprised to find a ghost here, of all places. I mean, this apartment complex is maybe three years old. There aren't any abandoned houses falling down or old battlefields or cemeteries or anything. It's not the sort of place you'd think would be haunted."

"Are you finished?" Anna looked amused, but her laugh was gone.

"Possibly." I coughed into my hand. "Look, do you want to come in out of the rain? I mean, I know it's going right through you and all, but that can't be comfortable."

"It doesn't really feel like anything," she said, "and I can't go inside. I'm not allowed to leave right here. It's nice that you asked, though. It's really sweet."

I pushed myself to my feet, painfully aware of the massive wet patch across my backside. "That doesn't make any sense," I said, and walked over to where she stood. "If you're not from here, why are you stuck here?"

She turned away from me, her shoulders hunched. "I don't know," she said in a small voice. "I don't know why I'm here, and I don't know what I have to do to get out." Abruptly, she faced me, and her eyes were bright. "I mean, it's a nice apartment complex, and I'm sure you've got a weight room and all that good stuff, but it's not where I want to be. I want to go home, Brian. I really want to go home."

Instinctively, I reached out to hold her, but she shrank away. "Don't. That just makes it worse."

"I'm sorry."

"Don't be. It's not your fault."

"Even so. Seriously, though do you have any idea why you're here?"

Anna didn't look at me. Instead, she started pacing back and forth, three steps in each direction and then a quick heel turn. Rain splashed through her and into the puddles underneath. "I told you, I don't know. It's not something I ever thought about until it was too late." She stopped, blinked, and finally looked at me. "Do you ever think about it? You should. Why are you here, Brian?"

I grimaced. "Cheap rent."

The ghost shook her head. "That's not funny, and that's not why you're here. Well, it's part of it, but it's not a real answer."

I felt a frown and a headache coming on. "Why is this about me all of a sudden?"

"Because I want it to be," Anna replied. "And I'm cold and I'm dead, and I'm tired of answering questions. Is that a good enough reason for you to answer one for me instead, or do you want to cross-examine me a little more?"

I turned and walked away a few steps. My shoelaces dragged on the wet asphalt behind me. "Fine. You win. What do you want to know?"

Her words drifted over my shoulder. "Turn around and face me." Sheepishly, I did so. Her eyes softened a bit. "Just answer one question for me, same as I did for you. That's all I'm asking."

"You want to know why I'm here?"

She nodded, and leaned down to pat her hand against the curb. "Right here. In this place, of all places, at this moment of all moments." She pointed to the apartment complex's rain-drenched sign. "In the entranceway to the Pine Meadows apartments, on a rainy night in Apex, North Carolina. Here."

"I don't know." It wasn't what I'd been planning on saying, but the truth of it couldn't be denied. I could see her face tighten, and I hurried to explain. "No, really, I don't know. I mean, I'm standing here because I was taking a walk until I ran into you. I was taking a walk because my apartment was just pissing me off, and my apartment was pissing me off because it's full of ten years of a temporary lifestyle. I've got a girlfriend in Ohio but she's got a good job and doesn't want to leave, so it doesn't make sense to be permanent here, but I don't know if I want to go there, either, because I might hate it and we might not work out. And maybe I like my job and maybe I don't, and maybe they'll blow me out the door in the fall when my project ends. But in the meantime I've got a place for my stuff and a place to sleep, and a way not to have to actually get on with my life."

She watched me. Her eyes were very large, and her lips were pressed together in a tiny "o". "Is that all?" she finally asked.

"I'm not sure." I thought for a moment. "It might be."

"I see." As she talked, she twirled a strand of hair around her index finger. "Why did you tell me that?

I blinked. "Because you asked."

"So I did." She looked thoughtful. "What do you expect to happen now?"

"I don't know," I answered. "I thought maybe telling you about my situation might, I don't know, might help with yours. That it might help you figure out what to do."

"I see," she said, and whatever bemused affection she'd had for me was gone. "Get out of the rain, Brian."

"What?"

She looked at me, looked through me. "You heard me. Go home."

I ran my fingers through my hair. "Why?"

Her eyes were full of pity. "Because of what you just told me. I think I'm waiting for someone, Brian. I don't think it's you."

"But I want to help." There was a whine to the words as they came out, and I hated myself for saying them.

"Do you really?" she asked.

"I think so," I mumbled, ashamed. "You shouldn't be stuck here."

"That's not what you're thinking. You're thinking that you shouldn't be stuck here."

"That's not fair." It was almost an apology.

She raised her hands to me. Water fell through them. "Neither is this."

"There has to be something I can do."

She laughed, bitterly. "Why? Why does there have to be something you, of all people, can do? You don't even know how to get yourself out of here, and that's just a matter of packing some boxes and writing a check. You don't have the right to try to help me, Brian. Not now. Not yet. Maybe not ever." She looked angry and scared and desperate, all at once, her eyes wild and her hair streaming out behind her in a wind I couldn't feel.

"I'm sorry. I'll go now." I took a few steps, then turned and looked over my shoulder. "I'd like to come back and talk to you, if I can, Anna. If that would be OK."

"Why?" she asked.

"Because I want to help."

She shook her head. "No, you don't. You just think you ought to try."

Her words hung there between us for a few seconds. "Maybe you're right," I heard myself saying. "But if that changes, can I look for you again?"

"If it does. Don't come by to ask me if it has, though. You'll know."

"And you'll be here?"

She nodded, once. It suddenly struck me that she was very beautiful. "I'll be here," she said, and I could see tears streaking her face through the rain. "Don't worry. I'll be here."

* * *

The light on my answering machine was blinking when I got back into the apartment. I didn't bother playing the message back. I knew who had called, and why.

The number I needed was on a scrap of paper next to the phone, the half-legible legend "hotel no." scrawled on top of it. I found it without any trouble, peeking out from under the pile of junk mail I'd tossed on the counter. Picking it up, I looked at the clock. It was after eleven, late but not too terribly so. Not later than I'd ever called before, certainly. Not later than she'd called me on occasion.

Reflexively, I dialed. I heard two rings, and then a sleepy, "Hello?"

"Hi." I said. "I have something important to tell you." There was dead air on the line, the hiss of a not-quite-perfect connection.

She waited a couple of heartbeats before asking. "Yes?"

I thought about it for a moment. Thought about what I was going to say, and what I might say to Anna the next time I saw her, if there was a next time. Thought about the apartment and the job and computer waiting for me in the corner, thought about how I'd gotten to this place and when I might someday leave it behind.

And I thought about Anna, trapped here, waiting patiently in the rain.

"I miss you," I said, and that was all.

Connecting Door

Santa Monica doesn't sleep at 3 AM.

Oh, it pretends to. It turns off the lights and shuts the doors, plays old Rush albums in the bars to drive the last drunks home, does a sweep of the streets to make sure that the homeless are tucked into their corners and the tourists are safely back in their hotels, but it doesn't sleep. You can still find a cup of coffee if you need it, or a bite to eat, or a few other things that maybe you're not supposed to be looking for, but that's between you and the man who's selling them, right?

That's what Ian Burgess found himself thinking at 3:02 on a Tuesday morning, tossing and turning and not at all asleep in the prefab comfort of a hotel room on Ocean Boulevard. It was cold in the room, or at least cold by California standards, and the late night street sounds drifted in through the window he'd opened six hours previously and then promptly forgotten about. That wasn't what kept him knotted, sleepless, in the sheets, though.

No, the source of his insomnia came from much closer at hand, from the other side of the pea-green wall he kept staring at with bleary eyes. There were people in there, people who were probably younger than he was and who were certainly having a much better time. He knew this, in part because he could hear every word they were saying — shouting, really — and they'd been at it for over two hours.

He looked over at the alarm clock. It read 3:03, now, creeping minute by minute toward the end of the night. From the other side of the wall, he heard the crash of something breaking, followed by laughter. At a guess, he figured that they'd just broken their hotel-provided alarm clock. If nothing else, it would fit.

There was another crash, followed by a chorus of voices calling "Fuck you." "No, man, fuck you!" in thick Jersey accents. Idly, Ian found himself wondering why none of the other guests had called the front desk about the rampaging goons next door, before realizing that they were no doubt asking the same thing about him.

"Goddamn idiots." He rolled back the sheets and thought about just throwing something at the wall, something breakable like, say, the lamp.

"Fuck you, man!"

"No, seriously, fuck you!"

More laughter. That's what did it, Ian decided. That's what pushed it all too far. He swung his bare feet onto the carpeted floor and hoisted himself upright. There he paused for a minute, listening, praying that somehow the sheer psychic force of the hatred he was generating would get the people in the next room to shut the fuck up and go to sleep before he actually had to do something.

No such luck.

"Like I told you, fuck you!"

"Go fuck yourself!"

"Aw, man, you are fucking hi-larious."

Hilarious, Ian thought, automatically correcting the pronunciation in his head as he shuffled across the floor. They were assholes and morons. Then again, they'd probably have some choice words for him, a flabby guy in plaid boxers pounding on their door in the middle of the night.

He'd thrown a t-shirt and jeans on the floor near the connecting door that led next door, but he ignored them. If he was lucky, he'd never need to see the schmucks, hence, no need to put on pants. Steeled by that thought, he scratched his balls reflectively, then used the same hand to hammer on the door. *Balls to you guys*, he thought, then said it out loud. It sounded good. It sounded tough. It sounded like the sort of thing you said just before kicking down the door in a seedy hotel and spraying gunfire at everyone inside.

Only, of course, he didn't have a gun. Wasn't going to kick down the door. Was hoping never to see the people he was pissed at, honestly, and wasn't quite sure where his jeans were.

"Balls to you," he muttered, one last time, then started pounding away with the side of his fist. It made a hollow, thudding sound that carried far less authority and displeasure than he wanted it to. There was a moment of stunned silence, and then, a chorus of comments, their volume mercifully lowered, their words split between "Shhh!" and "What the fuck, man?" There were maybe five distinct voices he could hear, all male, and with them the sound of people moving around a too-small room. It reminded him of the time a squirrel had gotten into the attic back home, a frantic scuttling with no point and no exit.

"Thank you," Ian said, in what he hoped was a voice just loud enough to be heard on the other side of the wall. In response, he got silence, and then muffled laughter.

As long as they keep it down, Ian told himself, and climbed back into bed. The clock now read 3:12. Outside, two drunks argued over whether Mike Piazza or Paul LoDuca had been a better catcher for the Dodgers, but their debate had a soothing quality to it. AT least they were arguing *about* something, Ian decided, even if the guy who was championing LoDuca was out of his mind.

Eventually, they drifted up the block, their voices fading with distance. Ian smiled to himself, mentally wished the two good luck in finding another bar somewhere, and closed his eyes.

"Shhh."

No, he told himself. This is not happening.

"Shh? Fuck!" A little louder now, punctuated by a cackle of laughter, quickly stifled.

"Fuck, we're being quiet. Yeah? Yeah."

"Shhhh!"

Ian groaned. Surely some of the other guests had to be hearing this. Surely someone else had to be losing sleep of this idiocy.

"Fuck, I hope we're quiet enough."

"Shhh, fucker."

"You shush, you fuck!"

That's it, he decided. No more Mister Nice Guy. He sat up, fumbling for the light and not finding it, but it wasn't as if he needed it. The connecting door stood out in the gloom, the source of sound and aggravation. Some genius had decided to paint it a couple of shades lighter than the wallpaper, and as a result it practically glowed in the thin moonlight that made it through the curtains.

If he looked closely, he could swear he could see it vibrating when the voices spoke, like some kind of a giant speaker.

"Enough of this crap," Ian muttered, and kicked his feet free of the blankets. He'd give them one more warning, then call the front desk and let them deal with this. It might get them thrown out on their asses in the middle of the night, but at this point, he was past caring. Let them try to find another place, blind drunk or high or whatever they were. All he wanted was a couple of hours of sleep.

"You think he's sleeping?"

"Fuck."

"Fuck, yeah."

"Whoo!"

They weren't even trying to be quiet now. The idea of keeping it down had become a joke, a sort of high-decibel sotto voce. Ian felt red rage bubbling up within him, and hammered on the door with the flat of his hand. "Come on, you assholes, cut it out! I need to get some sleep here." More pounding, hard enough to hurt now. "Would you please just keep it down, or so help me God, I'm coming in there and I'm going to kick your asses!"

There was no laughter now. No noise. No profanity. Just silence. Ian hit the door once more, mainly out of momentum. His hand made a weak, wet noise, a soft slapping sound. He drew it back, suddenly unsure of what to do next. Keep pounding? Go back to bed? Wait?

A sound came from the other side of the door then, a quiet, rasping noise accompanied by whispers and titters. It took Ian a moment to realize that it was the sound of the chain being pulled off the door on the other side of the wall. The noise from the street seemed to vanish. The door in front of him loomed larger, brighter, and more threatening. Suddenly, he was acutely aware of the weakness of his situation, of why a middle-aged man in his underwear should not threaten multiple obnoxious drunks in the middle of the night.

A creak told him the door was opening. Frantic, he checked the knob on his side. It was locked. Good. The chain? A quick look told him it was hooked through and secure. Even if the door on the other side were opened, this one would be secure. They wouldn't be getting in, no matter how many there were of them or how long the rest of the hotel ignored their shenanigans.

Underneath his hand, the doorknob jiggled.

He jumped back, swearing. The backs of his knees caught the edge of the bed and sent him tumbling into the tangled sheets.

"Shhh."

"Quiet!"

"Fucking A"

"Shhh!"

The doorknob rattled once, then a second time, much more fiercely. Ian stared at it, willing it not to open, praying that it wouldn't turn.

It didn't.

Instead, a slow, steady pounding started on the door, each one deeper and louder and more brutal than anything he'd managed.

THOOM

"Shhhh!"

THOOOM

"Keep it down!"

THOOM

"Quiet!"

THOOM

The chain rattled. The doorknob shook. The door quivered in its frame.

THOOM

Ian scrambled back, the cheap pressboard headboard cold against his back. The light switch was impossibly far away, the door to the hallway even further. Besides, if they were trying to get in through the connecting door, no doubt they had someone — or someones — outside, waiting for him to escape, waiting for the fat guy in his boxers to make a panicked run for it.

THOOM

For a second, he looked longingly at his jeans, strewn carelessly into a corner, armor that he'd abandoned. They, too, seemed out of reach.

THOOM.

"Fuck"

THOOM.

"Shh! I told you, shh!"

THOOM.

And suddenly, there was salvation, sitting placidly on the table on the other side of the bed. The phone. That he could reach. That would save him.

THOOM

"Oh yeah, real, quiet!"

THOOM

He threw himself horizontally across the bed, his outstretched hand slapping the table next to the beige plastic of the receiver. It hit with a loud smack, and sent a jolt of pain up his arm. His other hand caught the edge of the bed and he found himself pulling himself closer, desperate to be able to reach the phone's keypad and dial for help.

"Fuck, fuck, fuck!"

THOOM

Ian's hand scrabbled for the receiver. It slid across the tabletop, banging into the base of the phone and nearly knocking it off onto the floor. With his other hand he caught it, snagging it just as it tipped over the edge. He held it there for a second, his heart pounding as loudly as the fists on the other side of the door.

There was a bloom of orange light from the message indicator, and it rang.

Ian dropped the phone in shock. It hit the floor with a jangle, the receiver spinning away and bouncing off the wall. Distantly, he could hear a voice saying, "Hello? Hello? Mr. Burgess? Hello?" It sounded tinny and thin, exactly the way you'd expect a voice to sound when heard out of a telephone receiver at a distance.

Not the sort of thing you can hear when someone's pounding on the door, he realized dimly, and then he understood that the pounding had stopped. The cursing had stopped. Even the street noises were dim and distant, and the only sound was the increasingly urgent salutations coming out of the phone.

Leaning over the edge of the bed, he snagged the cord awkwardly and hauled the receiver in hand over hand. He could only imagine how ridiculous he looked, hanging over the edge of the bed with a phone to his ear and his ass in the air. All he needed now was to slip forward a little and crash face-first...no, best not to think about that.

"Hello?" he said, cradling the phone with his chin. "This is Mr. Burgess in 406, and — "

"I'm aware of what room you're in, sir," came the clipped voice of the night clerk. "I'm afraid I've received several complaints from other patrons about," and there was a pause, and the ostentatious ruffling of papers, "some noise coming from your room. Some, umm, shouting. And banging on the wall."

"My room?" Ian found himself blinking furiously, tears of anger blurring his vision. "They're talking about noises coming from my room? Jesus fucking Christ, man, I've been on the verge of calling you for an hour. There's noise, all right, but it's sure as hell not coming from my room. It's those assholes next door."

"Next door, sir?" The man's voice buzzed in his ear, a mixture of disbelief and polite disinterest. "Are you sure about that?"

He rolled over and pulled himself back onto the bed with his free hand. "Yes, next door. 404. Those guys have been yelling all night. I admit I may have raised my voice asking them to shut up, but they were making a hell of a racket before I said anything."

There was a pause. "I'm afraid there is no one staying in room 404, Mr. Burgess."

The phone felt heavy in his hand, and hot. The room suddenly seemed darker to him, the connecting door that had been such a beacon of menace a minute ago barely visible in the gloom. "That can't be right," he heard himself saying. "They were pounding on my door, for God's sake. They were laughing and cursing and I thought they were going to bust in here and — " He could hear the pitch of his voice rising, could hear himself getting hysterical, and it was only with a supreme effort of will that he cut himself off.

"Look," he said finally, "I don't know who was complaining, but they've got the wrong guy. I don't care what your records say, but there are a bunch of guys in 404 having one hell of a party, and I expect you to do something about it. Do that, and you won't have any more trouble out of *me*, I can promise you that much."

"Sir," the desk clerk began, but Ian simply dropped the receiver and, after a moment's deliberation, unhooked the cord from the wall socket.

"Noise from my room?" he grumbled. "Like anyone could actually hear me over the crap from next door." He rubbed his eyes and yawned titanically. Maybe the phone call had frightened the idiots in 404 into shutting up or going out. Maybe they'd finally be quiet. Maybe he could actually get some sleep. Maybe…

No.

There it was. A giggle.

"Shhh."

"Oh, fuck, he's gonna hear us."

"Fuck that."

"Hee! Hee!"

"Fuck!" The last one was Ian, louder than he'd expected. In return, there was a chorus of profanity from beyond the wall, each one echoing his tone and inflection, each one dripping with sarcasm and mockery.

"That does it, you assholes." With a grunt, he kicked the sheets off the bed and onto the floor. Heaving himself off the mattress, Ian landed at the foot of the bed and stomped over to the connecting door. Too loud, he thought, but only in a tiny, tinny voice that didn't really matter, anyway.

Instead, he reared back and slammed his fist against the offending door as hard as he could. "Hey! Assholes!" he roared, and hit the door again. "For the love of God, keep it the fuck down in there!"

"Fuck, fuck, fuck!"

"Man, he's fucking pissed!"

"Shhh!"

"That! Is! Enough!" With each word, Ian reared back and slammed his fist against the door. Something in his knuckles popped and sent a stabbing pain up his arm, but he didn't care, hammering against the door and ranting incoherently that whatever misbegotten sons of bitches were in 404, they needed to shut up right now or he was going to kick the door in and murder the lot of them.

The phone rang.

Ian paused, his arm halfway to the door and stopping so abruptly that something in his shoulder burned in protest. He could feel the throbbing in his fingers now. In the dim light, it looked as if he'd broken at least two of them. The whispers crawled under the door, but he ignored them, shuffling over to where the phone sat on the floor.

"Yes?" Ian tucked the receiver under his chin, picking up the base with his good hand.

"Shh!"

"Hee!"

"Oh fuck, oh fuck."

"He's on the phone. Fuck, fuck, fuck!"

More whispers came. He tried to ignore them.

"Mr. Bridges?"

Once again, the voice of the desk clerk came down the line. Ian found himself grinding his teeth, a perfect counterpoint to what sounded like scratching in the other room. "That's me."

"I'm afraid this is your last warning, sir." There it was, that supercilious, snotty tone that came with service jobs where no actual service seemed to be required. "We have received several complaints about the noise, and by all accounts it's getting louder."

He could feel his temper going and fought hard to rein it in. "I am telling you, it's not me. If you could just get the guests," — he nearly choked on the word — "in 404 to take their party somewhere else so I could get some sleep, I promise you this problem would be solved."

"And I told you, sir," The clerk's tone was sharper now, the sound of a man working himself up to call security. "There is no one staying in room 404, much less the party you describe. The only voice anyone is hearing right now is yours, and they're hearing it all over that side of the building. If you do not quiet down, I'm going to be forced to remove you from the premises."

"Wait, wait," Ian threw up his hand in a placating gesture, fully aware that the man couldn't see it but forgetting for a moment the agony the motion was likely to cause him. "There's no need. I'll just hold the phone up to the connecting door, and then you can hear them for yourself. How does that sound?" He could hear them even over the desk clerk's voice, the litany of catcalls and curses getting louder by the second.

"That would be fine, sir, if I can have your word that you'll keep your voice down."

"If you take care of these jerks, I'll be happy to." Ian walked over to the connecting door, the receiver held out before him like a talisman. "Just one second…here we are," he announced. "Now listen."

He listened. He heard them, each of them shouting "Fuck!" in a rising chorus or cackling like a madman in turn. He heard the whispers, the shrieks, the screams, and the whimpers, counting to sixty in order to give the man on the other end of the line an earful.

"Fuck."

"Fuck!"

"Shh!"

"Fuck!"

Grinning, satisfied, he tucked the phone back under his ear. "Are you there?"

There was a pause. "I heard nothing, sir. Please pack your belongings. Security will be at your room in roughly ten minutes."

There was a click. Ian stared at the receiver. "You goddamned little prick!" Unthinking, he took the phone and hurled it against the door, where it smashed in a welter of plastic shrapnel. "Fuck!" he shouted, and stomped on the largest surviving bits, heedless of his bare feet. "Mother fucking fucker! Of course he claimed he didn't hear anything. They're probably his buddies, or his cousins, or…oh, fuck!"

He stomped again for good measure, and his foot came down on a jagged piece of plastic four inches long. It tore easily through the skin, cutting a ragged line across the sole of his foot from the arch to the heel.

"Oh, fuck!" Ian could feel the warm gush of blood from his foot. He took a step back, and the wet, dark spot on the carpet was visible even in the dim light of his room. "Motherfucker! Fuck!" One handed, he reached down and grabbed the wreckage of the phone, the cord trailing out behind it like the guts of some eviscerated animal. He could hear them, even over his bellowing, could hear them matching him fuck for fuck, curse for curse, howl for howl.

Or was he matching them?

No! He was not doing anything like them. It was their fault, anyway. All their fault, and he'd tell security that when they arrived! He threw the blood-spattered mess against the window, which by some miracle did not shatter, and then stopped, staring, at the pile of parts it left on the floor.

The cord was there, strung out a good five feet from the main body of the thing, knotted in a couple of places and looped in over itself. The connector at the end looked to be in perfect condition.

Which, he realized, was because he'd detached it from the phone earlier, before the second time it had started ringing.

Ian blinked, and took a step back from the phone. The weight he put on his foot transformed into agony, the hand he held out to steady himself was laced with fire. "This isn't possible," he told himself. "The phone was unplugged. He couldn't have called. No one could have,"

"Hee hee."

"Fuck, fuck, fuck!"

"Impossible?"

"Fuck! Shhh!"

He took another step back. Somewhere, deep within the phone's battered electronic guts, a connection was made. A sound something like a ring choked itself out. A broken orange light bulb flared into life.

"No. Oh, no." Ian kept backing away.

"Fuck, yes!"

"Oh, yes. Shhh!"

"Fuck, yes, fucker!"

It rang, weakly at first, but then stronger. There were other sounds now, footsteps in the room above, someone banging on the wall from next door, muffled conversation from below. And above it all, he could hear the cackling profanity from 404, seeping in through every crack and crevice.

The phone rang again. He fled from it, desperate fingers scrabbling at the chain on the door to the room. No way was he staying in there, not any longer. He'd face the clerk, challenge the man, haul him up here if necessary to get him to see what was happening. To get him to hear what was being said.

The chain succumbed to his shaking fingers. He threw his weight onto the door handle and heaved it open, laughter following him out into the hallway. Stumbling, falling, he landed heavily on his hands, then collapsed to the carpet as an explosion of pain flashed in front of his eyes.

Behind him, the door back into his room slammed. The laughter quieted, but did not vanish. The hum of the ice machine down the hall drowned it out, soothing him with a blanked of white noise, and he lay there a moment to soak it in. Part of him was praying someone would come along and take pity on him, the bleeding, unclothed wreck on the floor. Part of his was terrified someone might.

An eternity of seconds later, he raised his head. The elevator was that way, a straight shot down the hall. All he had to do was hoist himself to his feet and stagger that far, bleeding foot and sagging boxers be damned. He propped himself up with his good hand, groaning, and stood. Off in the distance, he heard a ping. It was the sound of salvation, the sound of the elevator.

All that it would take would be to walk down that hall, right past room 404.

He closed his eyes and took a step forward. His foot came down with surprising force on the worn carpet, and he gasped as it his. The warmth of the blood leaking out was unmistakable. He was going to have to do something about that, he thought, even as the pain wrenched his eyes open.

404.

There it was. He was staring at it. And if he stood, and waited, and listened, he could hear them still. They were in there, still cursing, still laughing, no doubt mocking him for having been driven into the hall by their fun.

He tried to take another step and found that he couldn't. He could hear their voices distinctly now, drowning out the ice machine and the soda machine and every other damn thing on the hall.

"Fuck," he heard one of them saying.

"Fuck yourself," he growled back, and took a step toward the door. It was blue, he noticed, a slightly lighter shade than the carpet with a pitted brass number plate nailed into place right above the peephole.

"Shhh," came the sound from beyond the door.

"That's right, assholes, you'd better shhh." Another step, a raised fist, and he was almost there. He could smell blood now, no doubt his as he left a trail on the carpet. It didn't matter.

"Hee hee hee."

One last step, and Ian planted himself in front of the door, staring in through the peephole. "Yeah, laugh now," he shouted. "I'm coming for you!"

"He's here!"

It came in chorus this time, all the voices repeating the words in a fucked-up canon.

The elevator pinged again. There were voices down there, too, voices saying things like "disturbance in 406" and "think the guy's drunk." The owners of those voices, Ian knew, would be around the corner in a second, and they'd be looking for him.

There was just enough time, then. Ignoring the pain, he brought his fists down together on the door, centered and a little above the middle.

"You're in there," he shouted at the door. "I know you're in there. They say there's nobody in that room, but I know better! Show me your fucking faces, you hear me! Before they throw me out of this fucking hotel, I want to see who the fuck you are!"

There were footsteps around the corner now, coming quickly. They'd heard him, no doubt, had been called by someone to deal with the crazy man in his skivvies in the hall in the middle of the night.

"Fuck."

The door swung open. Ian glanced left and saw two burly rent-a-cops headed his way. They were advancing slowly but determinedly. Maybe they'd seen the blood, he thought. Wouldn't want any of that on them, no sir. But they didn't matter. 404 mattered. The people in 404 mattered.

And as he turned to look into the darkness and the voices pulled him in, he realized that the clerk had been right. There was nobody in 404. Then again, what was he? Another faceless business traveler, another piece of human baggage, another anonymous number checking in and out and in and out.

Another nobody.

"Fuck it," he said softly. The ones who were waiting for him the other nobodies, chuckled in appreciation. "Fuck it!" he bellowed, and stepped forward to join them.

The door slammed shut behind him. When asked later, the two security guards would swear that they had seen no one in the room, and that no human hands had touched the door to close it. And when they used their passkeys to let themselves in, there was no one in 404, and nothing except a single bloody footprint on the carpet to show that anyone ever had been.

* * *

They replaced the carpet in 406, and the hallway as well. In 404, they just covered it up, put a cheap throw rug over that one footprint and called it a done deal. It wasn't often the room was rented out, anyway. There was always a cancellation, or the hotel would run just under capacity, and lo and behold 404 would always be the room that somehow fell empty. Nobody complained, but nobody asked for it, and after a while the experienced clerks stopped offering it. Even with an oceanfront view, it got a reputation among the staff as a bit of an odd place, the room that nobody wanted.

Which was true enough, in the end.

Unhaunted House

They huddled in the bathroom on the second floor, a family of three, afraid.

Tap. Tap tap. Tap.

The sounds came from all over the house. Everywhere glass faced the outside, they could hear the delicate impact of small branches tap tap tapping, trying to find their way in. That was why they had chosen the bathroom to flee to. It, of all the rooms, had no windows.

Tap. Thump. Tap tap.

The Millers had bought the house two months previously, twenty percent down and the rest financed at five and a quarter percent. Their daughter, wide-eyed and fey at six years old, hadn't liked it much, but she hadn't liked any of the thirty-odd houses they'd seen, and this one had much to recommend it. High ceilings, a spacious kitchen, a master bath suite with a garden tub — and all for a pleasantly low price. The yard was unkempt, but the Millers figured that the previous owner simply hadn't had time to keep it up. Mrs. Miller asked the real estate agent, who talked about the benefits of the gas fireplace in the rumpus room instead.

Thump. Tappity thump. Crash.

"I don't like this house," the little girl had said, and tugged on the real estate agent's sleeve. "Is it haunted?"

He laughed, nervously. "The house? Absolutely not. I can promise you this house is not haunted."

Mr. Miller took his daughter's hand. "See, honey? No ghosts here."

"No ghosts in the house," the agent echoed.

The little girl looked at him. "Not yet," she said, and stared until he looked away.

"Kids," Mrs. Miller said with a laugh. "Such imaginations."

Thump. Crash tinkle tap tappity rustle.

The move had been swift and pleasant, and the installation of the Millers — father, mother, and recalcitrant daughter, too — had gone off without a hitch. Utilities were connected, services arranged, and neighbors nodded to, all in short order.

All that remained was the lawn, which Mr. Miller found himself curiously disinterested in working on.

Thump. Thump crash rustle tap. A different tap now, wood on wood, right outside the bathroom door.

"Dear, when are you going to mow the lawn?" Mrs. Miller had asked her husband on a cloudy and grim Sunday morning. "It's not going to take care of itself."

"Later," he had answered, and even meant it.

Later came. Later went. And that night, the little girl complained of branches tapping on her window.

Tap. Tap tap. Crash rustle crash thump.

Days passed. The tapping got louder, and more frequent. Mrs. Miller heard it now, too, though Mr. Miller swore he never did, or blamed it on the wind. The lawn stayed unmowed. Walking to the mailbox became a trick. Weeds stretched themselves across the sidewalk to trip the unwary. Branches seemed to swing low in the breeze to take accidental pokes at eyes.

Tap. Tap creak creak.

Neighbors tsk-tsked at the state of the property. Weeds grew up, thick and tall. Mrs. Miller stopped waving to the neighbors, and started nagging Mr. Miller about how unpleasant the house had become, even with new carpet and fresh paint in the upstairs bedrooms. Her husband pooh-poohed her. It was all coincidence, or something seasonal, or something to that effect. Of this, he was sure. The little girl listened to them debate over dinner, and shook her head.

"The house isn't haunted," she said thoughtfully. "The rest of the place is. That's why the lawn is acting funny. We should leave."

"We're not going to leave, honey," Mr. Miller said. "That would be silly. It's just the lawn. I'll mow it tomorrow. Or I'll hire someone to do it, and it will all be fine. You'll see."

"You do that, dear," Mrs. Miller said. "That would be very nice."

That had been yesterday.

Tap. Rustle rustle. Scratch, scratch, scratch, just outside in the hall.

Then, silence.

"How strong is the lock, honey?" Mrs. Miller asked, her arms around her daughter, her voice ever so slightly strained.

"I don't think it matters, dear," he replied, and held her as the first tendrils of green crept underneath the door.

Small Cold Things

It was the cursing, not the alarm, that woke Jenny on Monday morning. She sat up blearily, rubbing her eyes and wishing it wouldn't get quite so bright quite so early. "Is something wrong, honey?" she called out in the general direction of the bathroom, but she already knew the answer. Something was wrong. Something was wrong every morning. It was just a question of the details.

And if she understood the stream of profanity from behind the bathroom door properly, the location was the foot of the bed and the problem was the usual one: cat barf. A careful look over the edge of the bed confirmed her worst fear, and the culprit. Lucy, her Siamese, sat complacently next to an impressive pile of unidentifiable yellow chunks. The front half of the pile had been ground down into the pale blue of the carpet, a sure sign that Sean had stepped firmly in it on his way to brush his teeth.

"Bad cat," she said, but there was no heat in it. There never was.

Lucy looked up at her and purred, and with a sigh Jenny resigned herself to the inevitable. She reached down and gave the cat a quick scratch behind the ears, and Lucy leaned up and into it.

"That only encourages her, you know."

Jenny looked up. Sean had come out of the bathroom, a towel around his waist, head shaken in disgust. "You could at least say 'bad kitty' or something."

"I don't think she understands English." Jenny's reply was skittish, defensive. She swung her legs over the side of the bed, gingerly probing the carpet with her toes for anything that might have seen the inside of one of the cats. Finding nothing, she hoisted herself up and grabbed the roll of paper towels she'd learned to keep on the bedside table. Sean, arms folded across his chest, just watched her as she did.

From her knees next to the mess, Jenny looked up at him. "Why don't you go take the first shower, honey? I'll clean this up."

He glanced over at the clock, which blinked an ominously green "7:43". "I'll make it fast."

She shrugged. "You cleaned up the last time. It's my turn, that's all."

He grunted something that might have been agreement and turned back into the bathroom. This time, he didn't bother to shut the door, and she could see his towel fall to the floor as he stepped into the tub. Then the shower curtain — blue, like everything else he picked out — hid him from view, and the hiss of water rose up to drown out his muttering.

Wordlessly, she knelt down next to the lump on the floor. Lucy preened and rubbed her legs, but Jenny ignored her, dabbing disinterestedly at the pile of vomit. Both cats Ð Lucy and her mixed-breed playmate Sally Ð had been put on a special low-protein diet by their very intense, very persistent veterinarian. It was, Dr. Henshaw had insisted, the only way to prevent the urinary tract infections that had caused the cats to start using the downstairs as one giant litterbox.

Needless to say, Dr. Henshaw had been wrong. The random pissing had continued, and now both cats were taking turns finding new and exciting places to vomit up mounds of hideously expensive yellow chunks. Sean had voiced his suspicions that Henshaw liked cats a lot more than he liked people; Jenny thought he liked money more than he liked either. Regardless, the cats wouldn't even touch regular food any more, and that was another coal under the steady, simmering conflict between her and Sean.

Reasonably certain that she had as much of the residue up as she was going to get, Jenny walked over to the bedside trash can and dropped the soggy paper towel in. The entire bedroom reeked ever so slightly of used cat food, and no matter what she did to the carpet, the stink remained. Still, it was better than the downstairs, which was liberally doused with the scent of feline urine. They'd already replaced the living room carpet once, when the stench got too unbearable, but the relief that provided was only temporary. Within two weeks, both cats had been up to their old tricks. Now she was afraid the new carpet was doomed, too, despite the scent markers and shrieking motion detectors and other gadgets they'd lavished money on in hopes of keeping the cats in line. It was the only thing she and Sean fought over, but with all its permutations, they didn't need anything else. He'd walk in the door and make a complaint about the stink, or one of the cats would throw up on the bed, and they'd be at it again. It wasn't violent, just constant. Somehow the cats had become the only thing in their lives, and she could feel it strangling everything else they had.

The water in the shower shut off with an audible thunk, and a minute later Sean sauntered out of the bathroom. His black hair was still wet, and the towel tied around his waist didn't do much to hide that his physique was, if one were inclined to be polite, "peasant-like". He was a short, stocky man with the sort of bone structure and eating habits that suggested he'd be barrel-shaped one of these days. As he made his way over to the dresser, Sally darted out from under it. Her back paws landed on his bare foot, and as she sprung forward he grunted in pain.

"Stupid fucking cat," he muttered, and looked down. A half-dozen shallow gouges began filling up with blood. Jenny opened her mouth to apologize, but he put up a hand to forestall her. "It's fine," he said in a tone that indicated it wasn't, and started rummaging determinedly through the dresser drawers. "I need to get to work. It's no big deal. I'll see you tonight, OK?" He shrugged himself into his clothes and headed out, his subvocalized curses trailing down the hall.

"I love you," Jenny called out behind him. "Have a nice day." He didn't answer, unless a series of slammed doors counted as such.

In the bedroom, Jenny waited for the sound of his car to fade away before she let herself move. She shuddered once and headed for the bathroom. The last sound she heard before she shut the door was Sally, clawing at the furniture furiously.

* * *

Sean's car was in the garage when Jenny got home.

That was unusual; most nights, he worked an hour or two later than she did. She parked and sat for a minute, trying to find the nerve to get out of the car. Getting out of the car meant finding out why he was home so early. She imagined the scene in her head, imagined it ending badly twenty different ways.

It'll be fine, she told herself, hand frozen on the ignition. *He's just home early. It's nothing to worry about. Just go inside and talk to him.* And then, a minute later, *When this song is over.*

It was three songs and the end of the CD before Jenny finally killed the engine, and another minute after that before she let herself out. She stared at the door for a minute, then looked away.

Her eye caught something: a wet sycamore leaf plastered to the hood of Sean's Acura, dark against the white paint. I*'ll just take that off for him before I go in*, she thought. *He hates that sort of mess. It'll make him happy if I pull the leaf off.*

She walked over to his car. *I'll just grab the leaf and then we'll go in. That's all.*

The garage door grumbled shut behind her as she tentatively reached out to pluck the offending leaf. Her fingertips brushed the surface of the hood as she did so.

It was cool. He'd been home for a while, then, alone in the house with the cats. For no reason that she could fathom, that particular thought worried her. The leaf fell, forgotten, as she hurried to the door.

The mud room was dark as she turned the key, as was the hallway beyond it. Even the kitchen light, normally as constant as the sunrise, was off. "Honey," she called. "Are you OK?" The smell hit her like a hammer when she walked in the door, sharp and pungent. It was like this every day, but after a couple of breaths, as always, she found she could ignore it. Not Sean, though. He was a little more sensitive about it. It was hard for him.

"I'm fine," his words drifted back. "I'm just thinking."

"Is everything all right?" She drifted through the kitchen and into the den, barely spotting the silhouette of his head against the gloom. He was seated on the couch, lights out and television off, and a low purring told her that one of the cats was probably curled up in his lap.

"Everything's fine." His voice was low and even. He never got loud when he got angry; that was one of the things she loved about him. He never shouted. He just explained, relentlessly, how he was right and she was wrong and how it would be best if she just let him take care of whatever needed doing.

Most of the time, she simply did. The rest, she argued for a few minutes and then let him have his way anyway. Now, though, she suddenly wished he would. Instead, he turned and looked back at her over his shoulder. His voice was as soft and measured as ever, and he said, "We need to talk."

He's leaving. That was her first thought. He'd finally had enough and he was leaving. Hesitantly, she took the three steps that led her into the den.

"What's wrong?" she asked, and hated herself for the quaver in her voice. *He's not leaving. He can't be.* She stared at him, silently pleading with him to at least look at her, to face her when he dropped the bombshell.

His eyes strayed back to the floor.

"Look," he said, absently petting the Siamese curled up in his lap. "I like cats. You know that. I love cats, and I love your cats."

"Our cats," she corrected him, softly. "They're our cats. They love you, too."

He nodded absently. "I'm sure they do. When we first met, Lucy wouldn't have curled up in anyone's lap, would you girl?" He skritched the cat behind her ears, and was rewarded with a dull purr. "And now she likes sitting in Daddy's. But I can't take this any more. The house smells like cat piss, we can't have anyone over, my allergies are going berserk, and it's costing us a fortune. Every week it's another jug of that stain remover stuff, and it doesn't do any good. Thirty bucks a pop and we can't use the living room, and it hasn't even dried before the damn cats are in there peeing on everything again. I can't breathe, I can't touch you without one of them jumping up on us, and I can't walk through half my damn house because we've had to turn it into a minefield to keep the cats from pissing themselves under the coffee table."

"It's not their fault," Jenny protested weakly. "The neighbor's cat came into the house and marked the carpet. They're just trying to take it back. For us. It's their house, too."

Sean sighed, loud and long. Startled, Lucy leapt up from his lap. With a yowl and a venom-filled backward glance, the Siamese jumped down onto the floor, then padded her way to the cat door and out. Both of them stared after her.

"I thought we were keeping that closed," Sean said. "To keep the neighbor's cat from getting in and spraying the walls again. I even think it was your idea."

"I know, I know." Jenny stood and turned away from him. She hugged herself tightly and stared at the offending entrance. "I tried. But she was so miserable, and she kept yowling, and I was afraid if I kept her in here and she was unhappy that she'd start spraying because of that, and..."

"And instead the big marmalade tom got in again and peed on the bookshelves. Wonderful. Because what we really needed was a mixed bouquet of cat urine." Sean swung himself off the couch and paced back and forth in front of the fireplace. "This has to stop. I'm sorry, I know how much you love them, but it has to stop. I can't take it any more, and we just can't afford it."

"I know," she answered, without turning to look at him. "They're good girls, Sean. They don't want to do this. With the motion sensors and the alarms in there, I promise, it'll get better."

"It's not like they've helped so far, Jenny. We've paid three thousand dollars for new carpet this year alone. It was another grand on top of that in vet bills. We give them special food and special treatment and everything short of laminating the rest of the house for their benefit, and it just doesn't work." He reached her, put a hand on her shoulder. She shuddered at his touch, but didn't pull away. "They're just cats, sweetheart. We can't live our lives around them."

"I know, I know." Jenny's voice was barely audible. She took great gulping breaths, trying not to sob. "I can get rid of them, you know. That will fix things. That'll fix everything. I'll give them away tomorrow."

Sean spun away, jerking his hand back as if it had been burned. "I don't want that. They're something that's important to you and you shouldn't have to give it up. Besides, if you do then you'll just get mad at me for making you do it, and at this point I think you like the cats more than you like me, anyway. That's just not a solution, OK?"

"But it would solve the problem."

"You'd hate me for it. I said, it's not a solution."

She turned, staring at him. "Then what do you want to do? We can't keep them locked in the bedroom. What if they start peeing in there?"

"I don't know." He walked past her, into the kitchen, and took a beer out of the fridge. "I'll think of something. There are some people I can talk to about it, some friends of mine from work. They had an idea that I can check out. But it just can't go on like this."

"We can sell the house."

He whirled, slamming the beer down on the counter. "I am not going to be driven out of our house by your idiot cats."

"Then what do you want to do?" She stalked over to the kitchen table and stood there, fists quivering. "We can't shut them in, and we can't keep them outside, and we can't keep them from peeing on the carpet. You don't want to get rid of them, and I don't want to lock them up, and you don't want to sell the house, so I'm not really sure what options we have here."

"I don't know, all right? I just don't know. I'll think of something. I told you,

I'll talk to some people." Swiping the beer off the counter, Sean took a healthy swig, then started cursing as the over-excited liquid burbled out of the mouth of the bottle. It spattered loudly on the floor, and he stood there, watching, as it overflowed.

"Well?" Jenny asked softly.

"Well, fuck," Sean replied, his voice dangerously soft, and hurled the bottle into the sink. Somehow, miraculously, it failed to shatter, but instead spun crazily before landing, neck-down, in the disposal. Beer gurgled vociferously down the drain as Sean stood there, gaping. He glanced up at Jenny, who stood, one hand over her mouth to try to hide her laughter, then looked back into the sink, where the unbroken bottle stood as mute witness to the impotence of his rage.

"Fuck!" he bellowed, louder this time, then turned and stomped off into the living room. One by one, the motion sensors they'd set up went off, their piercing alarms clashing with each other in ear-splitting dissonance. She heard more cursing as he yanked the front door open, and then the sound of the heavy wood slamming behind him as he went out.

Jenny took a deep breath, then walked over to the counter to grab a paper towel. She'd never seen him like this Ð well, not often. But he'd come back. He just needed a little time to cool off, a little time away from the cats.

Sally peered at her from behind a kitchen chair as she sopped up the beer on the floor. It wasn't that much, she saw now, surely not enough for Sean to get really upset over. A couple of quick wipes and it was all gone. She turned and tossed the soggy paper towel in the sink. It hit with a wet sound as Jenny straightened and walked away. Sally followed her, closely.

* * *

"Honey."

Jenny stirred, frowning. The voice came again, soft and insistent. "Honey?"

She opened her eyes and was groggily unsurprised to discover that the room was still dark. The alarm clock on the floor told her that it was a little after three in the morning. She'd gone to bed at ten, still waiting for Sean to come back. The sound of the front door had awakened her an hour later, but he'd gone straight to his study instead of coming to bed. The sound of music coming down the hall told her that he was working on something Ð he always worked to music at home, usually loud and late at night Ð but after a while it turned into white noise, and she drifted off to sleep.

And now, he was there, sitting on the floor next to the bed with Lucy in his lap. Sally lay at his feet, her belly exposed and eyes closed. She wasn't purring.

"Sweetheart?" She half-sat up and groped for the light.

"No, no light," he said. "Don't bother."

"Sean? What's going on?" She was awake now, a cold tightness in her gut telling her that something she didn't understand was happening here. "You're not leaving, are you?" She winced, hating herself for having asked the question. "I swear, I'll make things better."

He shook his head, but his hands still held Lucy close. "No, Jenny. I'm not leaving. I'm not going anywhere."

"Oh good, oh God, thank you." The words came out of her in a rush. "I know it's been tough with the cats and everything, and I promise I'll do everything I can to try to make them behave better and won't you behave better, girls, for Daddy? Won't you?" She stared down at the cats, lip trembling. Lucy looked back into her eyes, unblinking, unmoving.

Sean smiled. "That's not necessary, honey. I've got a solution that's going to solve all our problems."

She sat up and blinked. "You do? That's wonderful, Sean. That's amazing. Did you find something online? Tell me!"

"Something like that," he said, and snapped Lucy's neck.

"Sean, no!" The words came out in a whisper, but to her they were a ragged shriek. She wanted to reach for him, to hurl something at him, to fling herself between him and Sally so he couldn't do her any harm, but her arms refused to obey and her body sat, frozen. She watched as gently, wordlessly, he laid Lucy's body down on the carpet and took Sally in his arms. "Shh, Jenny. It's OK. It's for the best. Trust me." His hands stroked Sally's belly once, and then closed on her throat.

Her eyes obeyed her, at least. She closed them so that only the soft crack of Sally's spine told her that the deed was done. *This is it*, she told herself. *I can't stay in a house with this. I can't stay with him. I'm leaving. Oh God, what if I'm next?*

She opened her eyes, looked down at him. He sat, cross-legged and smiling, a corpse on either side of him. "It's all right, Jenny. Everything is going to be just fine. I learned some interesting things tonight, you know."

"No, I don't know, Sean. I don't know what you're doing or why you killed our cats, but I'm leaving right now." *That's good*, she told herself. *Good, strong words. Now I just have to get up and move. But moving, doing had always been the problem...*

Sean put his left hand on Sally's head, his right on Lucy's. "I don't think so," he said conversationally. "I mean, you might if I gave you enough time to think about it and fret, but that would just be silly. Instead, I'm going to show you what I learned. It's going to solve all of our problems, honey. You'll have the cats but they won't do any of the things we hate, and you'll have them forever."

Her voice rose to a near-shriek. "You're going to *stuff* them?"

He laughed, softly. "No, I'm not going to stuff them. I'm going to give them back to you."

His eyes closed, and his mouth opened, and a fine mist poured out of it like water. It cascaded down, puddled in his lap and then spilled over. Tendrils of it twined around his arms and snaked around the cats, stroking them as gently as she herself had ever done. Gently, wisps of spectral smoke caressed the dead bodies' fur, slipped themselves into their mouths, and wove back and forth across their eyes.

And she watched. She watched as the last of the fog dripped from Sean's lips and his eyes opened, unseeing, as the wisps and shadows vanished into the tiny dead bodies there on the floor. She watched, and her hands tightened on the blankets. Inside, she knew, something was screaming. Something was cold and afraid and knew that things were very, very wrong, but it was buried deep down and she just sat and watched.

Under Sean's hand, Sally stirred. Rolled over. Opened her eyes, which now shone with the faintest hint of green. And started walking toward her.

She scrambled backwards, her muscles finally obeying her. "Sean? What's going on, Sean?"

"Everything is just fine, Jenny." He stood, Lucy in his arms. She swiveled her head with the faintest of grinding sounds and looked up, right into Jenny's eyes.

And purred.

"Oh, God, what have you done?" She looked away, even when a soft thump told her that Sally had jumped up on the bed, even when the cat's soft body rubbed up against her, even when the low rasp of Sally's purr let her know that she was demanding to be petted.

"They're fine, Jenny. Better than ever." Sean's voice was closer now, and she could feel the mattress shift as he sat down on the bed. "Here, take Lucy. She wants her mommy to skritch her."

Jenny shied away, her hands shoving Sally from her. The cat's fur was as soft as ever, the rumble of her purr still strong. She looked up at Jenny with hurt in her eyes, hurt and the unnatural gleam Sean had put there. "I can't do this, Sean. Take them away. Please, take them away."

"But they love you," he whispered, and put Lucy in her arms.

The weight was right. The feel was right. The purr and the tone and the texture of the fur against her skin were right. Only that soft rasp, the grinding of bone on bone, told her different. She felt the tears coming now, falling one at a time onto the thing she held in her arms. She felt her grip tighten reflexively, felt Lucy's head rub against her shoulder as she squirmed to get away from the water. The last reserves she had crumbled and she started weeping, stroking Lucy and holding her close. "I'm so sorry, girl, Mommy loves you, Mommy never wanted to hurt you, Mommy is so sorry."

"Shhh." Sean slid in beside her, wrapped his arms around her. "It's all right. Just a little pain for a moment and now they'll never hurt again."

Gently, he pushed her down to the bed, draped the cover over her. Lucy nested in her arms; Sally escaped to curl up on Sean's pillow. "We won't need to feed them any more. Won't need to clean the litterboxes. Won't have to worry about them when we go away. All of our troubles are gone, and you'll have them forever."

She sniffled and closed her eyes, feeling the weight of his body next to hers on the bed as he lay down beside her. "They're better off this way, honey, I promise. I love our cats. I love you."

Still weeping, she held Lucy close until felt the little body grow cold. Only then did she let the cat walk away.

The Road Best Not Taken

I got to Sam's place on the Carolina coast last that night, as was my habit. The others — Sam and Jeremy and Harris, the knights of our little college round table — had been there for hours, from what I could see, and had long since gotten the festivities going. They'd pulled up logs in a square around a bonfire on Sam's little strip of beach, and set up a cooler full of beer in easy reach. They sat there, waving me down from the driveway with gleeful and loving obscenities. I stalked down onto the sand to meet them, grinning like a fool. They grinned back, and the years started to fall away.

We spent the first few hours catching each other up on our lives. They'd all done well for themselves, it seemed. Sam was a little guy with too much energy for his frame, and big black eyes that darted around like a fish trapped in a too-small bowl. He'd taken that energy and made a fortune in software with it. Harris was in advertising in Atlanta. He was a tall, thin man with more chin now and less hair than I remembered, and hands that were always moving. And Jeremy, our resident cynic, had detoured from his literature studies into business school, and was currently climbing his way up the ladder with a credit firm in Richmond. He was as round as he'd always been, a soft-looking man with a sharp eye and a sharp tongue.

And that left me. They all wanted to know, and none would ask. Even back before graduation, I'd started drifting. They'd blamed it on a bad breakup, as friends are liable to do in those circumstances, and in a way they were right. But you could see the disappointment in their eyes when I told them what I was doing — teaching second graders in Raleigh, content on a small salary. No relationship, none for years now — that disappointed them, too. They asked questions, of course — did I like what I was doing, was I thinking of getting into school administration — but what they really wanted to know was what had happened with Jaimie. Oh, they weren't interested in her for her sake; they thought she was somehow responsible for my fall from grace and wanted to know why.

Sam finally asked, which only made sense. Sam had always been the direct one. We'd been digressing, talking about the sorry state of college basketball these days, when his head perked up like a bird's and he stared at me. "By the way,

Barry," he said, not even bothering to make a real question out of it. "Whatever happened to that redhead you used to date? The one you broke up with right before graduation."

Jeremy sucked air in through his teeth, and Harris winced. Neither of them turned away, though. They wanted to know.

"I could tell you what happened," I said, slowly, looking down at my hands, "but I don't think you'd believe me. Maybe it's best if you just think that the drive to Elizabeth City every weekend got the better of me."

"Oh, no." That was Harris, always second to the kill. "I'm not buying that for a second. You were crazy about her, man. She was gorgeous, she was funny..."

"She was hot," Jeremy interjected, and Harris swatted at him. He ducked out of the way, but mercifully shut up as he fell back onto the sand.

"She was good looking, and you two seemed happy together." Sam finished for all of them. "But all of a sudden it just went boom, and you started...drifting. So what happened?"

I shrugged. "Not what you'd think. There was no screwing around, no fighting, not even a Dear Barry letter. Just something strange that wasn't anybody's business but hers and mine. But," and I pointed at Sam, "If I tell you, will you let it go? It's not a story I want to tell twice."

Sam nodded. "We'll let it go, I promise." His eyes flicked around the circle, catching the others and holding them. One after the other, they nodded in agreement. "All of us. And if you want to stop, well, no one here will hold it against you." Jeremy murmured assent, and Harris slapped my knee in something approximating support. "We're here for you, man," he said. "Just get it off your chest."

"It's been fine where it was for nine years," I retorted, and shifted down my log out of kindly gesture range. The beer in my hand looked inviting, so I took a swig and stared into the open mouth of the bottle. It seemed easier than meeting their questioning looks.

But you can only stall for so long, once you've loosened the ties and started to let the cat out of the bag. "All right, then. The first thing you have to know, guys, is that this is only the second time I've ever told this story. The first time was talking to Jaimie the night it happened, and, well, that didn't turn out too well. So I haven't told a soul since then. Consider yourselves privileged to hear it."

"It all happened back when I was making those late-night Friday runs from Chapel Hill to Elizabeth City. I was doing it pretty much every week. Class would get out, I'd throw my duffel in the car and go. Jaimie's car was a piece of shit and I didn't trust it to make the trip without breaking down in some hick town in the country, so I ended up driving out there every weekend. The honest truth was that I didn't mind too much, especially since her roommate had some kind of internship in Charlotte and was gone three weeks out of four." There were nods of agreement around the circle, the unspoken suggestion that I continue.

"The last time I went out there was in late April. Everything around campus was an inch deep in bright green pollen, and I wanted to get the hell out of town as fast as I could before I sneezed my fool head off. But lab ran late that day, and the traffic was a pain in the ass, and the long and short of it was that I was two hours late getting on the road. So I did what any bright young fellow thinking with his dick would do. I turned up the music too loud and drove too goddamned fast, praying the cops were looking the other way."

I stopped for a minute to catch my breath. My chest was oddly tight, and my lips were suddenly dry. Nine years of silence about what had happened that night was a lot to overcome, more than I had realized. Part of me wanted to tell them all that nothing had actually happened, that we'd just gone our separate ways. But it was too late. I'd started. Something in me needed to finish, needed to tell this story tonight. A half-dozen times before I'd tried to do this with friends and acquaintances, starting and stopping in a stutter-step that made me look foolish but revealed nothing. *Not tonight*, I decided. *Tonight, I tell the whole damned thing.*

With a deep breath, I continued. "An hour east of Raleigh, I hit construction. This was back in the days when the orange traffic barrel was the state flower of North Carolina." "Still is," Harris stage-whispered, but I ignored him and plunged on. "Anyway, I was running late already, and I didn't want to sit in some made-up traffic jam for another ninety minutes, so I jumped off the highway and went looking for a shortcut."

Sam laughed. "Dumb thing to do, man."

I nodded in agreement, slowly. "Yup. Didn't realize how dumb for another hour, though. I mean, it looked like a good idea at the time. I'd pulled out the map and there was this little spaghetti pattern of county highways on it that would get me where I was going, if I was careful. It didn't seem to be *that* stupid."

I could remember it, of course — sitting in the car in the empty roadside. I could see myself, hunched over with the overhead light flickering and the stereo turned low, tracing tiny lines of black with my finger on an outdated map crumpled in the passenger seat. One streetlight burned up ahead, beckoning me along the road. Otherwise, it was dark enough to count stars by the hundreds. Behind me, a closed gas station had hunkered down against the night; in front of me was only asphalt and a lonely yellow light staring down on the road. I'd been afraid, of course. The thought of trying to find my way along a half-dozen back roads in the middle of the night had my gut twisted in a knot, but I thought about Jaimie waiting for me and put it all down to city boy nerves. There had been one last look at the map, a soft recitation of route numbers I had to look for, and then I hit the gas.

A minute later, I turned up the music. I think it was to make me feel brave.

I didn't tell the guys any of that, though. They wouldn't understand it, or maybe the would and they'd laugh at me for it. Sam would say I was retro-fitting my emotions to what happened later, and Harris would tell me I was just full of crap, and Jeremy, well, Jeremy would just want me to cut to the chase to see if I nailed the redhead in the end. No, it was better just to tell them the basics. It was all they wanted to know, in any case. Armed with a fresh batch of rationalizations, I reached for my beer, took a sip, and continued.

"I had what I thought was a pretty good route, and there was no other traffic on the road. Not surprising, really — we're talking two lanes of bad paving cutting across swampland. No wonder there was no one else out there. The locals had all gone to bed, and strangers just didn't use those roads. Not unless they were stupid, or desperate, or lost."

Out of the corner of my eye, I caught Jeremy nodding. "I've been up that way. It's dense stuff. Lots of swamp, lots of trees, no lights on the road. The only times I've been through there, I made sure I had plenty of daylight. I can't imagine what it'd be like after dark."

"Scary as all fuck," I replied, and took another sip of beer. "You can't imagine. The trees start maybe two feet from the road. There's no shoulder, no signs to tell you where you are or where you're going, and the branches on the pine trees are so thick overheard you can't see the sky. It's like a big tunnel to the middle of the swamp, with nowhere to turn except onto these tiny dirt roads that the mapmakers never heard of. It stinks to high heaven of rot and standing water, and it's got a sound to it like you've never heard anywhere else. Frogs and bugs and birds and God-knows-what crashing off in the bushes, all mixed together to let you know you're not wanted there, and the stink's so bad you have to roll down your windows. If you didn't, the smell would just get in the car and stay there."

"Good thing you had the music going," Sam offered.

I shook my head. "No, I turned it off. It felt wrong, somehow, like it wouldn't be tolerated."

Harris laughed. "Come on, man. You got lost, got spooked, and freaked out. Big deal. It happens to everyone."

I looked at him, my eyes meeting his. "You weren't there," I said, as calmly as I could, and he quickly looked away. "But that's just setting the stage. That isn't what happened."

Sam coughed, softly. "So what did happen?"

"I drove," I said. "I drove for half an hour, found the first crossroads I was looking for, and turned right. Then I drove some more, found another turn that I was supposed to make, and got myself lost. Really lost, as in help-me-Jesus-I-think-I'm-gonna-die-out-here lost." Someone chuckled, and I looked balefully around the fire. "You can laugh, but you know how it is. Your brain may tell you that you can't be more than a few dozen miles from bright lights and strip malls, but your gut's going nuts because you're alone in the dark and you don't know where the hell you are, and every turn takes you further in."

I paused for a moment, and all I could hear was the fire crackling and the slow waves rolling against the beach. No wisecracks from Harris; he was holding onto his beer bottle like it was a talisman against the darkness I'd conjured. Sam's eyes were as big as I'd ever seen them. He sat still, taking tiny sips of air like he was afraid breathing too loud might let the world know he was there. Jeremy, for his part, was just taking the occasional look over his shoulder, making sure nothing was coming up out of the dark to listen with us.

I didn't blame him. I was half-convinced something just might.

It was time to take a deep breath, so I did so, and clapped my hands together once. I'd done that the night I'd gotten lost, clapped like that to tell myself it was time to stop screwing around and try to find a way out. This night felt a lot like that one had, though God knows, I couldn't tell you why.

"The swamp's a dark place," I said, and coughed before I continued. "Road signs get covered up pretty fast by kudzu and vines and whatever else, and there's no good place to put a light unless you want to sink concrete thirty feet down in the muck. That meant it took me a long time to figure out for sure that I was lost, and even longer to find a place to stop so I could look at the map. Eventually I found a flat place that was kind of sandy, where the trees backed off from the road a little bit, and I pulled over. I killed the motor — didn't want to get stuck out there with no gas — flicked on the light, and pulled out the map. And that's when I realized something was wrong."

"That you were lost?" I raised my eyebrows and looked over at Jeremy. You could see it in his eyes. For all his joking, he'd built his own version of that swamp in his head and gotten lost in it, and now he was counting on me to lead him back out.

I spat into the fire. It sizzled away in an instant. "Nope. I already knew I was lost. Of course, once I got a look at the map, I realized how lost I was. Couldn't find anything that looked vaguely familiar on there, but my best guess told me that I was a half an hour away from anything like a way out. But as I finished looking at the map and folded it back up, it hit me that I was worse off than I thought."

"I could hear the map fold up, you see." They nodded. They could see. "Every pop and crackle of that piece of crap road map — I could hear it, and there's no way I should have been able to. Not above the frogs and the crickets and the grasshoppers and the damn swamp noises. But it had all gone quiet, every little bit of it. No wind, either, so you didn't hear the swoosh of the branches going back and forth. All that there was came from the map, and my heartbeat, and one other thing. Something was out there, crashing around in the dark. I could hear branches snapping, loud pops like you get from a stick an inch thick when it breaks. This wasn't a deer or a bobcat or, God help me, a cougar."

"There haven't been cougars in the eastern part of the state for a hundred years," Sam interjected weakly. "It couldn't have been one of them."

"They haven't caught one for a hundred years," I reproached him, and he shrank back on his log. "But it wasn't a cougar. A cougar doesn't break branches, he moves through them. Nothing natural moves like that. Nothing natural's big enough to move like that, or at least nothing you'd think of as natural."

"It started getting closer, the sound did, and I decided that I didn't care where I was going. I just wanted to be out of there. I didn't think it would go over too well with Jaimie if I missed our rendezvous because something ate me out in the swamps. So I turned the key in the ignition, with every intent of getting the hell on my way somewhere big critters didn't blunder around in the dark."

"And the car didn't start?" I turned to look at Harris, who'd asked the question, and shook my head.

"Of course the damn thing started. I told you before, this story's true. None of this made-up horror movie crap where the car stalls out at the worst moment, just because it can. I took care of that car, and it turned over nice and easy and started up for me. I put my foot on the brake, shifted gears, and got ready to pull out, and that's when I smelled it."

"Smelled...whatever was making that noise?" It was Sam again, shrunk in on himself and a little bit afraid. I gave a smile to show he was right.

"I think that's what it was. It had gotten close enough for me to smell it, and if you thought that swamp stink was foul, you'd keel over when you got a whiff of this. It was like rotten eggs in a blender with ten pounds of roadkill. It hit like a hammer, too. One minute it was just the swamp air, and I'd almost gotten used to that. The next, the stink of the thing was in my lungs and my eyes were watering from the strength of it. Something told me that if I sat there much longer, I might get more than a snootfull of the thing, so I hit the gas and peeled out of there in what I thought was a good direction."

"And that's when I heard it." I pushed myself to my feet, and warmed my hands at the fire. Suddenly, it seemed very cold, and I wanted to be as close to light and heat as I could. "So help me God, I'd never heard anything like that before in my life, and I never wanted to hear it again. It was a howl and a moan and a promise all at once, sad and lonesome and mean. It went up from the woods near where I'd just been parked, and you could all of a sudden hear the birds fleeing out of the trees. I'm telling you, no human throat ever made that sound, and no animal I'd ever heard, either. It went on for maybe thirty seconds, though it felt like longer, and then it died away for a minute. Then it called again, and again, and I put the hammer down on those dark and tiny roads just to get the hell away from it."

"Jesus," Harris whispered. "You must have been in that thing's lap, whatever it was."

"Too damn close," I agreed. "But the worst thing was, I heard other calls, out in the dark, answering it. I heard four, five different calls out there, all versions of the same thing."

Nobody said anything for a moment. Sam reached into the cooler and got me another beer, and I took it from him gratefully. The waves sounded further away; the tide was going out. I'd been talking longer than I thought.

"So was that it?" Jeremy finally ventured. He'd pulled up close to the fire, too, and Harris had taken some initiative in throwing a few more logs on the embers. It blazed up now, good and bright, and we all took strength from it.

"Yeah, is that all?" Sam finally asked. "You got lost, heard this thing, and ran?"

"No." I popped the lid on the beer and took a good, long swallow. "Jesus help me, I wish that were all the story I had. Hell, if I'd only heard the thing and smelled it, I'd be a happier man." I took another swig of beer, and wiped my mouth with the back of my hand. "Probably be married to Jaimie now, too. *That* story, she might have believed."

"You...saw it? Whatever it was?" Jeremy was asking like he didn't want to know the answer. I chuckled, and he suddenly flushed.

"Hell yeah, I saw it. I saw it and then some. You want to hear the rest?"

Jeremy said, "Yes." So did Sam. Harris paused for a minute, and then said, "I think so."

Truth be told, Harris always was the brightest one of us. I raised my bottle in his direction, a little bit of a toast to him, and continued.

"I told you those roads were dark. They were also pretty narrow, and they run from nowhere to nowhere. There was nothing along the route — no gas stations, no doughnut shops, no houses, nothing. God alone knows why those roads were even built because they didn't serve man's purpose at all. But with nothing out there, you can put your foot to the floor and run like hell, and that's exactly what I did. I put the high beams up, the pedal down, and the stereo blasting to keep me from hearing anything like that call again. I didn't care if it was running right alongside the damn car, I didn't want to hear it. I didn't want to know. I must have been doing 90 through those woods, and I was begging the car for more."

"Those roads twist, you know. Not often, and not hard, but once in a while they twist. You'll be cruising along a straightaway, hell bent for leather, and then all of a sudden the road jumps rightwards and you need to cut the wheel and pray, or else you're going to end up off the embankment and gone forever in the underbrush. That's what got me in the end. One of those curves. A stupid, stinking little curve."

Harris unwound himself and stood, facing me. "I remember," he said faintly. "I remember you fucked up your car on one of those trips. Is that what happened? You wrecked in the swamp while you were running?"

"Sort of," I admitted. "It's been a long time, but you might recall the car still ran. No damage to the front bumper, no damage to the hood. It got messed up a few other places. I stayed on the road, for whatever that was worth. At least I managed that much. But I came around that bend and what do my lights show me but a man crossing the road. Tall son of a bitch, too, hunched over and walking across the highway in the middle of the night like he owned it. As soon as I saw him I yanked the wheel left. He turned and looked at me, and in that half second before my fender clipped him, his eyes caught the light. He looked at me. So help me, he looked at me. And then the fender hit him with that awful thump you only get when metal meets flesh going way too fast, and he went down. I hit the brakes and stopped, maybe twenty yards down the road. After all, I'd hit a man. I needed to get out and see if he was OK. That's the right thing to do, the human thing, not to mention the legally appropriate thing. I mean, that's what you do, right?"

I looked around, drained the last of the beer in one long swallow, and threw the bottle down the beach. It hit the sand with a soft sound. Everyone stared at me. I'd have to finish, I knew. Nothing for it now, I had to tell the end. My fingers flexed into fists once, twice, a third time, and I had to swallow back the urge to run. Nine years since I'd told this story, nine years since it happened, and it still turned my knees to water and my guts to sand.

A hand landed on my shoulder, gently. I jumped, breathing hard, and then turned to see it was Harris. "You don't have to finish, man," he said quietly. "We understand."

"No," I said thickly, and brushed his hand off me. "I do have to finish. Just because. You see," and I turned to face Harris where he stood, "I knew. Even as I was stopping the car, I knew. Because when my headlights hit those eyes, they shone red. Human eyes don't do that, Harris. I didn't hit a man crossing the road. I hit — you know what I hit."

Sam made a choking sound and stared at me. "You can't be serious, Barry," he said. "You can't mean that." Next to him, Jeremy shook his head slowly, like a man in a fog.

I looked away, because I didn't want to see his face when I told him. "I mean it, Sam. I hit that thing from the woods, or one of his kin, and even as I stopped the car it was peeling itself up off the road. I'd only winged him with my fender, and he was a big fella. He'd rolled a dozen yards and then hauled himself up, and when he did, he screamed. I swear, I pissed my pants when I heard that sound. It was that same call from before, but up close and personal and full of hate for me. And then he started running, running best as he could right at the car. I'd cut the engine and opened the door before I realized what he was doing, but I slammed that door right fast and put the key in the ignition. And all the while it's howling and running at me, and just as I get the car started, something hits the trunk like an angel dropped a ton of bricks out of the sky. I look in the rearview and I see him. It. Whatever it was. It's on my trunk, got both hands dug in, and it's looking right at me. It's huge and it's covered in hair and it's close enough to human to scare the shit out of me, and it's decided it wants to kill me. One of those big hands went up, and then it came down and smashed the rear windshield. Glass went everywhere. The car was full of its stink and its roaring, and that hand was going back up for another punch, so I hit the gas and cried like a little girl."

I sat down, breathing hard. All their eyes were on me; I could feel it.

"So what happened?" Harris finally ventured.

I shrugged. "He held on for about another hundred yards. Beat the living shit out of my trunk and kicked out both of my taillights. I got the car up to ninety and kept it there until I reached some one horse town on the edge of the swamp that had an insomniac cop. He pulled me over. He probably thought I was on drugs."

"You told him what happened?" Sam was incredulous.

"Hell, no," I said tiredly. "I told him I'd hit a cow. He looked at me funny and said that he didn't know any beef or dairy farmers around those parts, but since he didn't smell any beer on my breath and he let me off with a warning for the speeding and the tail lights. He even gave me directions up to Elizabeth City, after I stopped shaking enough to ask, and he led me to a gas station that had a men's room I could use to freshen up. I ended up reaching Jaimie's place around 3:30 in the morning. Rang the doorbell and when she answered it, there I was — dirty, stinking like piss, and driving a certifiable wreck. She asked me what happened, so I did the damn fool thing and told her. And, sensibly, she didn't believe me. She told me I had to come up with a better excuse if I was going to get into bar fights, not that I blamed her for thinking that way. That night, I slept on her couch, and two weeks later I was single. You know the rest, I think." As I finished, my shoulders slumped and I stared down at the sand between my feet. All the energy had gone out of me with the telling. I was cold, and my throat was sore from too much talking, and I was very aware that all the beer I'd had wasn't doing a damn thing except sloshing around in my belly.

"Wow," said Sam. Harris nodded. And Jeremy, well, he smiled.

"Bullshit," he said, his eyes just a little too bright.

"I beg your pardon?" I asked him, knowing already what he was going to say. Harris might have believed me. Sam probably did. But Jerermy? He bought it all, every last word, and that scared the hell out of him. And because he was afraid, he was going to do the same thing scared men had been doing since caveman days. He was going to laugh, and he was going to laugh loud enough that he couldn't hear those little voices in his head whispering to him that it was true.

"This is bullshit. The whole story — pure and unadulterated crap. You sit here and tell us you ran over Bigfoot when he was jaywalking in a North Carolina swamp, and you expect us to believe it? Oh, you're good, man, you're very good. You had me going for a minute there. But Bigfoot? Come on. Save it for the second graders, Barry. It doesn't fly here."

I blew out a deep breath. "You can believe it or not," I said simply. "It doesn't matter to me. I told you what happened, and you can do with that story what you like. Enough people have seen something in the woods that I'll take my chances with what happened to me. I heard *something*. I hit *something*. *Something* punched through my windshield and did its honest best to kill me. But if you don't believe me, well, I just think you'd do well to stay off those roads. I know I have, ever since that night"

Jeremy laughed then, a high and brittle sound. He laughed at me, and I just didn't feel like taking it any more. "Goodnight, Sam, Harris," I said, and stood. "Good to see you again. Sorry about the beer bottle I threw down there — I owe you one for the cleanup."

Sam looked at me, then looked at Jeremy. He knew, and he knew why I was leaving. "Let me walk you to your car," he offered.

"I'd like that," I said, and headed back toward the house. Sam fell in behind me. Back on the beach, I could hear Harris and Jeremy arguing in low, furious tones, but I didn't care. In the morning, maybe it would have meant something, but morning was a long way away.

Neither Sam nor I spoke as our footsteps crunched onto the gravel of the driveway. We walked past Sam's cars, then past Jeremy's motorcycle and Harris' lovingly restored Jaguar. My sedan sat last in the line, unprepossessing. Sam patted the hood and grinned at me. "Looks like this one's had better luck."

I smiled back at him. "So far, yeah. Look, I'm sorry, Sam, but I really don't think I can — "

He held up his hand, silencing me. "It's cool, Barry. Really, it is. I don't know what the hell to think about that story you told, but it's clear that telling it took a lot out of you. And to have Jeremy just laugh in your face, well, that was uncool. I understand if you want to get out of here. I wish you'd change your mind, but I won't be hurt if you don't, OK?"

"OK," I said, and shook his hand. "Thanks, man. It was good to see you again."

He clasped his other hand around mine. "It was too long. We'll have to do this again soon, and I promise, I'll have Jeremy gagged when we do." He laughed, and I caught myself laughing with him.

"Deal," I said, and stepped around to let myself into the car. Before I did so, Sam stopped me.

"Barry," he said, "I have to ask. Was it true?"

"Yeah," I said, and slid past him into the driver's seat. "It was true. I never went back — not to Elizabeth City, and not through those swamps. I'd drive an hour out of my way to make sure I didn't risk getting caught in there. And yeah, people have seen something strange up in that part of the state, more than once if I've been told right. Be careful in these woods of yours, all right? Don't let Jeremy wander off on his own. He might see something that would make him stop laughing."

"I will," he said, oddly serious, and stepped away from the car. I started her up, did a three point turn in the driveway, and headed home.

It was funny, I decided as I navigated the maze of local highways leading me back toward the interstate, that I'd come out here tonight to tell that story. I'd told Sam a half-truth on leaving; I hadn't been anywhere near the coast in nine years. There were too many memories, too many nightmares that still had me waking up in a cold sweat. Jaimie hadn't understood, of course, and I didn't blame her. I would have laughed, too, if it hadn't happened to me.

Pondering opportunities lost, I drove on. The trees closed in over the road, kudzu hanging down off their branches in a green shroud. A thin ribbon of sky showed overhead, a finger's width, maybe two. Shaking my head to clear it of ghoulish thoughts, I stomped down on the accelerator. The car leapt forward, and I found myself thinking about Jaimie. Maybe nine years was enough time gone by. I could look her up, see how she was doing, nothing more. Of course getting back together with her was out of the question. It had been years, after all, and she'd no doubt moved on with her life. Gotten married, perhaps, or moved out of state. But maybe, just maybe — no, it was best not to think about it. I chuckled a little at myself for letting the romantic fantasies out of the box where I'd been keeping them for so long. Maybe telling the story tonight had done me some good after all, no matter what Jeremy said.

Still smiling, I took the left that should have taken me onto a county highway leading to the interstate. Instead, I found myself heading out of the trees, past head-high swamp grass and occasional pines, down a road that occasionally forgot it was paved. "God damnit," I muttered, and looked for a place to turn around. None was forthcoming, but the grass got taller and the pines got closer, and the road started doing drunken doglegs between them. Backing up was out of the question, so I flicked on the high beams and pressed the pedal ever so slightly closer to the floor. The faster I drove, I told myself, the sooner I'd find a place to turn around, or at least to pull off and look at a map. Meanwhile, though, my lead foot just took me deeper and deeper under the trees. The ocean smell faded and that old familiar stink started wafting in through the radiator vents — rotting logs and dead frogs and all the other smells that made for a swamp's unique odor. With a grimace, I flicked on the internal circulation button on the AC's control panel, but it was too little, too late.

"Marvelous," I groaned, and, just to prove that I could affect my environment in some small way, I killed the power to the radio. Outside, cicadas and crickets set up a dull roar that crested over the sound of my rushing tires on the mud and gravel and occasional asphalt of the road. Once in a while, I could see old homesteads back off the roadside, roofs falling in and vines crawling in through the empty windows, but there were no driveways, and no crossroads, either.

Finally, I spotted a patch where the pine trees shimmied back away from the pavement far enough to make a decent shoulder. "At last," I told myself, and stopped composing "Hi, how are you?" emails to Jaimie in my head long enough to pull the car off the road. The wheels sank into the soft mud of the shoulder, and I cursed. The last thing I needed was to get stuck out here, in the middle of another slice of North Carolina nowhere. My cell phone helpfully told me that it was out of its service area, so I tossed it in the back seat, cut the engine to save gas, and opened the glove box. The directions to Sam's I'd downloaded that morning were rolled up in there, and I grabbed them irritably to see if there was a hope in hell of figuring out where I'd gone. After all, there couldn't be too many roads snaking off this far into the hinterlands. I should be able to pick up my position without too much of a hassle.

Unrolling the paper, I squinted a bit and then stopped every damn thing I was doing. The sound of the paper had been very, very loud. Too loud; no insects or frogs could be heard over it. I looked up and flicked on my headlights, praying I'd see nothing.

For a second, I did. Then, down the road at the tree line, I could see two red eyes staring back at me. They started moving closer, bobbing up and down at a limping giant's pace.

"Oh Jesus," I said, and started the motor. He kept coming. I threw the car into reverse and stomped on the gas, and heard nothing but my wheels spinning on mud. He kept coming, and I slammed it into drive. No luck; the tires spun and kicked up dirt like they were getting paid by the pound.

I could see the thing's face now, and I thought, just for a second, that maybe that wounded critter, that skunk ape or whatever it was, had decided to avoid those swamps, too. Maybe he'd started looking for a new home after that night nine years ago, someplace down south that was a little safer. Someplace where a damn fool wouldn't drive too fast along a dark road in the middle of the night.

And then both of us, each knowing the other, screamed.

For The Autumn Queen, Where She Rests Among the Fallen

To Tommy, it was just a leaf.

Oh, it was a beautiful leaf, to be certain, five-tined, like a maple, and blood-red at the edges with lines like yellow and orange flames in the center. And when he saw it on the sidewalk on his way home from school, resting among the dead and withered brown husks, he knew he had to take it home. He'd press it in wax paper, he thought. He'd preserve it.

He'd save it.

Behind him, the dead dry leaves rattled and rustled and made sounds like bony hands shaking a pair of dice as they skittered across the sidewalk. There was no breeze to move them, not on that sunny fall day, but that was not Tommy's concern, not when in his hands he held the most beautiful leaf in the world.

Tommy, you must understand, was six at the time. What he knew of magic was what all six year olds know, if they are allowed to. He knew that there was magic in the world, though he couldn't tell you where it was. He knew that strange and wonderful and special things could happen, and that Dracula and Bigfoot went out for cheeseburgers together when the moon was right, and that there really were dragons off the edge of the map and monsters under the bed.

What he did not know, what he could not know, was that in his hand he held the Autumn Queen, born best beloved every spring and adored through the dying time in the fall, most royal and exalted of the leaf-spirits whose existence is a secret even to six year old boys who know something about the way the world really works.

And so even as he hurried home, the better to preserve his find before any of her glory faded, word spread from leaf to leaf and branch to branch, limb to limb and tree to tree. Winds picked up leaves in ranks and blew them down the street after one small boy. Thousands upon thousands of leaves let go their last, painful grip on the branches that had given them life, and let themselves be carried away after the kidnapper, the defiler, the one who even now held the Autumn Queen between two fat and indelicate fingers.

He reached home ahead of the swirling winds, slamming the door behind him the face of a cloud of pursuers. They slammed themselves against the door and walls of his house, dashing themselves against it again and again until they battered themselves to pieces, and a thin smoke born of their passing filled the air. And even as one fell, another arrived on the breeze, or skittered along the sidewalk when it thought no one was looking, or dropped out of the clear blue sky to continue the assault.

Tommy, for his part, did not notice this, or if he did he ignored it, for he had better things to do. There was a leaf to preserve, after all, Fall's finest colors to save so that they might be cherished all through the winter. Carefully he made his preparations, studious and careful in the way of small boys intent on a task that they know in their bones to be the most important thing in the world.

At least, it's the most important thing in the world, until another thing comes along, such as your mother telling you to play outside. It was, she told him, a beautiful day, and he ought not to be inside.

"Just a minute," he told her. "I just have one more thing to take care of."

* * *

They found Tommy in the back yard, his mouth stuffed impossibly full of leaves and his face blue. On his hands and arms and round little-boy face were a thousand tiny cuts, the sort that might have been paper cuts, or scrapes from falling down on too-rough concrete, or a thousand other things, but weren't. His mother cried and his father stood stoically while the ambulance took him away, at least until the nice policeman suggested that they go inside and get out of the wind that was whipping the unraked leaves in their backyard every which way. And so they went inside, and poured out their grief, and told the policeman what they knew, which, in the grand scheme of things, was nothing at all.

Outside, the leaves still beat at the windows and at the doors, at the walls and at the roof, for while they had achieved vengeance, that was all that they had done, and it was not enough.

And inside, the Autumn Queen sobbed unheard where she lay, alone and imprisoned, in the silence and desolation between pages 234 and 235.

Come Quietly and No One Gets Hurt

Scott was thirteen when he found something that would drive *them* away.

Thirteen had already been a magical summer for Scott. It was the summer of baseball, the summer of long bike rides along paths he thought were hidden from other eyes, and the summer of finally noticing girls.

Most important of all, though, thirteen was the summer of music. Music had always been there before in his life, leaking from the radios of passing cars and dripping from the overhead speakers at restaurants when his parents took him out for dinner. Then, however, it had just been noise, and he'd hated it. It had seemed loud and obnoxious, shouty and rude.

Now it suddenly meant something. The shouting wasn't just shouting, it was rage that he could feel in his tendons and bones. The angry screech of the guitar was a shout of defiance, the jackhammer thud of the bass drum a line drawn in the sand.

In other words, Scott discovered rock and roll, and it spoke to him. The money from his allowance went to buy a record player, and then to purchase records themselves. At first he asked for music for his birthday and Christmas, but the gifts he received weren't exactly what he was looking for. They were his parents' choices, music they thought he should like, and it bored him senseless. His parents were nice people, and they liked nice music, and they wanted him to be nice, too.

The problem was that nice wouldn't keep *them* away.

Scott could not remember a time when *they* had not been there. The sound of them scuttling across his bedroom floor was one of his oldest memories; as far as he knew, they'd always been there. He didn't know what they were, nor did they offer the information. They were just dark shapes, almost human enough to be mistaken for his shadow, not quite perfect enough to pull off the lie. Scott had long ago given up trying to discover their true nature. He knew that *they* were simply *they*, and *they* were not to be mistaken for anything else.

They were curious when he was young, spending their hours poking around his bedroom to see what they could see. Mostly, they saw Scott.

The older he got, the more they crowded close. He could see them in public places sometimes — ducking behind a seat in a half-empty movie theater, or scuttling under a car in a dim parking lot — but he never told anyone. Scott had seen other children ridiculed for being different; and had no wish to join them. As much as he was *theirs*, *they* were his, his secret, and together they held a shared bond of silence. Without words he nevertheless understood that they wanted him for some unknown purpose, but that they couldn't take him yet, and that his complicity helped keep things that way. Someday, though, they would come for him. Of that he was quite sure.

But when he was thirteen, Scott found a weapon. The first time he smuggled a radio up to his room and flicked it on, they scuttled for cover, hiding behind the dresser and peeking out from behind the closet door. They voiced no sound, made no cry of protest or scream of pain, but instead skittered like cockroaches to the edge of the noise. He could feel them staring at him, hurt and angry and afraid.

Slowly, deliberately, he turned up the volume.

They fell back, scampering and sliding along the floor. "Go away," he said, and turned it up further. A Led Zeppelin tune, anthemic and forgettable, screeched at them. They retreated, ran, and finally vanished completely.

Scott smiled.

A rough pounding managed to pierce the din. "Scott Doherty, you turn that noise down this instant! Your father and I can barely hear ourselves think." It was his mother's voice, of course, strained and angry and normal, interspersed with the arrhythmic thuds of her fist on the door.

"Yes, Mother," Scott said, and turned the music down. "Sorry, Mother," he added, and kept his smile. Even when he turned the radio down to a whisper, *they* did not return.

So began a new phase in Scott's relationship with *them*, an angry peace. *They* finally came back after a few days, openly hostile and much more cautious. Scott retaliated by keeping the radio in his room and by playing it all night long, the volume turned up as loud as he dared make it. Some nights, it was barely audible, and he could feel them crowding close. Other nights the fear of *them* was so great that he turned the volume up louder and louder, risking the pounding fist on the door to keep *them* away. When the first cassette players became affordable he saved up for one with auto-reverse, so he could put a tape in before he went to bed and trust it to protect him endlessly as he slept; too often the songs on the radio had been interrupted by commercials or disc jockey prattle. He dreamed about *them* now, but dream was all he did, and his nights were guarded by The Clash and Cheap Trick and Blue Oyster Cult.

College was much the same, though Scott drove away a succession of roommates before finding one who loved music as much as he did. He acquired a reputation for being a bit odd, if harmless. Women were flattered by the tapes he made for them and insisted on playing in their presence; men who liked him simply appreciated the vast collection from which they could borrow, and accepted his eccentricity as relatively minor, all things being equal.

As for *them*, well, *they* kept away as long as Scott had the music. Only occasionally could he feel *them*, lurking on the fringes of perception, their hatred for him building day by day. Usually he'd let *them* stay there, on the outskirts of his view. *They* couldn't harm him from there.

Only once during his college years did Scott truly fear *them*. The occasion was a late-night power outage, inflicted on the campus by a thunderstorm. His fellow residents lit candles and drank bad wine to drive the dark away but Scott huddled under the covers, terrified. All around, he could hear *them* getting cautiously closer, not daring to believe their luck. Minute by minute, *they* crept nearer, their footsteps deliberately dragging across the floor to let him know *they* were there. Scott turned off the flashlight he held in his sweaty hands, knowing it would do him no good. Almost seeing *them* would only it worse.

The seconds dragged on, and *they* drew closer. He could hear the footfalls on his bed, feel them on his pillow. *They* were close now, closer than they'd been since he was a child.

And suddenly, miraculously, the lights stuttered back on, and with them, the music. *They* fled silently back into the shadows.

The next day, Scott bought a portable CD player and a carton of batteries for it. He kept it under his pillow when he slept, its music a constant low murmur in his dreams.

Scott went back home after he graduated. It seemed the sensible thing to do. His parents were glad to have him back, and he found work in the area soon enough. He moved out of the room that had been his as a child, though. There were too many memories there, and too many nightmares. Instead, he took the basement, which was larger and darker and more soundproof. These were all things he — and his parents, who still had no ear for his music — liked.

Scott's parents retired a few years after he started living in the basement, and they began to travel. This left Scott alone in the house for a few days at a time, and then stretches of weeks or even months. Uncomfortable with his supervisor's dislike of music, he started working from the house, in his basement with no dark corners for *them* to hide in. For their part, Scott's parents were just as happy to spend time in places that were quiet, or at least quieter than a house with Scott in it could be.

In the basement, Scott kept his records and tapes — most of them worn to scratchy irrelevance — and compact discs. He kept a stereo with a 500 CD player, a computer loaded with MP3s, and a portable CD player with a stash of batteries, just in case. Occasionally, there were power outages, and Scott would switch on the portable until they passed. On rare occasions, the blackouts lasted long enough that he had to switch the batteries. And always, when he did, he could feel *them* waiting for him on the edge of sight and hearing. *They* would come for him someday, he was now sure, and *they* would not be gentle. If ever the music failed, *they* would come for him.

The power died one night when Scott's parents were off on a cruise, gazing at melting glaciers in Alaska. Scott sighed and cursed and flicked on the portable, then proceeded to save what he had been working on. Grumbling, he shut his computer down before the power left his UPS completely, then sat back to listen to the portable sing to him. The Small Faces howled out of the device's small speakers, and Scott smiled down at it, content. "Six packs of batteries," he said to himself. "That ought to be enough." And putting the CD player on auto-repeat, he fell asleep in his chair.

An hour before morning, the explosion came. The sound woke Scott from his sleep. It was still dark; no light came in the basement windows from neighboring houses or overhanging streetlamps. "Substation," he said to himself, remembering other times it had blown and been quickly repaired, and fell back asleep. The music was still playing as he closed his eyes, and that soothed him.

He carried the CD player with him the next morning when he went to explore the rest of the house. The power was still out, and remained out all day. Scott carefully conserved the fading cold of the refrigerator, cursed the fact that he'd not be able to get any work done, and sat on the porch with his music playing. Occasionally, he changed the CD. Less often, he changed the batteries. The sun went down, neighbors drove home, and still the lights stayed off. Scott heard snatches of conversation from nearby houses. Power would not be coming back on that night, it seemed. Something had wrecked the substation, and wrecked it thoroughly. Repairing it might take days.

Days.

Mentally, Scott tallied his battery supply. It might last days. It might. All around him in the gathering dark, he sensed *them*, and suddenly knew what had wrecked the substation. "Oh no you don't," he said, and switched from CD to radio. A moment's static gave them hope, and then Scott found the right place on the dial. Music surrounded him, music protected him.

They went away, more slowly than usual.

Nine hours later, in the middle of something Scott dimly thought was by Styx, the music vanished as well. A knife of silence descended, cutting off the song mid-note. Nerves screaming with panic, Scott scrabbled for the tuner. Long seconds passed before found another signal, static giving way to talk to blessed music. A cascade of drums told Scott he'd found salvation, and he gave a sigh of relief. "Must be a problem at the radio station," he told himself. "They'll be back on air soon."

After six hours, the second station went off the dial as well. Neighbors who had stayed home from work discussed the sudden disappearances of the two stations as they strolled out in the neighborhood. *Very strange*, they called it. Scott nodded to them as they passed, the portable clutched tightly in his hand.

As he listened, the third station vanished. Then a fourth, and then a fifth. By midnight, they were all gone.

AM and FM, Scott scanned the dial. There was nothing. Resignedly, he flipped the portable back to CD mode, listened to the motor spin up to speed, and counted his batteries.

Two thirds had gone missing, small tears in the empty packaging showing where tiny dark claws had snatched them away. He'd been a fool, he realized. He'd left the batteries behind when he'd gone upstairs to sit and chat. And while he'd been gone, *they*'d done their work. There were just enough batteries left to get him through another night. If he were conservative, it might last him the day as well. That was all.

In the recesses of his home, Scott could sense *them* laughing, silently. *They* were laughing at him.

"The hell with you," he said, his voice shaking only a little. He threw the empty packages of batteries into the trash and stuffed the remaining cells into the pockets of his jeans.

Holding the CD player close, he slept.

Morning came, and with it, no power. Scott trooped up out of the basement, haggard. His sleep had been fitful, full of bad dreams and silence. He needed fresh batteries. Ordinarily, this would not be a problem. He would order them in bulk from an office supply store, or ask his father to pick some up when he went out. But his father was not here and the mail had stopped coming, and these circumstances were anything but normal.

For the first time since that terrible night in college, Scott was afraid.

He'd never learned to drive, and that had never been an issue before. There had always been someone to pick him up or run his errand as a favor. As such, he didn't even have a set of his parents' car keys. His mother's Acura sat in the garage, silently. He'd laughed when she first bought it, and told her that the stereo system she'd insisted on was too good for the music she insisted on playing. Now those fine speakers, that oh-so-delicate equalizer lay locked away behind windshield glass. He'd find no help there.

Furthermore, there were no stores within walking distance. His parents, Scott recalled bitterly, had viewed that as a benefit. He stalked outside, looking for someone who could give him a ride.

Most of his neighbors had fled the area temporarily, discouraged by a report that progress on the substation was slow. A strange mood was in the air, one that made men decide to slide the extra bolt on their front doors and send their children to bed early. Gossip leapt from shuttered house to shuttered house. The radio stations, the stories said, had been destroyed by something monstrous. Bodies had been found inside, horribly mutilated bodies, and every tape, disc and record had been smashed. Police said there were no suspects, and no clues.

It had been *them*. Scott was sure of it. His steps quickening with panic, he went from door to door, searching for a neighbor who'd save him, who'd give him a ride, who'd take him somewhere to buy the life-preserving batteries that were the key to his rescue, or at least his endurance.

Doors slammed in his face, or didn't open. Whining apologies came faintly through peepholes. Scott heard them all, moved on, kept trying. Finally, he found a man who would listen, and who wanted to get out of the neighborhood as badly as Scott did, even for a little while. "Wife's driving me crazy," the man said. "Be happy to help you out, Scott. I know how you kids feel about your music."

"Thank you," Scott replied, and got in the car quickly.

They rode out in the man's blue sedan, Scott's radio humming softly in his lap. "Nothing on the radio, I'm afraid" the man had apologized, and Scott nodded. For the rest of the drive, neither said a word.

The first store they found was stuck onto a gas station as an afterthought, but it had power. Scott's neighbor filled up the sedan's gas tank while Scott dove into the mini-mart like a starving man chasing a rabbit. Inside was chaos, a clerk bellowing at another clerk, who cowered and cringed at every word. As Scott entered, they stopped and looked at him. "Yes?" the taller one, the one being yelled at, said. His voice was thin and nasal.

The words came tumbling out. "Batteries. I need D batteries. Now."

They looked at one another. "They're all gone," said the shorter clerk. Behind him, the tall one held out his hands, helplessly.

Scott looked at them in disbelief. "Sold out?"

The short man shook his head. "I said gone. Stolen. Taken. The whole damn display was ripped right out of the wall. Same thing in every store in the city, I hear. Hell, they're starting to report it across the river in Jersey."

"Someone's hoarding," the tall man said solemnly. The shorter one turned to him, scolding.

"Don't go saying that. People will think we're hoarding them."

"I don't think that at all," Scott said quickly. The two men stared at him. He turned, and pretended to study a bag of circus peanuts. "Do you mind if I hang out here for a while."

"I don't — " the taller man started, and then with a snap, the lights went out. The hum of the refrigerators faded. Outside, dimly, Scott could hear his neighbor cursing at the half-finished fill up. The pumps, it seemed, had died as well.

"What the hell just happened?" the short man said. "There's not supposed to be any more blackouts."

"I'm sorry," Scott said, and walked out. Behind him, the clerks' arguing voices were like the buzzing of bees. Up and down the block, the power was gone. Instinctively, he turned down the volume on his CD player. Maybe that would make it last a little longer.

Angrily, Scott's neighbor thrust the nozzle back onto the pump. "Let's go home, Scott," he said. "We're done here."

"Yes," Scott said, and climbed in. "I'm sorry," he added as he slammed the door shut.

The drive home was quiet, and Scott barely mumbled a "thank-you" before slipping into his house and back down into the basement. He could hear the fading grumble of the engine as his neighbor drove home against the angry sunset. "Please," Scott whispered. "Get out. Run." Scott had whispered it like a prayer, but of course the man couldn't hear him.

An hour later, the sounds began outside. They didn't last very long, punctuated every few seconds by the tinkle of glass being smashed. Doors slammed open. People shouted. There were screams, at least for a little while.

Scott stayed in the basement and changed the CD when the occasion demanded it. Another dawn came, and he walked around the neighborhood to see the night's devastation. The walk didn't last long. A few houses were all he needed to see. Dogs had been at some of the bodies, it seemed. *Something* had chewed on them. He didn't bother reporting it. Trees had been felled across the nearby streets, one after the other. The neighborhood was cut off, isolated. Now Scott knew why emergency vehicles had not come to pick through the carnage the past night, had not tried to stop the screaming.

Besides, Scott was sure they had been busy elsewhere this past night. This place, it seemed, had been forgotten by the rest of the city. He didn't even try to call a taxi, knowing as he did that it would never come.

The day drew toward its close. Scott returned home, and put the last set of batteries in. He went down to his basement, his home, and waited. The music was kept low now, barely loud enough to hear, and Scott could sense *them*, waiting.

They had done this. They had done it all, to get to him. He knew that now. He just hoped it would end with him as well. If he'd gone quietly, perhaps all of the others would have been spared...but it was best not to think of that.

The last light faded. Silence descended as the last of the batteries bled themselves dry. The basement was dark now, and within it, darker shadows moved. Scott sat in the center of the room, in the center of his world, waiting. The tired CD player rested in his lap. He cradled it instinctively, like a talisman or a child, against the darkness.

They were coming now, pouring in from all sides. Scott could see their shapes in the shadows, long and angular and cruel. They had no eyes, just deeper pits of blackness into which he could not look for long, and they moved in slow, careful steps, like spiders walking delicately along a single razored thread.

He did not try to run. There was nowhere to run to, just a world full of things like *them* in the silence *they* loved.

They made a ring around where he sat, still fearful, perhaps, of a last burst of song. He smiled at them, almost gently, and popped the lid on the disc player. Slowly, he reached in and removed the CD — which one it was, he could not see — then tossed it aside in a gesture of surrender.

"You win," he started to say, but suddenly there was a dark finger on his lips, and cold hands clutching at his arm. And as the light faded for the last time, he heard a single whispered voice say, for the first time, a single word.

"Shhhh."

Losing Altitude

Are you comfortable?

I'm fine, honey.

Do you want the window seat? We could switch?

It's fine. Really. It's great.

OK. If you change your mind —

Honey? Sit down. We're taking off soon.

Yeah. I can't believe we got tickets on the one flight going out.

You did great at the ticket desk, honey. I'm very proud of you.

Thank you. Hard to believe they're only opening up the airport long enough to let a couple of flights out.

And we're on the only one going west to New York.

Lucky indeed.

Put your seat belt on.

Yes, dear.

. . .

Why did they open up the airport for just a few hours?

There was some kind of break in the ash cloud. Some kind of weird wind pattern east of Iceland and it punched a hole in the cloud clear across England.

That's good, I guess. But it's closing again?

Not until we're past Iceland and on our way home.

That's good. I'd hate to get caught in that. It sounds nasty.

It is. You know what happens when a plane flies into that stuff?

What?

Well, volcanic ash is really tiny pieces of rock and glass. So when a plane sucks that into its jet engines, it's basically sandblasting the turbines.

That sounds bad.

It is bad. And then it gets worse.

Worse?

Yeah. The ash melts and then sticks to the engine when it hits. The more ash the plane flies through, the more molten rock gloms onto the engine, until it finally can't handle it any more.

What happens then?

It stops.

The plane?

The engine. Of course, all of your engines are getting the same treatment, so —

I don't want to hear any more. I'm just glad we're not going through any of that cloud.

Me too, honey. Me too.

. . .

What's that?

What's what?

Out the window.

It's a cloud.

It's a really dark cloud. Are we over the volcano?

We shouldn't be.

But are we?

I don't think so.

It looks like the cloud's getting bigger. We're heading towards it.

That would be ridiculous. Why would we do that?

I don't know. It's a weird airline. I never heard of them before today. Maybe they do weird things.

Maybe. . .

We'll be fine. It still beats being stuck back in England, right?

I guess so.

It'll be fine.

. . .

The captain just said something about flying into the cloud.

I only caught part of it. Something about "brief transit" and "nothing to worry about."

So this is the ash cloud we're in.

It seems like it. But I'm sure we wouldn't be flying through it if there were any danger.

You're sure?

If we crash, the airline gets sued right out of business. They're not going to take any risks.

Wow, that's so comforting.

Logic rarely comforts. But it works.

Uh-huh. Then why are we flying into the cloud, genius?

I have no idea.

. . .

It's dark out there.

Mostly dark. You can see some lightning.

Lightning? Not lava?

We're way too high up for lava. But you get a lot of lightning in eruptions like this.

Is it dangerous?

Only if we get hit.

I'm going to pull the shade down now.

That's a good idea. Try to get some sleep.

I can't sleep. Not in this.

Try anyway.

OK. I love you.

I love you too.

...

What did the pilot say?

He said we've lost an engine.

That's bad, right?

Yeah. But not too bad. These things can fly just fine with only one engine going.

How many engines does this plane have?

Four. Well, three now. At least for the moment.

What does that mean?

It just means three are working, and we're fine.

You're sure?

We're fine.

...

Have you seen any flight attendants?

Not since we took off.

Shouldn't they be going through the aisles telling us to be calm now?

Or at least bringing us tasty beverages.

It's not funny. Don't joke.

I'm sorry. You're right. It's weird we haven't seen any. I wonder where they are.

I wonder if there are any. You said this was a cheap airline.

I don't think it's possible to be that cheap. Is it?

...

There's the captain again.

I hate these plane PA systems. You can never understand anything they're saying.

Yeah. About that...

What is it?

We're down two more engines.

Two more? That means...

We've only got one left, yeah.

But we can fly on one. You said we could fly on one, right?

That's what I said, and it's true. But just to be safe, the pilot said he's going to turn us around and bring us back in.

Where?

I don't know. Spain, probably. Or Portugal. I think they're closest now.

We can make it that far, right?

We could make it to New York on one engine, honey. This is just a precaution.

It's quiet all of a sudden. Why is it quiet?

The last engine cut out about a minute ago.

....

Yeah.

We're going to die. That's why the captain's not saying anything, isn't it? We're going to die!

Shhh. Not so loud.

What do you mean, not so loud? We're going to die and you're telling me to shush?

Look, the last time this happened, a British Airways jet lost all its engines in an ash cloud. You know what happened to that plane?

It crashed and everyone on it died?

No. The pilot flew it like a glider out of the ash cloud and then the engines restarted.

They didn't die?

No. Nobody died. They had to repaint the plane, though.

Hah. I can see that. How far did they have to glide?

I think they lost something like ten thousand feet of altitude.

Ten thousand? That's a lot.

Yeah, But if you're starting at thirty thousand, like we are, you've got plenty of room.

So you're sure we're going to be OK?

I'm positive. As soon as we get out of the cloud, the engines will restart.

...

How long has it been?

Since what?

Since the engines quit?

I don't know. Five minutes, maybe?

Five minutes? How much altitude can we lose in five minutes?

I don't know. I mean, it's thirty two feet per second per second if we're just falling until you reach terminal velocity, but we've got the wings so we're gliding in a controlled descent, and we had forward momentum, so —

Stop it. Just stop it.

OK, fine. You wanted to know.

I didn't want to know all of that. How long did it take us to reach cruising altitude?

Maybe twenty minutes.

And that was going up. So it would have been slower than going down, right?

I…think so, yeah. You're probably right.

So we've got less that fifteen minutes to get out of the cloud and get the engines started before we hit.

Less than, probably.

That's not a lot of time.

No. It isn't.

…

Look out the window. Are we out of the cloud yet?

No. I can't see anything.

It wasn't supposed to be anywhere below fifteen thousand feet. We've got to break through the bottom soon, and then we'll hit clear air.

Are you sure?

I'm positive.

Why isn't the captain saying anything?

He probably doesn't want to scare anyone.

Well, I'm scared anyway!

You've got me.

Heh. You make a lousy flotation device, honey.

…

How long has it been?

Ten minutes? Twelve?

We should have come out of the cloud by now.

Any minute now. Any minute now…

…

Honey?

Yeah?

It's been twenty minutes.

Are you sure? Time sense is one of the first things to get weird when —

I'm sure. I've been checking my cell phone every ten seconds. It's been twenty minutes.

So we should have hit by now.

We should have come out of the clouds, at least.

Maybe the pilot's really good at gliding.

It's a giant metal tube with wings. It's not going to glide that well.

You're not helping.

You're not being realistic.

Realistically, we should have gotten the engines started by now.

Or died.

Or died. But we haven't.

So what does that mean?

I don't know.

I wish the captain would say something.

Yeah. Me, too.

...

What did you see?

What?

You just sneaked a look out the window. I saw you. What did you see?

Nothing.

Nothing?

Nothing. It's all...gray out there. Nothing but gray.

So we're still in the cloud.

I guess.

That's impossible.

Yeah. I know.

What do you want to do?

I want to scream. But I don't think that will help.

Why isn't anyone else screaming? I mean, people scream on airplanes all the time and that's with all the engines working? Why isn't anybody screaming now? Huh? Why not? What's going on?

I don't know. Maybe they've all decided to be calm. Or they're asleep. Or —

All of them? Every last one? That's impossible. Somebody's got to be up. Someone's got to have noticed.

Hah.

What?

Look. The "Fasten seat belts" light just came on.

Just now?

Yeah. Just now.

That's a good thing, right? It means someone's there to turn it on?

Maybe. Or it's a short circuit.

Don't say that. Just...don't.

...

We're still falling.

Yeah.

How long has it been?

I don't know. I thought you were keeping track.

I gave up after an hour.

An…hour?

An hour. That's not possible, right? We should have hit the ocean before now. We should be dead.

We should have come out of the bottom of the cloud before we hit the ocean. We should have gotten the engines restarted. We should have been fine!

But none of that happened.

No! None of it happened! And it has to have happened!

Something happened.

Yeah. Something. I don't know what.

…

How long has it been?

I don't know.

My cell phone battery is dead. I don't have a watch.

We're still falling, aren't we.

Yeah.

We've got to hit something, right?

Something. Yeah.

I'm scared, honey.

I'm scared, too.

But hey, we're still alive, right?

Yeah.

That's something. That's something good, right?

Yeah. Yeah, it is.

OK then. Let's just hang on to that.

Hang on to me.

We're still falling.

Hang on to me.

Minus One

Tom had been in Paris for three weeks when he'd first noticed that the numbers in the elevator were wrong. There were two elevators out of the lobby in the residence hotel his company had assigned him to, and for the first twenty days of his stay he'd always used the one on the left. There was nothing to that, no preference or superstition. The left one had just always arrived first. He'd gotten on, pressed the button for his fourth floor flat, and thought no more about it.

And then one night, the other elevator had gotten there first. He'd stepped in with a still-warm *baguette* in one hand and his briefcase in the other, more occupied with the logistics of getting a finger free to press a button than anything else. The slender woman at the front desk gave him a desultory "*bonsoir*" and went back to reading her magazine. He'd mumbled "*bonsoir*" back, and been relieved when the door slid shut so there was no possibility of further conversation. His French, all twelve words of it, sucked.

The elevator was empty save for him, narrow and deep and done up in white tile and aluminum panels. It claimed to hold thirteen people, but twelve of them would have to be made out of pipe cleaners in order to fit. Enjoying the solitude, he put the briefcase down and did his usual travel ritual — pat the right pocket for the wallet, the left one for the passport, the belt for the smartphone. Three bulges under his fingers reassured him that they were all there. Then and only then did he extend a finger to punch the number that would take him up, and in the midst of doing so, he froze.

The 4 wasn't where it should have been. Instead, it had jumped from the left-hand column of numbers to the right.

"Son of a bitch," he muttered, then shifted his aim to nail the proper button. It lit up, the number shining out in green, and the elevator promptly lurched upwards.

It took maybe twenty seconds to make the uninterrupted climb from lobby to fourth floor, long enough for Tom to scan the control panel to see why his button had migrated. The change went all the way up to the top, where the 12th floor had suddenly gone from being the last number on the right to standing alone at the top of the column on the left. That meant the change was the bottom, and even as the door pulled open he found the new button, the one that he'd never seen before.

It read, in the same font and style as all the others, –1.

He blinked.

Gently, he ran his finger over it. It was cool metal, and it felt the same under his fingers. He let the pad of his finger rest on it a minute and frowned. Elevators didn't just sprout new numbers. Half of him wanted to press it, to see where it went. The other half wanted no part of it. He stood there, poised in indecision.

"Ahem."

Tom turned. Standing there was a middle-aged tourist couple overdressed for dinner.

"Is this elevator taken," the man said in a voice heavy with impatience and a thick Georgia accent. "Because if not, my wife and I would like to use it." Beside the man, the woman stared at him impatient disdain.

He felt himself flushing. "Sorry, just getting off," he said, picking up the briefcase and jostling the man slightly as he got out. "What a rude — " he heard behind him, and then heard no more as the elevator door slid shut. That, Tom reflected, was probably the longest conversation he'd had with any of his neighbors since he'd arrived

The hotel was like that, though, he knew. This was a place for people to be stored temporarily while they were useful, and when they were done, they could be moved out without leaving any trace of themselves behind. Everyone was transient and everyone knew it, and so everyone avoided talking to anyone else. *Bonjour* and *pardonnez-moi* in the lobby, and that was it. Why bother getting to know your neighbors when they might be gone tomorrow? You just stopped seeing them in the hallway one day, and assumed they'd been reassigned or gone home. Then you just let them vanish from your memory as well, and thought no more about them.

The same way they'd forget all about Tom once he left.

"You're cheerful tonight," he told himself as he let himself into his room. A room it was — one room with a bathroom and a countertop that was supposed to serve as a kitchen, random lightswitches everywhere and a bed that folded into the wall. There weren't enough electrical outlets, the chairs were mismatched, and the sofa was a pull-out sleeper with nowhere to pull out to.

It was, he had decided on his first night in, a singularly depressing place to come home to, and the calendar on the desk bore mute witness to that. Two more weeks and then he'd be flying back home to the States, and thank God for that. A mere fifteen more days in this place and he'd go crazy.

He dropped the room's keycard on the thin slice of wood that passed for a desk. The thin wand of bread he placed more gently on the kitchen counter, between the two burners and the coffee machine. There was a clean glass in the sink; he grabbed it and filled it with Diet Coke from the mini-fridge, and threw himself down on the couch to think about what he'd seen.

Minus one. He was pretty sure he'd never seen that before anywhere, and this was his fifth trip out here. He took a sip of soda and coughed, as he always did at the excessive carbonation. Outside his open window, he could hear the foot traffic going to and fro, commuters returning home and tourists scurrying out, eager to find their destinations on the Metro before the scary foreign night closed in.

The thought goosed him into action. He'd seen something odd and foreign, and here he was letting it drive him nuts. Schoolgirls on exchange programs and nervous housewives from Kansas City acted like that. World-weary business travelers didn't.

World-weary business travelers like Tom called the concierge instead.

It took seven rings before the woman at the front desk answered. "*Bonsoir*?"

"Err, *je non parle Français*."

"Yes, sir?" she answered, in accented English.

"I have a question."

"We are here to help." She sounded bored. "What can I assist you with?"

Tom cleared his throat. "Tonight, in one of the elevators, I noticed something odd."

"Do you want me to have maintenance look at it, sir?" Even more boredom, now mixed with irritation for those damn demanding Americans who kept on insisting everything be like home. He didn't even need to see her face to know what she was thinking.

"No, no, that's not it. It's just I saw a negative one on one of the elevator buttons tonight, and I'd never seen it before. I was wondering if you could tell me where that goes."

There was a pause, and then contempt. "I believe you call it a basement in America, sir. If you look at the card on the desk in your room, you will notice that we have a laundrette available for your use. It is located on that floor. Only one elevator can access it. Are there any other questions I can answer for you?" *Any other stupid questions*, he mentally corrected her.

"No. Thank you very much."

"*Bonsoir*," she said pointedly, and hung up.

The laundry. Of course. He walked over to the desk and picked up the card she'd mentioned, a laminated three-parter with a short list of services the hotel did provide and a longer list of the ones it didn't. There it was, a brief mention of the coin-operated laundry available to guests. He hadn't noticed, as he'd been using the dry-cleaning service and billing his employer for the privilege, but sure enough, there it was.

"I feel like a moron," he announced, and walked over to the door. He could go check it out right now and confirm for himself that there was nothing sinister about going to a floor labeled –1.

He could. He thought about doing so. And then he turned and walked back to the couch, kicked off his shoes, and turned on the television.

Tomorrow. He'd check it out tomorrow.

* * *

Briefcase yes, *baguette* no. That made wrangling the door easier in the morning, which Tom appreciated. He took the walk to the elevator quickly, confidently, and trying his best not to think about the button which had disturbed him so the previous night. *Just the laundry*, he told himself. *Nothing strange there*. He pressed the call button for the elevator.

The right one arrived first. The door rolled open.

He stood there. Watched it for a minute. Let the doors close and the grind of cable on pulleys announce that it had moved on.

And then he pushed the call button again.

It took another minute and a half for the left-hand elevator to arrive. With a silent sigh of relief, he stepped in. *Idiot, idiot, idiot*, he raged at himself mentally. *It's just the laundry*. Tom shook his head and went to push the lobby button, the one labeled "0".

Next to it was one marked "–1".

Tom blinked. Took a step back and banged his briefcase into the wall behind him. "That wasn't…" he started, and took a deep breath.

Maybe it was there yesterday. Maybe he'd mixed up his elevators. It was no big deal, and he wasn't going down to –1 anyway. It didn't matter. He wouldn't let it matter. Deliberately, he pressed the zero, right in its center. It lit up like a smile.

Tom kept his back against the elevator wall, though. Just in case.

There was a different woman at the desk when he exited into the lobby, just a little bit faster than usual. There was always a different woman. Three weeks here, and he wasn't sure he'd seen the same desk attendant twice. He walked past the smooth black reception desk, hesitated, and then turned.

"*Bonjour, monsieur*," the woman said brightly. She was short and dark-skinned, her head covered in a brightly-colored scarf.

"*Bonjour*. I have a question?"

"Yes?" She was all smiles, eager to help.

"Last night the woman at the desk told me that only one elevator went down to the laundry level. Today, I saw that both elevators go down there. Was I… confused?"

She blinked at him. "*Monsieur*? Both elevators have always gone down to the *lingerie*…the laundry level. What you were told last night, it is incorrect."

He smiled. "Thank you. I guess the woman who answered my question last night was misinformed."

"I will leave a note for her so she does not make the same mistake again." The woman ducked behind the desk, then reappeared a moment later with what looked to be a cleverly disguised work schedule. Her finger ran down the page, and her face crumpled into a puzzled frown. "M'sieur is absolutely certain he spoke to a woman last night?"

Tom nodded. "Yes, she was at the desk when I came in. A tall, thin woman." He paused. "She was actually kind of rude."

"That is odd," the woman said. "According to this, Monsieur Gaudet was here last night. See?" She shoved the paper forward.

"I'll take your word for it," Tom said, and stepped back. "Maybe he called in sick and she was his replacement?"

"Maybe," she said. She didn't sound convinced.

"Don't worry about it." With a wave of dismissal, Tom was already halfway to the door. "Thank you very much for your help. Uh, *merci*."

* * *

The front desk was untenanted when Tom finally came home. Work had run late, followed by a mandatory dinner meeting with the European sales staff, followed by mandatory drinking sessions with the survivors of dinner, and before he knew it Tom was making excuses about how he had to leave in order to get home before the Metro shut down. It was bad office politics, he knew, but he was tired, and bored, and unpleasantly buzzed besides.

The door to the room behind the reception desk was closed, he saw as he waited, and it sounded like someone was puttering around in there. No doubt that was where the clerk was hiding. One mystery solved. Now, for the other.

The left elevator opened first. He stepped in, but reached back with one hand to hold the door open.

One receptionist had told him one thing. Another had said something different. The hell with both of them, he was going to check for himself.

A quick look confirmed the presence of the aberrant number. This elevator would in fact go down one more level. Frowning, Tom punched the button for the eleventh floor, then stepped back out into the lobby. The door slid shut and the number on the lintel started climbing. Satisfied, he hit the call button again.

The elevator on the right opened up almost immediately. This time, he stepped all the way in and counted down.

There it was. Minus one. Both had it. Mystery solved.

He put his finger on the button for the fourth floor.

Held it there.

And pushed the button marked "–1". It lit up, cherry red instead of green.

* * *

It took five long seconds to go down that one floor. The elevator door opened. Tom looked out.

Floor minus-one had the same off-white tile as all of the other floors. It had the same white wallpaper. But somehow it was lit differently. The shadows were sharper here, and darker as well.

Grabbing his briefcase, Tom stepped out and looked up. *Fluorescent bulbs*, he thought. *No need for pretty sconce lights down here.* He looked around. A corridor ran off to the left, while another, wider one ran straight ahead. Affixed to the wall at the corner was a sign with two words: *Laverie*, and underneath it, *Toilettes*. Both were next to arrows that pointed to the right.

Tom went left. The heels of his shoes clicked on the tile floor. On the right, he passed a succession of doors, all marked with French that he assumed meant "Do Not Enter". The last was a set of swinging double doors marked *Lingerie.* Hot air seeped out from it as he stood there, and he could hear machines working. This was the hotel's laundry, then, the place where the staff washed the sheets and towels on whatever arcane schedule they followed.

At the end of the hall was a door labeled *Sortie de Secours* — emergency exit. The handle was lime green, the sort of color little kids probably felt compelled to lick. Tom just stared at it for a moment.

Behind him, a bell and the whoosh of a door announced the arrival of an elevator.

He turned, panicking, explanations for why he was in the wrong part of the hallways half-forming in his head.

No one was there. The door waited a moment, then closed itself.

"Easy, son," he said aloud, and winced at the flat sound of his voice. "I'll just go check out the other side, then go up to my room and go the hell to bed already."

He marched determinedly around the corner. The signs did not lie. On the right, two doors marked with the peculiar French pictographs for Men and Women waited for anyone who felt the need to relieve themselves mid-rinse cycle. On the left was a closed door marked *Laverie.* Taped to it was a warning that the hotel would not refund change lost in the machines.

He read it, raised an eyebrow, and eased the door open. Inside, it was dark except for a few LEDs on the appliances. He felt along the wall for the light switch, found it, and flicked it.

Nothing happened. Shaking his head, he opened the door wider to let the hallway light illuminate the scene.

There wasn't much to see. A couple of washers sat next to a lone dryer, and over them hung a sign announcing the outrageous price for a single load. It seemed perfectly normal. Regardless, he decided to go all the way in. He was here; he might as well explore his mystery thoroughly and in doing so, set it to rest.

But doing that would take more light.

Pushing the door open all the way, he dropped the briefcase right in front of it and shoved them together. A moment's testing made sure it wouldn't slide, and then walked into the dim *laverie.*

The room itself was shaped oddly, all corners and angles. There were no chairs or tables for folding laundry, and Tom felt certain that the entire setup was designed to encourage use of the staggeringly expensive dry-cleaning service. Nothing seemed sinister or out of place, though. Nothing felt suspicious at all.

Satisfied, he turned and walked out. The elevator came within seconds of his call. Smiling, he got in, pressed the button for 4, and let it shine green as the door closed.

* * *

Tom was half undressed for bed before he realized he'd left his briefcase in the basement.

The case itself wasn't worth much, bought for durability instead of flash. What it held, however, was irreplaceable — business plans, sales orders, things that hadn't yet been backed up or duplicated. Cursing himself loudly, he threw on a t-shirt and sneakers without socks. Keycard in his pocked, he hurried back toward the bank of elevators.

Jamming the call button hard enough to make his finger hurt, he stared at the door and then jammed it again. Minutes ticked by, or felt like they did. He thought about the stairs, realized he didn't even know where they were, and then punched the button angrily a few more times.

Finally, leisurely, the elevator on the right made its appearance. With a low hum, its door hummed open. Tom stomped inside, breathing hard, and stabbed at the –1 button on the control panel.

–2 lit up instead.

He stared at the panel. Where –1 had been was now the next number in the sequence. It shone red in the dim light of the elevator, a perfectly normal button on a perfectly normal panel.

Except that it had not been there ten minutes earlier. Tom's lungs felt tight, the air in them hot. He slid his thumb onto the –1 button and pressed it. *Just a mistake*, he thought. *I read it wrong. Just a mistake.*

The elevator plunged downward. The –1 refused to light up. He swore, then made a fast stab at 0. It wasn't quick enough. He shot past the lobby and down, taken far longer than the journey one additional floor should have taken.

Tom backed away from the door. It opened anyway. A billow of steam wafted in, hot and stinking of bleach. The light that shone down was pale and flickering, and the steam was shot through with the sickly green of the emergency exit sign.

"What the hell?" he said, and ran his fingers over the elevator buttons. None responded; none lit up. The elevator didn't want to go anywhere.

And now he saw there was a –3 button. That one, he didn't dare press.

Pleading, he hit the "Door Close" button. That didn't work, either.

If he wanted to go back upstairs, he knew, there was only one way out. Walk out onto floor minus-two, and look for another way out.

Five minutes passed between this realization and his first step onto the floor. The tile was slick with moisture, the walls positively dripping with it. He took a deep breath and nearly gagged. The bleach smell was stronger now, the air hotter. Cursing himself for a fool, he brought his back foot out of the elevator.

The door slammed itself shut behind him, and the sudden roar of the motor told him it had shot up like a rocket. Without him.

His hand trembling, he pressed the call button.

It lit up.

Long minutes later, it was still lit. Tom stared at it, pushed it again a few times, and stepped back. Nothing.

He looked around for another way out. The green glow still flooded the steam, but he would be damned if he could see where it was coming from. Still, if he could see the light its source had to be around here somewhere. Cautiously, he picked a direction and moved. Right seemed as good as any; he had a vague memory of the *Sortie de secours* being off that way.

Slowly, hands out in front of him, he shuffled forward. There were noises now, hisses and clanks and whirrs, all coming from up ahead, and he didn't want to accidentally stumble into one of the machines responsible for those sounds. His hands touched nothing. The steam grew hotter. He inched forward, sweating profusely but not daring to pull a hand back to wipe his brow. How long had he been plodding forward? Five minutes? More? How, in a corridor just fifty feet long?

With a jolt, his hands hit the smooth paint of the emergency exit. Breathing shallowly, he pressed his face against the cool surface and ran his hands up and down, looking for the push bar. His questing fingers found it, tensed and waiting. He thought briefly of the explaining he'd have to do when the alarm sounded, and decided the hell with it. He leaned forward on it, ready to dash through and up whatever stairs lay beyond.

It didn't budge. "Stuck," Tom told himself, and pushed harder. His feet nearly slid out from under him on the slick floor, and he staggered. The door remained immobile, mocking him.

"Open, damn you!" He could hear what sounded like laughter now, mixed in with the machine sounds and the hiss of the steam. He didn't care, pounding on the push bar with both fists. His footing gave way and he slipped, landing hard on his knees but never stopping his assault on the door.

Nothing happened in front of him, but behind him he heard the chime of the elevator.

"No!" Wide-eyed with panic, Tom tried to stand and turn all at once, succeeding at neither. He sprawled out on the floor, hot moisture soaking through his t-shirt and jeans as he scrabbled forward. "Wait! Don't leave me down here!" Half-running, half-crawling, he stumbled back toward the elevator. He couldn't tell which one had arrived and he didn't care. One was here. That was all that mattered.

The door was closing as he finally reached it, sliding shut with impersonal smoothness. Instinctively, Tom reacted, shoving his hand into the doorway to stop it from closing completely. The door bumped against his wrist, pressed against it for a moment, and then drew back.

Tom let out a sigh of relief and pulled himself to his feet, his hand still guarding the doorway. The call button light was green now, he saw, unnecessary confirmation of arrival.

And the door rushed back.

He heard it before he saw it and froze, torn between throwing himself forward and just pulling his hand away. In the end he did neither, and the door slammed against his hand like a runaway train. He heard rather than felt the bones crunch under the impact. *There's supposed to be a rubber guard there*, he thought crazily. *I have to report this elevator as unsafe*. Then the pain hit him and he dropped to the floor, his hand still pinned.

The door ground against him for a minute, then pulled back for another run. Tom fell forward, shrieking with pain as he landed on his damaged hand. Terror struck him as he realized he was halfway across the threshold, and then the door started sliding closed again.

He reached forward with his good hand, trying for any purchase on the wet tile of the elevator floor. There was none.

The door tapped him once, softly, letting Tom know it had him. Slowly it drew back, humming to itself as it did.

He rolled on his back and planted his feet against the floor. There was a little traction there, a little push, but it wasn't enough. He wasn't going to make it all the way, not before it caught him.

It gave a little shake and started forward.

And Tom reached up under the side paneling with his shattered hand and pulled. He could feel muscle pulling away from shattered bone, but it gave him enough. He pulled his legs forward and into the elevator as the door slammed hungrily shut behind him.

Disbelieving, he stared at it for a moment. It showed no signs of opening again.

"And stay closed," he said weakly. Using his good hand, he hauled himself up to the control panel. With careful deliberation, he pressed the button for the lobby, careful to look at no other buttons, especially not ones that might shine red. *Let housekeeping get the briefcase*, he thought. He was done with negative numbers.

Amazingly, the 0 button lit up. The elevator glided into motion, then eased to a halt. The door opened, and Tom stumbled out, clutching his hand.

The woman he'd spoken to the previous night was at the reception desk, wearing a nametag that announced her as Cecile. She looked over at him with haughty grandeur. "Can I help you?"

"Yes," Tom said. "I would like to make a complaint."

She looked him up and down. "You do realize, sir, that we have a dress code for our guests? There might be a complaint against *you*."

He looked down at himself, stained and soggy and mangled. One of his sneakers had slipped off at some point; he had no memory of it happening. He could only imagine his face, white with pain and dripping with sweat. Not a pretty picture, no, and the absurdity of her criticizing him for it whipped his agony into anger.

He leaned forward, smearing the counter with water and sweat. "I don't care if anyone complains. I want someone to go downstairs to the *laverie* to get my briefcase, and I want to go to the American Hospital, and I want to know what the hell is going on here."

She looked at him, unperturbed. "If you read the card in your room, *monsieur*, you will know that we do not pick up — "

"Fuck the card in my room, and fuck you. You don't even work here, do you?" He shoved his ruined hand in her face. "This isn't on the card, either. I don't know who you are or what you're doing to me, but it ends. It ends right here, and it ends right now. And tomorrow morning I am checking out and moving to the *Sofitel* across the street, and someone at this desk will make that reservation for me as well. Am I understood?"

Her face might have been made of carved stone. "I am very sorry you feel that way, and that your stay has not been as pleasant as you would have hoped for. We will of course take care of everything. Now, would you like me to call an ambulance or a taxi for you?"

He looked at his hand again and nearly puked all over the desk. It wasn't a hand any more, just a bunch of bones in a bag at the end of his arm. The pain was so intense he could barely breathe. "Ambulance, I think," he said unsteadily.

"I'm going back up to my room to put some shoes on and get my wallet. And I still don't think you work here." The pain surged up his arm, putting a grey haze in front of his eyes and slowing his thoughts. He backed away from the reception desk toward the elevator, eyes still locked on the woman who sat there. "Make the call. I want to see you make the call."

She nodded graciously. "Of course." She picked up the phone and dialed. "'Allo? I need an ambulance for a guest at the *Suites du Bercy*. A broken hand, I think. No, he does not want a taxi. Very well, thank you." With a shake of her head, the woman hung up. "They will be here in twenty minutes, if you want to go get your identification from your room. They will not admit you without it."

"Fine, thank you." His back bumped against a wall. *Elevator bank*, he realized muzzily. *Got to get upstairs, there are no stairs.*

"Are you all right, sir?" the woman at the desk asked. There was no concern in her voice. "Should I have someone get your things while you wait here?"

"No!" He reached back and found the call button, pressed it and held it until it was slick with sweat. "No one's going in my room but me. Just have them get the briefcase from the laundry and…and we'll discuss the rest when I get back."

"Of course, sir. *Bonsoir.*" The elevator on the left chimed and its door opened. Tom stepped back into it, staring at her until the door slid shut and hid the reception desk from view. Blindly, he reached out until he could feel the 4 under his fingertip. He pressed it. Warmth told him it was lit. He could hear the pulleys start up, the signal that the elevator was beginning to move. *Good*, he thought. *Finally working right.* He sank down to the floor and closed his eyes. *Tomorrow I'm gone. Maybe tonight I can sleep at the hospital. Maybe…*

And as his eyes closed, he realized that all the numbers were bright, and that they were all shining red as the elevator went down, down, down.

The Deep End of the Shallow Water

We got out of the car just before sunset, a half-mile down a gravel service road that we shouldn't have been able to access. The spot where we'd stopped was a pretty one, a clearing in the second-growth pine woods that ran up the edge of the body of water we'd come to investigate. Soft dirt gave way to sticky clay down by the shoreline, and tree roots and tufts of grasses marked the bank all the way down. I could see reeds poking up through the water, stands of them here and there in places where the bottom was muddy enough to support plant life that ambitious. Across the way I could see the other side, red dirt and green grass underneath a purpling sky. It didn't look terribly far away.

"What do you think?" Lester said, and grinned. His boots crunched on the white rock of the road as he moseyed around to the trunk, the better to pop it and get out the equipment. "Is this spot perfect or what?"

I stared at him for a minute, then pointed at the water. "Lester," I said, "That is a pond."

He nodded. "So it is, Tyler, so it is." The trunk squealed open and his head disappeared inside as he began rummaging around.

"Let me try this again," I said, and took a couple of steps closer to the water. "Lester, this is a pond. Moreover, if I am reading that sign there correctly" — I pointed to an innocuous piece of metal that proclaimed the pond to be "Flood Control Structure #32 — "it's a man-made pond. Constructed, I might add, in 1966."

His head popped out for a moment, now adorned with night-vision goggles. "Is it, now?"

I took a deep breath, counted to ten, and let it go slowly. No sense letting Lester drive me crazy this early in the evening, I thought. He'd have all night to do it, if I let him.

"Lester," I said in my most reasonable voice, "stop that. What we are looking at is an artificial pond so small I could swim it without kicking my shoes off first. Hell, it's so shallow I could probably walk it, and never have to hold my breath. If there are any fish in there, they were artificially introduced when this thing was built. There is maybe enough biomass in that whole thing to support one moderately anorexic snapping turtle as the local apex predator, and that's it."

"Really." He sounded distracted, or at least he did until he straightened up too fast and bounced the back of his head off the inside of the trunk lid. "Owww."

"Oh, for God's sake." I stomped over to the car and relieved Lester of half the armload of equipment he was carrying. It was all there, the usual gear for this sort of trip: NVG, infrared cameras, motion sensors, microphones, and more. There was also a sealed thermos marked "rotten fish" in Lester's wife's handwriting, more proof that she was the most patient and sainted of women to walk this earth, and what looked like 250 feet of 50 pound test line with no other fishing equipment in sight. "You all right?"

"Yes, yes, fine. Just…put that down over there." He waved vaguely toward the water. "Ow."

"Don't think self-mutilation's going to get you out of answering me," I told him, even as I did what he said. "You still haven't told me why the hell you think we're going to find something here."

"Because it's there," he said, as if it were the most reasonable thing in the world, and slammed the trunk with casual malice. "That's the reason we go everywhere, right?"

I shook my head. "Lester, we go where there are genuine, verifiable sightings of cryptozoological specimens, not hysterical impossibilities."

He joined me at the top of the bank and deposited his load of gear next to mine. "You're absolutely correct, and again, that's why we're here. Give me a hand down?" Without waiting for me to answer, he slid down the muddy slope. His heels gouged long, smooth lines in the clay as he went.

I waited for him to find his footing, then started handing pieces of gear to him. "Les, we did not have a genuine, verifiable sighting here. We had a couple of drunk teenagers with a cell phone camera."

"And the images they recorded clearly show something in the water. Which is why we're here."

"For God's sake, Lester, where's the breeding population going to come from? Old packets of sea monkeys?"

He shook his head, and brushed his hands on the well-worn fishing vest he always wore on trips like these. "You're missing the point, my friend. Come on down here and I'll try to show you."

"Show me what?" I grumbled suspiciously, but by then I was already moving. "Another cell phone video?"

"No, not quite." My heels hit ground and I skidded backwards. Only Lester's hand caught me, stabilizing me from going over while I lurched to my feet. He said nothing until I was upright and steady, then gestured toward the far shore. "Now, look out there. What do you see?"

I peered out into the gathering dusk. Overhead, the sky had settled to a shade of deep-bruise purple, warning us that we were running out of light. The water's surface was still, an indigo mirror reflecting featureless heavens. Across the way, a single heron picked its fastidious way along the shoreline, pausing every so often to stab at something small and unseen. Frogs, maybe, or minnows.

"I see a pond," I said.

Lester shook his head. "No, you don't. You know there's a pond here, a crappy little hole in the ground they poured some water into, so that's all you'll let yourself think there can be. But what do you see?"

"Lester — " I started, but he shushed me.

"You see a flood control structure. Those kids? They saw a pond that's been here all their lives, dark and scary and with something they've never seen the bottom of. Maybe their older brothers told them that it had a monster in it, and they believed."

"Then they're idiots," I muttered, but Lester was rolling now.

"How deep is that water? What moves underneath it? What might have been buried, asleep in the muck for centuries before the return of the waters awakened it? From here, we don't know; they certainly don't, or they do, and their answers have nothing to do with what the engineers might say. Us? We can't know. All we see is that — " he waved out at the smooth surface of the pond before us — "and that reflects all our thoughts back at us. It's impenetrable, and beyond it lies whatever we can imagine living in those murky depths. Why shouldn't there be monsters here, if those kids want there to be some?"

"Because there can't be," I said weakly. "Because there's no room, and no food, and no history. There's a million reasons there can't be anything bigger than a catfish in there."

"Ah, but there can, if we want it to be there badly enough. That's the thing about monsters, you know. They come when they're called. When they're possible. When they're told that they've always been there."

I opened my mouth to tell him that he was crazy, that we'd agreed to do scientific investigation only, that I was done with this partnership if he was going to sprinkle magical pixie dust over everything I'd thought we'd stood for.

And from across the water, there was a splash. I looked up, just as Lester did, just in time to see the heron disappearing in a spray of black water. Its wings beat frantically against the water's surface for an instant and then it was gone. A handful of feathers floated into view, bright against the dark outline of a vast shape moving slowly to deeper water.

For a moment, neither of us said anything. Lester looked at me. I looked at the ground.

"Did you...see something," I heard myself asking.

Lester sounded noncommittal. "I might have."

"Right." I kicked a pebble toward the water. It hit with an audible thunk, then sank out of sight, instantly. "Why don't I go set up the equipment?"

"Why don't I help you?"

I shook my head. "Why don't you keep an eye on the water?"

Suburban Sprawl

Eight and a half hours to JFK, two more hours to Raleigh-Durham International, and the twenty-five minutes home were the hardest part of the trip back from Paris.

My bags were jumbled in the back seat of Lisa's car; I'd practically thrown them in there in my hurry to get home. She was driving, window down and long black hair whipping in the nighttime breeze. It was warm for October and the leaves were procrastinating on their annual change. I loved it, rolled down the window and took a deep breath. It smelled like home.

Lisa eased the car off the highway and onto the local road that would bring us to the house. It was a narrow two-laner, just twisty enough to make it interesting and overhung with pine trees that seemed to make the road their personal business. Here and there we passed houses set back from the road, sometimes so far into the dark that a mailbox was the only sign that they were there. Intersections were infrequent, equally local roads crossing one another on their own business, and if you didn't know where you were going, you had no business driving them.

"It's good to have you home," Lisa finally said, and flashed me a quick smile. "I missed you."

"I missed you, too," I told her, and meant it. "Accounting is going to have puppies when they see the phone bill."

"Accounting can go screw itself. Eight weeks in France with three days' warning? Paying for some phone time is the least they can do."

"It's a start," I agreed, and stretched. "Man, my back is killing me."

She chuckled. "Poor baby. When we get home, I'll rub it for you."

I grinned back at her. She was beautiful in the dark, the soft light from the dashboard giving her a luminous glow that was halfway to a halo. "If I tell you something else is stiff, would you rub that, too?"

"Depends if you ask nicely," she said primly, and sat up straighter. Up ahead, the headlights swept across the trees as the road curved left. Then, suddenly, the trees were gone. The lights passed over red earth and a white trailer, holding for a long instant, and then moving on.

"What's that?" I said, and pointed out to the right.

"Hmm?" She spared a half-second's glance, and then turned her attention back to the road. "I'm sorry. I thought I'd told you about that."

"That", I saw when we went past it, was an empty slash of red clay a quarter mile long and God knew how deep, stretching off into the dark. A single white trailer squatted along the roadside, and past it I could see the silhouettes of things that were either earthmovers or dinosaurs.

"That whole chunk of land. When I left, it was trees. What happened?" We sped past, but my eyes were glued to sight of dark earth in the moonlight. I turned and watched behind us, until a bend in the road put it out of sight.

Lisa thrummed her fingers against the steering wheel a couple of times before answering. "They're developing it. The sign went up two days after you left."

"I wasn't gone for that long," I said, incredulous. "Eight weeks shouldn't be enough time to chop down — "

"A hundred acres of forest, yes." She sounded irritated. "Apparently, it is. The signs went up, the trucks came in, and the trees went down. A week later, they pulled out the stumps. I give it a month before the first Subway opens for business." She flicked on the turn signal with more force than was strictly necessary. "And I'm glad to see you, too."

Something between a sigh and a cough forced its way out of my mouth. "I'm sorry, honey. I really am glad to be home. To be with you." My hand drifted over to her leg, settling just above her knee. With one finger, I started tracing small circles. "It's just, you know — when you're away for a while, you get a mental picture of home, and when it's not like that it's kind of jarring."

"I know," she said, and took one hand off the wheel to pat mine. "Honestly, I was kind of upset when it happened, too. We moved out here because there wasn't any development."

"And three years later, it shows up anyway." My fingers closed around hers as the car curved left onto the road that led to our house. "Inevitable, I suppose."

"I suppose," she said neutrally. Up ahead, I could see our mailbox shining in the headlights, the house beyond it obscured by a wild growth of shrubbery and tree. "And it's going to get worse. They'll put one mall in, then another, and then the whole area's going to be built up before we know it."

The car glided to a stop. Lisa let it idle as she looked over at me. "We could sell, you know. Do it now, before it gets too crazy, and buy something further out."

I squeezed her hand. "And in three years it happens all over again, and in the meantime we're going nuts on the commute. I don't know, babe. Besides, this is home."

She smiled. "Yeah, it is. Welcome home, sweetheart." She leaned forward and kissed me, soft and slow and a million other ways that reminded me that it was good to be back in the hinterlands of Creedmor.

We left my bags in the car. There was nothing in them that couldn't wait until morning.

* * *

Sunday I slept in, and let jet lag have its merry way with me. The bags came in, and I was vaguely aware of Lisa doing laundry-type things as I dozed. It was good just to hear the ordinary household rhythms, the comfortable sounds of home. It was also pleasant, I decided, to have someone else do the laundry for a change, and not to have to dig through my pockets for Euro coins in order to do so, but I decided to keep that observation to myself. Instead, I closed my eyes and let the noises lull me back to sleep.

Around eleven, Lisa marched into the bedroom, her coat on and her keys in her hand. The cats trailed in behind her, yowling their displeasure. "You still asleep?" she asked.

"Not anymore," I answered, and pulled the sheets up over my head. "Have some pity for a man who's still six time zones away."

"You're supposed to be six hours ahead, lazybutt. You should have been up hours ago." She grinned, and poked my foot under the comforter.

"I adjust quickly," I told her, and sat up. "I'd almost been over there long enough to forget you were a morning person, you know."

She gasped in mock horror. "It's a good thing you came back, then. Who knows what else you would have forgotten if you'd stayed much longer." The keys went into her jacket pocket, and she started the process of buttoning up. "I'm going to the supermarket, honey. There are a few things I didn't keep in the fridge when you weren't here."

I swung myself out of bed and stretched. "Like?"

"Beer, for one. Milk, for another. Just don't go into the kitchen until I get back, or you might decide to get back on a plane."

"No chance." I shambled over to where she stood and kissed her on the cheek. "Hurry back."

"I will," she said. "I'm glad you're home."

"Me, too." She turned and left. A minute after that, I heard the front door close with its distinctive hingey squeal, and I made my way over to the window. Lisa had already gotten to her car by the time I reached the sill, and I watched her drive off through the patchwork green.

An hour later, the phone rang. Against express orders, I'd wandered into the kitchen and ransacked the fridge for something edible, though the wall of soy milk cartons on the top shelf didn't offer much hope. Elbow-deep in the cheese drawer (the contents of which failed to include any actual cheese) and intent on my quarry, I ignored it until the answering machine picked up, and Lisa's voice came over the line.

"Sweetheart? Are you there? I hate to do this, but I need you to come pick me up. I've got a flat. It's terribly embarrassing and I'm sorry to ask you to — oh, I'm at the Winn Dixie on Pettigrew — but if you could come get me I'd really appreciate it. You have my cell number if you need to get a hold of me. Bye."

"Son of a bitch." I straightened up and shoved the drawer closed with one slippered foot. A strategic sniff told me I didn't need to bother with a shower before heading over. Pants, however, were a different story, and it was five minutes before I had my car out of the garage and rolling. The radio, which hadn't had its station changed off the local sports talk station since I'd bought the thing, yammered at me as I let reflex guide me back to the market. Some caller from Fuquay was very upset over something to do with something he'd seen at the State game the day before, and the way he was carrying on, you'd think it was the end of the world. Linebackers were involved, I think.

A minute gone, I went past that empty spot where the trees had been. "I don't know what they're thinking," the man on the radio announced. "It's like they don't know what they're dealing with here, or how important this is."

I shut off the radio and drove the rest of the way in silence.

* * *

Lisa's car was in a prime spot, three rows up from the front door and sagging badly on the driver side. Lisa herself stood next to it, arms crossed and eyes scanning the lot anxiously. When she saw me pull in, a smile of relief grew out of her worried frown, and she waved. I waved back, and found a spot not too far away and walked over. "What's the problem?"

She pointed. "Driver's front tire is flat. I noticed when I came out. And look at this." She beckoned me over and knelt down beside the wheel in question. "Bent rim," I said, and it wasn't a question. Something had given the wheel a hammer blow, to the point where a section of the rim was visibly flattened. No wonder the thing couldn't hold a seal or take a fix. "We're going to need to replace that."

"I know," she said, and stood. "How much is that going to cost?"

I shrugged. "About three hundred. Depends on the car, really." I scratched my chin and decided to shower and shave once I got back. "This wasn't a problem last night, was it?"

Lisa shook her head. "No, and it was fine this morning when I got into the car. I hit a pothole just past the intersection with Sheppard. Do you think that could have done it?"

I'd seen the pothole she was talking about on the way over. It was an axle eater, pure and simple, and it sure as hell hadn't been there when I left. "Yeah," I answered slowly. "If you hit it with any kind of speed. When's that monster getting fixed, anyway?"

"When the construction's done," she answered. "That's why the road looks like a pizza. The trucks have really torn it up, but there's no sense repairing the road if they're going to keep wrecking it."

"Beautiful." I turned and walked a few steps toward my car. "So in the meantime the rest of us get to play pinball with the roadbed." I sighed, straightened up, and turned around. "Here are my keys," I said, fishing in my pocket. "Let's move the groceries to my car. You can take them home. I'll change out the flat for the donut and get this over to a tire place."

"Are you sure?" She took the keys.

"Positive. Come on. We don't want the beer getting warm."

* * *

Monday morning meant rolling out of bed early, since I needed to get Lisa to work before heading in myself. I'd found a garage that was open on Sundays, but they needed to order the wheel to replace Lisa's bruised one, and that was going to take a couple of days.

So instead I found myself piloting my car toward Lisa's office, with her in the passenger seat fiddling with the CD player. "An all-star tribute to Johnny Cash? Supertramp? Live Styx? Honey, we really need to talk about your music collection."

I shrugged, and made a right. The nagging bare spot went by on the left, somehow looking even more naked and raw in the morning daylight. There had been showers around midnight, and the earthmovers sent up reddish blasts of mud as they maneuvered back and forth.

"I know that's fascinating, sweetie, but eyes on the road, please?" I jerked my attention back to the pavement in front of me, just in time to see the back end of a muck-encrusted dump truck looming up at me. Slamming on the brakes, I managed to avoid rear-ending him, but only barely. Lisa braced her hands against the dash and bounced once against her seat belt; I just cursed.

In front of us, unconcerned, the truck continued along.

"Jesus Christ," I spat. "How fast is he going? 20? 25, maybe? Isn't there a speed limit on the bottom end, too?"

"Easy, honey." Lisa was pale, but composed. "I forgot, you weren't used to that. It's pretty standard traffic around here now. They've got some houses going up on Maitland, and..." Her voice trailed off. I took a deep breath and stepped on the gas, gently. "Sorry. I should have warned you."

"No, no, you're right. I should have been paying attention." I turned the stereo down in the gesture of all frustrated male drivers since time immemorial, and tried to get a hold of myself. "I just wasn't expecting it, that's all."

"It's only going to be about a mile before he turns off for Maitland," she said softly.

"Until they start putting more stuff up here. Or the strip mall decides to expand. Or they cut down a bunch more trees and declare they're building Pine Manor Estates."

Carefully, Lisa nodded. "And that'll bring in more traffic, and the roads will still be lousy."

I stared straight ahead. "You're serious about moving, aren't you?"

"I don't know." The catch in her voice told me she most certainly did. "I guess the people who lived out here before they put up our neighborhood felt the same way about us. But that was just one development, and they kept a lot of trees. This is just...rapacious."

"It's all second-growth forest," I said, trying to keep my voice even. "This all used to be farmland. The woods came back. They could come back again."

"I don't want to wait a hundred years for that to happen," she snapped, and looked away.

Ahead of us, the truck slowed and farted a column of black exhaust into the air. Gingerly, it began the torturous process of a right turn, the driver belatedly throwing his turn signal on in case any cops were watching.

I waited until he was halfway around the corner, then floored it and swerved around him.

"Let me think about it," I said. "I'd like to be home a little while before it's not home any more."

"I know," she said. She didn't smile.

* * *

Midnight, and Lisa was asleep. I sat on the edge of the bed, watching moonlight fall through the window and wondering what the hell to do.

She was right, of course. Once the buildup started it wouldn't stop. They'd pave the area within an inch of its life, then move on down the road and do the same thing all over again. The shiny new buildings around here would be forgotten in favor of the shinier, newer ones up the strip, and aesthetics aside, the property values would go through the floor. After all, who wants to live near the mall people used to go to?

The logical part of my brain said to sell, to move further out and hope the builders went in another direction. The longer commute would be worth the saved aggravation, and the pleasure of seeing actual trees, as opposed to carefully landscaped Bartlett pears, every time I looked out the window. But part of me wanted to stay, wanted to stand our ground. We'd put years into this house, thousands of dollars and buckets of sweat, and I didn't want to just hand it off and run because some lozenge-shaped developer decided that two miles was too far to go for the nearest crafts store.

Besides, moving was a hell of a lot of work.

If only they hadn't started here. I thought about that ragged gash in the forest. It stood for more than the imminent arrival of convenient shopping, or even the annoyances of sharing the road with construction equipment and new neighbors. It was the opening salvo in the barrage being fired on the area.

Suddenly, wandering over to take a look at it seemed like a very good idea. I stood and shrugged myself into jeans and a t-shirt. The shirt drawer creaked as I slid it shut, and Lisa stirred.

"Mmmm?'

She rolled over, groped sleepily toward my side of the bed. I caught her hand in mine, leaned down and kissed it. "It's OK, sweetheart. I'm just going for a walk. Go back to sleep."

She tucked an elbow underneath her and half-propped herself up. "It's 3 AM," she protested muzzily. "It's dark."

Gently, I let her hand go and walked around the bed. "Mind the cats," she mumbled as I dropped down to my haunches in front of her.

"The cats are fine. I'll be fine. I just can't sleep, that's all. So I thought I'd go for a walk because that way I wouldn't wake you up."

She smiled. "Oops."

"Oops," I whispered back, and kissed her forehead. "Go back to sleep, sweetheart."

"Come back soon," she said, but her eyes were already closed and arms wrapped around her pillow. Within seconds, her breathing dropped into the slow regular pattern that told me she was dreaming.

I stared at her for a moment. Hair tousled, covers half-kicked off, a tiny puddle of drool on the pillow underneath her — she was the most beautiful thing I'd ever seen. She'd liked the trees when we came out here, liked how there were just a few islands of houses in a sea of green. Now the sea was draining away.

"This is for you, sweetheart," I murmured once I was sure she wouldn't hear me, and walked away.

Ginger was waiting for me at the bottom of the stairs, her tail fluffed out and her eyes expectant. "No playing now, kitty," I told her, and scritched under her collar. She meowed her frustration, and trotted back into the kitchen in hopes I'd follow her to the treat jar.

Instead, I shrugged into the jacket I'd left hanging on the banister and opened the front door. It creaked, as it always did, and Ginger yowled an answer to it. "You tell it, girl," I said, and then went out into the night.

The moon was just past full, which meant it was still riding high in the sky as I stepped out onto the street. Thin wisps of cloud gave it rakish stripes, with a double handful of stars for accent. I nodded in appreciation and started walking toward the future site of Westwood Commons.

What I was going to do, I had no idea. Piss on an earthmover, maybe, or throw a few rocks into the middle of the tidily scraped field. What else could I do? The trees were done, the stumps cleared, the land leveled, and even if someone suddenly drove a dump truck full of money up to my house, I wouldn't be able to purchase the land and let it grow wild again. Besides, next month they'd find another parcel down the road a ways and do the same thing all over again.

But, I told myself, I had to do something. Something to show that not everyone approved, that some of us didn't want another shopping center three minutes closer than the last one.

Something to tell the trees that they'd be missed.

The rubber of my sneaker soles slapped the pavement as I turned the corner. On the right, an unbroken line of trees waved gently in the breeze. On the left, the row of treetops only went halfway. The cutoff was savage, a vicious, arbitrary swipe into the green. It seemed abrupt somehow, half-finished, like they'd come back later and finish the job.

Come to think of it, they probably would.

A lone car sped past me with one headlight out, going too fast and weaving. It wasn't followed, not by police, not by anybody. Nobody came out this way in the middle of the night. There was no reason to, at least not yet. No doubt that would change soon enough, too.

A hundred steps, counted silently in my head, and I was halfway there. I could hear the trees creaking gently in the breeze. Frogs and cicadas went at it in the distance, both of them sounding vaguely alarmed. Otherwise, the only sounds were my feet on asphalt and the rush of blood in my ears. Every step I took got me madder. Why they hell would they do this? It's not like they'd make that much more money. It's not like we needed another EB and Subway and Office Depot six blocks from the last one. And they'd keep on doing it, too — leapfrogging shopping center after shopping center, further and further out and leaving abandoned, empty ones behind. No doubt they'd all meet sooner or later — lines of mini-malls marking the demarcation between cities, and all in the name of convenience.

Well, fuck that, I decided. Maybe there wasn't anything I could do. Maybe there wasn't anything anyone could do, not against the almighty dollar and the lure of cheap land. But that didn't mean they could pretend everything was all right. That didn't mean they could pretend that everyone liked what they were doing.

I stepped off the road, and onto the bare red clay of the cleared acres. I was on the makeshift "driveway" the trucks had moved, the ground rutted deep with the marks of their tires. On the right was the trailer they'd set up as a temporary office, no light shining from its windows. The trucks were parked dead ahead, lined up like soldiers awaiting inspection. And where twenty acres of second-growth woodland had been, there was nothing. Just flat red earth with tiny flags sticking out of it, no doubt marking where concrete slabs and sewage pipes would need to go. It was sterile. It was ugly. And I didn't imagine a string of chain bistros and pet stores improving it any.

The clay was hard-packed under my feet as I walked over toward the earthmoving equipment. The weight of the trucks had no doubt mashed it flat. The closer I got, the more I realized how huge the vehicles were — tires taller than I was, cabs ten feet off the ground. If you were going to fight the forest, you needed titans on your side, and here they were, resting. They looked harmless in the moonlight, big kids' toys left abandoned after a hard day of play.

I looked right, and they didn't seem so harmless.

The border between the cleared land and the forest was sharp, marked by a moraine of stones and branches that had been shoved off the developers' property. I walked over to it. The stones were fist sized and larger, inconveniences to the progress of the project.

They were, however, small enough to throw. I bent down and hefted one. It felt good in my hand, a little heavier than a baseball. No throwing a slider, then, I told myself, and heaved it.

It bounced off the side of a bulldozer with a clang, and fell to the ground. The sound was loud in the night, too loud. Cicadas hushed, frogs stopped chirping in the trees, and the noise echoed out over the empty land.

I dove across the line into the trees, half expecting searchlights to stab out and sirens to wail. Crouched behind the inadequate cover of a pine tree, breathing loudly enough that they could probably hear me in Chapel Hill, I waited.

Nothing happened. Nobody came by. No alarms went off. Somewhere in the distance, a dog barked a couple of times, then stopped. Slowly, the bugs and amphibians got back in their groove.

And eventually I got the balls to step back out there. Gingerly, I advanced toward the bulldozer. I wanted to see what I'd done. I wanted to see the mark I'd made, the symbol of my defiance.

Twenty feet away, and I couldn't see it. I edged closer. Ten feet. Still no sign. Five. Two.

And there it was, a tiny chip in the paint on the door of the driver's compartment. The rock, the one that had felt so good and heavy in my hand, lay on the ground nearby. There was a fleck of yellow on it. One fleck, and that was all.

I let out an expletive and tossed the rock back into the woods. It hit the brush with a pitiful thump, no doubt scaring the hell out of a rabbit or opossum or something equally furry and nocturnal. One chip in the paint. That was all. That was my big gesture.

That wasn't nearly enough.

I unzipped my pants, suddenly not caring if anyone saw me, and pissed on the tread. Absurdly, I found myself wishing I'd had another beer with dinner, so I could leave more of a mark. It ran down the side of the tread and puddled on the ground, pungent enough that it might even get noticed in the morning. Good, I thought to myself and zipped back up. Let some hardhat step in that first thing. It'll ruin his whole day.

I looked around to see what else I could do. Throwing rocks through cab windows was one possibility. Doing something to the trailer was another. And then my eyes swept across that empty, perfectly flat space, and I knew.

That's what I had to mess up. That's what I was looking for.

The dirt was perfectly smooth, soft and precise in its patterns. Someday there'd be storefronts rising from it, but not yet.

And if I were lucky, I'd be delaying it a little longer.

I ran, full tilt, out onto the field. I could feel my shoes sinking into the dirt with every step. Each stride marked it, made it impossible to lay a concrete foundation on, threw a delay into the work that would be done here. I ran in zig-zags back and forth, jumping up and down for emphasis until my breath was ragged in my lungs and my legs ached from the effort. I stood in the middle of the field, and surveyed my works.

The smooth clay was no longer smooth. Footprints were everywhere, stomped and gouged into the soil. It looked like an army of drunken ants had been through here, or a third-rate marching band. The field, in other words, was trashed.

Covered in footprints.

My footprints.

Cold sweat broke out on my forehead. My heart pounded. There were footprints, all right, hundreds of them, all of them matching the shoes I had on. They'd be noticed in the morning — that was the whole idea, after all — and the cops would be called, and plaster casts would be taken. And they'd ask around the neighborhood to see if anyone heard anything suspicious, and Lisa would tell them that I might have because I had taken a late-night walk, and then things would just get ugly.

"Oh, hell," The words just hissed out of me. Maybe I could tell Lisa what I'd done. She'd be furious. Maybe she'd lie to cover me. Maybe she wouldn't. It wasn't the sort of thing you should ask of your wife, though. After all, she'd liked the idea of closer shopping.

Without thinking, I dropped to my knees. Great, I thought, dirt on my jeans. More evidence. Despair flooded through me.

In the trailer, a light went on.

My breath caught in my throat.

The blinds at the rear window moved. Someone was in there, looking out.

I threw myself down to the ground, praying the earth would swallow me up and hide me. I could see it all now — the arrest, the humiliation, the need to pay for the extra work the company would do.

A shadow moved against the venetian, back and forth slowly. Someone was pacing. Someone couldn't sleep.

Pressing myself against the earth, I willed myself to lay still. The clay was cold against my cheek. I could feel it, could feel every inch where it touched me. It crumbled up inside my socks, got in between the buttons on my shirt, pressed into my ear and nose. I could taste it on my lips.

The latch on the trailer door clicked. Something creaked open. I swallowed in fear.

And suddenly, I could feel more than just the dirt against me. All of it spoke to me. I could understand its anger at being mashed down, its fear at the asphalt and concrete that soon would be coming. There was energy and power here, something angry and old and unable to help itself, and it was talking to me.

Use this, it said. Do something.

I closed my eyes and thought. Footsteps clunked down the wooden stairs at the trailer's front. Someone was coming down. A sharp sound told me a shotgun was being racked; whoever was coming was taking no chances.

I could feel something else in the soil now, something tiny and bright. They shone green in my mind's eye, brighter than the stars and sharper, too. It took me a long second to realize what they were, and then I understood.

Seeds.

A blink, and I knew them better. The land had been plowed over and sprayed and abused, but still there was life here. Here I could taste pine, there locust and sycamore. There were thousands of them, more than I could count or imagine. Each shone bright with potential, with the life they'd never had once the foundation slabs got laid down and the parking lot set up.

A shadow came around the side of the trailer. "Hey!" I could hear someone shout. "What are you doing out there?"

Everything, I thought.

I took the power the earth was offering me. Live, I told the seeds. All of you, live now.

And I let the power go.

The earth groaned. I could feel it shaking underneath me. In the distance, the man from the trailer raised his gun, the barrel waggling in silhouette as the ground twisted underneath his feet. "I'm warning you!" he shouted, and brought it in line to fire.

The ground exploded underneath him. A thousand explosions, each louder than the last, echoed across the space as red clay shrapnel burst into the air. Half-blinded, half-deafened, I curled in a ball and wrapped my hands over my head in a feeble attempt at protecting myself. What have you turned loose? I asked myself.

A second later, I knew.

The trees had come back. Stabbing out of the ground like the spears of a conquering army, they shot up into the night sky one after another, from street to property line and back again. Where they came up under the bulldozers and logging trucks, they grew broad and strong until they could just shrug the equipment away. Tortured metal gave shrieks of surprise as, one after another, the vehicles toppled over. Showers of glass burst out as saplings punched through cab windows, threading the needle from one side to the other and arching skyward. Chassis caught between the rapidly thickening trunks were crunched and crumpled, disappearing behind the greenery in seconds. Underbrush curled up and around, filling the spaces between the trees and hiding the broken, flattened, abused clay. I couldn't help but think of a blanket thrown over a nude and abused body, a desire to hide nakedness and shame, to cover up the bruises and scars.

The trailer was torn apart from the inside, a dozen branches bursting out on every side and flinging the cheap aluminum away as they burst through. For a moment, I saw the fragments carried up into the air as the trees grew, rushing toward the heavens as chunks of it tumbled heavily down.

As for the man with the gun, I heard him fire once. That's all. I don't think the trees were very happy with him.

Eventually, it stopped. By my watch, it was three minutes later. It had felt like three hours. And looking around at the trees that surrounded me, it looked like I had been there thirty years, maybe more.

"You're back," I whispered, and pulled myself to my feet. Every inch of me was covered in red mud — ground in, spattered, smeared, and crumbled. It was in my hair, on my face, and I could swear I felt crumbs of it in my ears. But it was nowhere else to be seen. Green was everywhere, softly whispering in the wind. A stranger would never know that the trees had been gone.

The neighbors would, of course. So would the construction company, and presumably the investors, and the insurance people, and God knows who else. They'd probably come back and try it again, but this time I didn't think the landscape would be quite so forgiving.

Around me, there was a clear space perhaps six feet from side to side. Only grass grew within it, though I could see creepers and thorn bushes at the edge, quivering. They wanted in, I think. They wanted me to leave.

So I obliged them. The path was just wide enough for me to get through, paved with moss and grass that the shrubs and vines swallowed after each step I took. I knew better than to look back. I don't think I would have liked what I'd see.

My feet hit blacktop, and I could hear the rush of the vegetation behind me.

The trees were gone from my mind now. I'd done what they'd — what both of us — had wanted me to. There was no need for further communication, not so much as a "don't come back" or a "thank you".

Right was home, I reminded myself, and started walking. I suddenly ached everywhere. Some of the red on my skin wasn't from the mud, I knew — the clay had hit like shotgun pellets, and I was going to have to spend some quality time with peroxide and Bactine before I did anything else. Cringing in anticipation, I dragged myself home.

By some miracle, Lisa was still asleep. I cleansed myself as quietly as I could, keeping the cursing to an absolute minimum. On the way home, I'd decided that if she asked about what happened, I'd answer — but that I sincerely hoped she wouldn't ask. And if I could wash up and slide back into bed without her waking, well, so much the better. She murmured something that might have been words as I pulled up the covers, something else as I draped my arm across her so that my hand cupped her breast.

"Don't worry, my dear," I told her. "Everything's taken care of. You'll see in the morning."

"Hmmmm," was all she said then, and for that I was grateful.

That night, I dreamed of explosions.

It was the shrieking that woke me up. Lisa was there, two fingers pulling the curtain on the bedroom window aside so she could see out into the street. Her other hand was over her mouth, and she was screaming wordlessly.

I threw myself out of bed. "What is it, babe? What's wrong?" Two stumbling steps got me to the window, and I yanked the curtains away.

Outside, there was green. Where the street had been, a jagged palisade of second-growth forest wove its way off into the distance. Trees spread out away from the road, where the houses and swing sets and decks of our neighbors had been. A couple of chimneys poked up through the pine and black locust, but that was all. No roofs, no driveways, no cars or lawns or decorative Bartlett pear trees planted for artistic effect. Just acres and acres of trees, as far as the eye could see.

Except around our house. The border of the property we'd bought was razor-sharp, free and clear of any growth I hadn't been ignoring for months already. No new trees here, no invasion of the forest or reclaiming of the land. The seeds buried underneath the cheap sod of the lawn and cheaper concrete of the driveway were going to stay there.

"My God." I could hear Lisa whimpering next to me. "My God. My God. My God. What happened, Jase, what happened out there?" She sagged into my arms. I held her, stroked her hair and told her it was going to be all right, that we, at least, were going to be fine. And all the while I stared out at the sea of leaves and pine needles that we indeed would be fine, the two of us. Everyone else in the world was screwed, but not us. Oh, I could see it. The trees I'd woken up had whispered to their neighbors, and to the seeds dreaming in the soil, and the notion had spread. They didn't need me any more. I'd just had to do it once. They'd take it from there. And now, no doubt, the trees were rising up everywhere, spreading out from that one lot in every direction. Raleigh was probably gone now, and Durham and Chapel Hill would follow. It would go up I-85 and out I-40, down the side streets and along the state roads and it wouldn't stop. When it got to the deserts, seeds on the wind would carry it across. When it got to the oceans, the currents would bear it, and the sargasso would repeat the knowledge to the algae on the side of each passing ship.

But not here. With cold certainty, I knew that we were safe, that we would always be safe. I'd set the avalanche rolling, after all — kicked the first pebble down the hill.

And the trees wanted to say "thank you" after all.

Fat Man on an Airplane

"I can make miracles," said the fat man in the aisle seat, sadly. "Small ones only, you see. But miracles nonetheless."

"That's...very interesting," Janice responded, and silently wished like hell that the plane would go faster. They'd sat on the tarmac at Dallas-Fort Worth for an hour before taking off, adding yet another delay to an already interminable trip. Four days in San Jose for a conference had left her with a small mountain of acquired business cards, a throbbing headache, and a deep disdain for her professional peers. She was in no mood for conversation, particularly not with a guy who clearly used anyone next to him as a shrink. His habit of slopping his forearm over their shared armrest didn't endear him to her, either. Grimacing, she slid herself a half-inch to the left and prayed for a sudden emergency landing.

"It's quite true, I assure you." She felt, rather than saw him nod, and despite herself, turned to face him.

Her first impression of the man was that he'd been made like a snowman, globes of various sizes all rolled up and stuck together under sweaty pink skin. He was going bald, and his attempt at a beard didn't do much to hide his chins. What was left of his hair was black, like his shirt, a polo with a bland corporate logo over the left breast. Janice *thought* he was wearing jeans, but wasn't willing to look closer in order to resolve the issue.

"Beller. Adam Beller," the man wheezed, and extended a large pink hand in her direction. Gingerly, Janice took it. His skin was soft and smooth, and his handshake weak. His palm, Janice noticed, was moist, and she surreptitiously wiped her hand on her skirt after he let go.

"Janice Vance," she replied, wondering why she'd given her real name.

"It is a pleasure to make your acquaintance, Janice," Adam wheezed. "My apologies for taking over the armrest. These seats aren't built for people like me."

"And there's not enough leg space for anyone," she replied in her best make-nice voice. *Now, now*, her conscience told her. *At least he's trying to be polite.*

Beller chuckled, a liquid sound that seemed to shake all of his loose, flabby flesh. "Too true. For me, air travel is balanced somewhere between boring and painful." He paused and neatly snagged the elbow of a passing flight attendant. "More water, if you please," he puffed, and released her. She scurried off toward the galley.

Janice looked after her in envy, but then Beller started speaking again, and she felt compelled to meet his eyes.

"I do work miracles," he said, and shook his head sadly. Wattles of flesh shook in sympathy. "The catch is, I can only do small ones."

"Small...miracles." Janice's thoughts came to a screeching halt. She debated demanding another seat right now, contemplated laughing in the fat man's face. "I'm not sure what you mean," was what finally passed her lips, and she winced as she realized this meant Beller would likely launch into a fuller explanation.

"Miracles," he said, and waggled his fingers for effect. "Things that happen that should not happen. Some people call it magic, but I prefer not to be mixed up with the rabbit-in-a-hat crowd. People ask me to do something, if they know what I can do, and I make it so. Sometimes."

"I've been called on to do a few miracles in my day, Mr. Beller." She felt the annoyance creep into her voice but didn't much care. "Most of them involved shaking loose deliverables from people who swore up and down that they didn't exist."

"Those aren't miracles," Beller said, and pointed a fat finger at her in reprimand. "That's just good work. Or bad work on their part, though I'd prefer to give you credit. But I'm talking the sort of thing that can't be explained, Miss Vance. Water into wine, though in my case it would probably be a wine cooler."

He laughed then, and the whole row of seats shook with him as he did.

* * *

Down in the dark, Gary ran. He wasn't a thin man anymore, but now he ran like a deer. Breath burned in his lungs. He didn't care. Over fallen logs, through thickets and thorn bushes, he ran.

Because something was behind him. Something was hunting him.

Something was gaining.

* * *

Janice turned her face to the window. *That's it*, she told herself. *You tried to be nice, but he's certifiable. No good deed goes unpunished.* She'd had enough of Beller's ravings; looking at him would only encourage him. For the rest of the flight, she'd stare out the window and count the street lights down below.

They, at least, were silent.

Beller caught the hint, it seemed. He said nothing more to her, but thanked the flight attendant noisily when she returned with his water. Occasionally, she could hear him slurp at it.

She tried to ignore him, tried to pretend she didn't feel his eyes boring into her back. It didn't work. His presence was inescapable.

Below her, as if conspiring with Beller, thin wisps of cloud wove themselves into thick sheets. They drifted across her view, shrouding the lights below.

Outside the plane, there was nothing to see. Inside, there was nothing but Beller.

Janice shrugged, took a deep breath. Only then did she turn.

Beller was looking at her. He was smiling.

* * *

A stump Gary didn't see caught his foot as he ran. The impact knocked him to the ground and sent stars of pain shooting out behind his eyes. He hit hard, shoulder first, and rolled a dozen feet down the wooded slope. Behind him, the thing that chased him let out a howl. Wolves might have howled like that, Gary thought, ten thousand years ago.

Big wolves.

Gary got up and started running again.

* * *

"Fine, fine." Janice threw one hand in the air; the other would have smacked against Beller's flesh if she'd tried. "You do miracles. Whatever."

"But dear lady," Beller said in a tone that suggested he was deeply hurt, "it's true. As much as I wish it were otherwise — that my talent were more useful, or nonexistent — it is what it is. And that is the knack of making small miracles."

"Really." Janice set her lips in a thin line. "That's the sort of claim that usually gets followed by a demand for proof."

Beller chuckled. "Well, for one thing I can make a cloud appear where none is supposed to be, or make it go away just as suddenly."

"Right."

The fat man flung his hands up in the air. "I have no reason to lie. Look out your window, Miss Vance."

She looked.

The clouds were gone.

* * *

Each breath Gary took felt like it cut sideways in his throat. He cursed himself for his idiot idea of going camping alone, for his double-idiot idea of setting up way the hell and gone off in the woods. His tent and his gear were probably miles behind him. He'd never find them again, even if he escaped.

It had come out of the woods just before midnight, a dark shape against the darker trees. It had sniffed the air. Snarled. And started walking towards him.

He couldn't tell what it was then, just what it wasn't. Not a bear; too big. Wolf-like was the best word for it, but it wasn't a wolf, either. Wolves didn't stand six feet tall at the shoulder, or flow like a hungry cloud over the forest floor. It was just a shape in the darkness.

Darkness.

Somewhere in his brain, something sparked. The thing, whatever it was, stuck to the shadows. Even as it chased him, it avoided the tiny patches of thin moonlight that made it through the trees.

Maybe...

Maybe if he found light, that would hold it off.

There were access roads in the forest, he knew. Some of them had light posts. Some of them had lights.

Up ahead, Gary thought he saw something shine. He ran faster.

* * *

"That's not a miracle," Janice said. "That's meteorology, and a fast-moving plane."

Beller took another loud sip of water. "That's one possibility," he said cautiously, "though in this case, not the right one." He sighed, and shook his head ponderously. "I'm going to have to provide a demonstration, aren't I? All right. What do you want me to do?"

Janice exhaled sharply. She'd hoped to shut Beller up. Instead, he seemed disappointed but serene.

Like he'd known it would come down to this.

She rubbed her eyes. Fine. He wanted a request, she'd give him one.

"Down there," she said, and waved toward the window. "One of those lights. Make it go out. Now."

Beller heaved his bulk toward her, his face craning toward the window. "The area we're passing over isn't exactly a bustling metropolis. There aren't a lot of lights down there," he said. He sounded worried. "You might miss your proof, even if I provide it. Are you sure this is what you want?"

"Absolutely." Janice felt herself nodding. "Not a lot of lights means that I'll notice the one you plunk — if you do it. Trust me, if it works, I'll see it."

Breath exploded out of the fat man. "Fine." He sounded tired. "A dead light it is."

He closed his eyes. Janice looked out the window, surprised at how anxious she was.

Below her were a handful of lights, scattered across the landscape like a gemcutter's leavings. "That one," she said, even though she knew Beller couldn't see her. "That one," she repeated, and tapped the glass.

* * *

The light was up ahead. Gary could see it. It was sickly yellow and buzzing like a nest of hornets, but as far as he was concerned, it was the sun, the moon and the stars all rolled into one. The thing pursuing him knew he was close, too. Its howls got more frequent, more vicious, more *hungry*.

A few more steps.

Into the light.

Almost there, he told himself. *Almost there*.

With a final burst of speed, he stumbled onto the dirt road. The light post stood overhead, its lamp casting its benediction down on him.

"Safe," he wheezed to himself, and stood there, panting. "I'll just stay here til morning. Safe."

He sank to the ground.

The light went out.

Something growled.

* * *

Far below, the light chosen winked out. Janice let out a small cry of surprise, then felt her face flush with embarrassment. She quickly sagged back into her seat, away from the window, and looked over at Beller.

The fat man looked unhappy. He opened his eyes, then turned to look at her. "You have your proof now," he grunted. "You picked one out. I made it disappear. Simple, really, though not much use in everyday affairs."

Janice nodded, suddenly overwhelmed with sympathy. "Are you sure?" she said. "I mean, if you could do that..." Her voice trailed off.

"Unimportant wishes are all I can do, you see." He fumbled in his pocket, then drew out a sweat-stained handkerchief to mop his brow. "Small miracles, that's all."

"Ah," she said. "I'm sorry I doubted you," she added, softly.

"Everyone does," Beller replied, then closed his eyes. Janice watched him for a moment, then turned back to the window, and to the spot where that light had been.

Now it was just darkness, sliding away behind her.

* * *

Gary stood.

It was close now. There was no more sense in running. *Might as well try to fight here*, he thought, and raised his fists to defend himself.

Overhead, he could see the lights of an airplane, passing by. They shone brightly against the night sky for a moment, then passed behind the stand of trees that lined the road and were gone.

Let the House Sing Me To Sleep

To: The_Real_Dennis
From: Oldgent34
Time: 05/08/09 19:42:06
Subject: Where R U?
Hey, Dennis:

How's it going, bro? I haven't seen you online for a while. What's the matter? Afraid the wife will see you get pwned and lose interest?

Drop me a line when you get a chance, or throw me a game invite next time you're on. Everyone misses kicking your ass.

– Barry

To: Oldgent34
From: The_Real_Dennis
Time: 05/08/09 11:13:47
Subject: re: Where R U?

Dude. Nobody says pwned any more. What are you, 14?

Sorry I haven't been on a lot lately. Chrissie's travel schedule is about to pick up, and when she's home, I like to spend as much time with her as I can. Apparently the Portland office is a complete charlie foxtrot, and she got picked to clean up the mess.

So the bad news is that my wife is probably going to be on the road half the time from now on. The good news is that I should have more chances to frag while she's gone.

See you online.

To: The_Real_Dennis
From: Oldgent34
Time: 05/10/09 16:32:04
Subject: re: Where R U?
Y0.

We're playing tonight @8. Danny's hosting. Just letting you know.

To: Oldgent34
From: The_Real_Dennis
Time: 05/10/09 11:13:47
Subject: re: Where R U?
Chrissie took off this morning, so I'll be there. Thanks for the heads-up.
btw, why the fuck are we still playing PC? Console's where it's at.

To: The_Real_Dennis
From: Oldgent34
Time: 05/11/09 23:09:55
Subject: U Suck
Consoles are for whiny teenagers whose balls haven't dropped. PC is for grownups. Leave your midlife crisis out of this.

Also, you have been two-fisting tallboys of suck, my friend. Doctor Barry prescribes a serious dose of single-player action until you get your chops back. I haven't seen you raped like that since you were a n00b. What's the deal?

To: Oldgent34
From: The_Real_Dennis
Time: 05/12/09 00:31:42
Subject: Sucking
You wouldn't believe me if I told you.

To: The_Real_Dennis
From: Oldgent34
Time: 05/12/09 10:49:22
Subject: Re: Sucking
Try me. The clan needs you at your best. So talk to me. Maybe I can help straighten your shit out.

To: Oldgent34
From: The_Real_Dennis
Time: 05/12/09 17:09:25
Subject: It's Just st00pid
Ah, don't worry about it. I'm just not getting a lot of sleep these days, and it's throwing everything else off. Chrissie's out of town and I have to take care of everything while she's gone, and stuff's just, I dunno. Off.

Screw it. I'll be fine. 2100 HRS — team domination, right? See you then.

To: The_Real_Dennis
From: Oldgent34

Time: 05/12/09 17:17:18
Subject: St00pid is as st00pid does
D00d. Take a nap. They have pills for this sort of thing, you know?

To: Oldgent34
From: The_Real_Dennis
Time: 05/12/09 18:02:37
Subject: Whatever
She'll be home in three days. I'll be fine.

To: Oldgent34
From: The_Real_Dennis
Time: 05/14/09 18:27:53
Subject: Wh00ps
OK, she's not coming home. They extended her trip by a week. Tonight I try Tylenol PM, tomorrow night, Gentleman Jack.

I'm telling you, though, it's just weird. I never have any trouble sleeping when she's home. But when she's gone, I dunno. The place just feels different. It's too big. It's empty, and it knows it.

Screw it. I'm a dumbass. Forget I said anything.

To: The_Real_Dennis
From: Oldgent34
Time: 05/14/09 20:56:04
Subject: MEOW MEOW MEOW
Correction. You do not sound like a dumbass. You sound whipped. There's a difference.

To: Oldgent34
From: The_Real_Dennis
Time: 05/14/09 21:47:14
Subject: Thought You Might Say That
At least I'm getting some from somebody besides Rosie Palm, on those occasions when the wife unit is actually home. Don't be jealous. It makes you sound petty.

I tell you, though, it's not just the fact that she's out of town. There's something weird about the house when she's not here.

To: The_Real_Dennis
From: Oldgent34
Time: 05/14/09 23:57:44

Subject: Excuses, Excuses
EOM

To: Oldgent34
From: The_Real_Dennis
Time: 05/15/09 01:04:00
Subject: Fuck U 2
She's due back on Saturday, so I'll be AFK for a while. Say hi to your favorite bottle of lotion for me. I'm sure you two will have a lovely time together.

To: Oldgent34
From: The_Real_Dennis
Time: 05/16/09 16:32:33
Subject: Game 2 Nite?
So, what maps are we playing tonight?

To: The_Real_Dennis
From: Oldgent34
Time: 05/16/09 18:12:21
Subject: WTF?
I thought wifey was back in town and you weren't allowed to play until you got your fill of sweet loving? WTFU w/ that?

To: Oldgent34
From: The_Real_Dennis
Time: 05/16/09 18:19:42
Subject: Re: WTF?
She's back in Portland. Some kind of software emergency, apparently. Real sudden. And since she's gone and I'm not going to get any sleep tonight, I figure I might as well get out some of my aggression wasting punk-ass n00bs.

To: The_Real_Dennis
From: Oldgent34
Time: 05/16/09 19:13:53
Subject: Re: Re: WTF?
Does this mean your house is still acting all weird and crap when she's gone?

To: Oldgent34
From: The_Real_Dennis
Time: 05/16/09 19:17:12
Subject: Dunno

But I'm going to find out tonight, I guess. See you online.

To: The_Real_Dennis
From: Oldgent34
Time: 05/18/09 09:44:12
Subject: So?
EOM

To: Oldgent34
From: The_Real_Dennis
Time: 05/18/09 10:26:19
Subject: It's All Fucked Up
To answer your last question, yeah, there's still something screwy going on in the house when she's gone. I called her about it last night, but she said it was cute how I missed her, and that she had to run. Some kind of business dinner, I think.

To: The_Real_Dennis
From: Oldgent34
Time: 05/18/09 22:58:01
Subject: Your House
Define "fucked up" for your old college buddy, would you? I'm getting st00pid in my old age.

To: Oldgent34
From: The_Real_Dennis
Time: 05/19/09 03:14:35
Subject: Re: Your House
You really want to know? OK, but you're going to laugh your ass off at me.

I know this sounds crazy, but just hear me out. You know how a house makes noises at night? After a while, you get used to the noises the place you're living in makes. You know what the water heater and the pipes and everything else sound like, and you get used to it, right? Right.

Except our place makes different noises when she's gone, and it's freaky. I know what the house is supposed to sound like at night, and it doesn't sound like that when she's gone, and the whole thing just gets on my nerves. I'll be right on the edge of falling asleep, and then all of a sudden there's a thunk or something I wasn't expecting, and I'm wide awake again.

So there it is. You can start making fun of me now.

To: The_Real_Dennis

From: Oldgent34
Time: 05/21/09 12:07:25
Subject: Dumbass

I was wrong, you are a dumbass. How's this for a theory: You can't sleep without your slamp at home, so you stay up later, which means you're hearing the house at a different time than usual. That means you hear different things and, since you look for crap to freak out 24/7, you're freaking out about it.

Get your drink on before bed. It'll knock your ass out and you won't worry about this crap any more.

To: Oldgent34
From: The_Real_Dennis
Time: 05/24/09 13:15:41
Subject: Hahaha

I married her, man. She's not a slampiece once you put a ring on it.

Which reminds me — I need to ship some of her clothes out to her in Portland. It's now an official "Extended stay assignment." With attached bonus, I might add, but it's still a pain in the ass.

To: The_Real_Dennis
From: Oldgent34
Time: 05/25/09 13:57:01
Subject: You sound real thrilled...

Isn't her company supposed to, like, buy her clothes and crap? Maybe you should take the stuff out to her. You know, surprise her. Let the house make noise to itself for a little while.

And you can take the laptop with, so you can still get some gametime in. Just don't play any shooters while you're on the plane — that "tango down" shit freaks the stewardesses out.

To: Oldgent34
From: The_Real_Dennis
Time: 05/25/09 14:41:32
Subject: Not a bad idea

"Cabin crew." They're cabin crew now.

Thanks for the suggestion, Barry. I'll talk to you from Portland.

To: The_Real_Dennis
From: Oldgent34
Time: 05/29/09 20:05:46
Subject: So...

How's it going? Was she surprised to see you? When are you going to stop screwing like bunnies and get back online? We need you, man.

To: Oldgent34
From: The_Real_Dennis
Time: 05/30/09 01:47:52
Subject: Tell you what…
I'm gonna mail you a shovel, and when you get it, start digging up.

The short version: I got to Portland. Took a cab to her hotel. Thought I'd surprise her.

I did. Surprised the guy in the room with her, too. Apparently he's the Portland office sysadmin. They fell in love over a server upgrade.

Fuck. Fuck fuck fuckity fuck fuck fuck.

We playing tonight or what?

To: The_Real_Dennis
From: Oldgent34
Time: 06/01/09 09:34:11
Subject: Well, fuck
I'm sorry, man. I'm really sorry. If I knew, there's no way I would have told you to go out there to see her. Or something. Fuckity fuck fuck fuck says it pretty good.

Let me know if I can do anything, OK?

To: Oldgent34
From: The_Real_Dennis
Time: 06/02/09 02:11:09
Subject: It's fine
Better to find out now, you know?

I got myself a lawyer. Hopefully we can settle this all friendly, what with her having found someone new and everything. Did I mention she wants to stay out in Portland?

I'll tell you one thing. The house is definitely sounding weirder since I got back. More thumps. Louder ones, too. It's like they're getting closer or something.

To: The_Real_Dennis
From: Oldgent34
Time: 06/02/09 11:23:05
Subject: Duh
If you weren't sleeping before, you ain't sleeping now. And if you're associating those noises with her not being there, it doesn't take a genius to see where this is

going.

But just for shits and grins, tell me what the noises sound like.

To: Oldgent34
From: The_Real_Dennis
Time: 06/03/09 00:34:21
Subject: You Really Wanna Know?

They sound unhappy. Angry. Like the vents are wheezing and coughing, and something's splintering up in the walls, and something's banging on in the inside of the sheetrock. And once in a while there's this crack like a gunshot, and it wakes me right up. Or there's creaking that sounds like someone walking along the upstairs hallway. I know it's just the house settling, but it's freaking me the fuck out.

Only when she's not there, though.

Which means all the time now.

To: The_Real_Dennis
From: Oldgent34
Time: 06/04/09 09:54:01
Subject: OK that's freaky

And it doesn't make these sounds when she's home? You *sure* it's not just you staying up later and hearing different crap?

To: Oldgent34
From: The_Real_Dennis
Time: 06/13/09 23:14:07
Subject: Yes I'm sure

She came home to get her stuff.

The noises stopped. The house seemed — I don't have a better word for it — happy.

She stayed a week. I thought we could work things out. We even slept in the same bed. But at the end of the week, she told me she'd filed for divorce and that she was going back to Portland to be with Armand.

Can you believe it? I lost my wife to a guy named fucking Armand.

Oh, and she said that it wasn't my fault and that I was a very sweet guy and that she was hoping that the divorce would be amicable. Just fucking great, you know?

I drove her to the airport on Sunday.

Sunday night, the noises came back.

They were louder. A lot louder.

To: The_Real_Dennis
From: Oldgent34
Time: 06/14/09 11:17:41
Subject: Man that's messed up
You've got it bad, bro. No wonder you're hearing things.
I recommend you start playing again. Frag yourself blind. Just don't mope and shit.

To: Oldgent34
From: The_Real_Dennis
Time: 06/15/09 01:55:19
Subject: I am not hearing things
Or if I am, the things I'm hearing are real.
Couldn't get any sleep last light. The house was making noises all night long. Every time I shut my eyes, there'd be a sound like one of the support beams going, or footsteps on the roof over the master bedroom, or the hot water pipes slamming themselves around inside the walls. When the heater starts up now, it makes a sound like a gun going off. I had a guy in to look at it yesterday and he said it's fine, that it should be good for ten more years. But every night, the place sounds like it's tearing itself apart.
I don't know. Maybe it misses her.

To: The_Real_Dennis
From: Oldgent34
Time: 06/16/09 14:33:04
Subject: Wrong
No. /You/ miss her. This is all in your head.
I'll tell you what. You've got a mic on your system. Download a recording ap. Set a timer to start up recording in the middle of the night. Then take a listen in the morning.
You know what you're gonna hear? Nada. Trust me on this one.
Btw, how's it going with the lawyer?

To: Oldgent34
From: The_Real_Dennis
Time: 06/19/09 01:28:43
Subject: I need to stop taking your advice
So I followed your advice, which was fucking stupid, as usual. I set up the rig to start dumping to audio file precisely at 1 AM. You know, dead hour of the night, wee hours of the morning, all that good crap. Meanwhile, I'm laying awake in bed like a dumbass, waiting for the show to start.

It hits 1. I hear the computer start up. I hear the house go batshit. I wait 20 minutes, long enough to get a decent sample, and then I go to shut the system down.

Guess what? When I get there, the fucking hard drive is fried. Won't even spin up. I'm writing from the old beater rig I never got around to throwing out when I upgraded. So there goes your proof and my tax records. Happy now?

In better news (not), my lawyer says everything's fine and I should get whatever I want. She doesn't seem inclined to contest. The best news to come out of that is that if we divide assets down the middle, we sell the house and split the proceeds. Then this place becomes someone else's problem.

To: The_Real_Dennis
From: Oldgent34
Time: 06/21/09 11:49:52
Subject: Calm Down

A fried HD does not mean your house is haunted. It means you need to replace that POS rig you've been running on for the last three years. You DID make backups of your tax records, right, Einstein? And why the hell should you sell the place? Suck it up, Spartacus. It's your house. Live there.

To: Oldgent34
From: The_Real_Dennis
Time: 06/23/09 01:21:28
Subject: Interesting

One of our IT guys at work took a look at the drive and managed to extract the data off it. The sound file was mostly intact. It's too big to mail, but I've posted it on the private page on my site. Password is SUCKITBARRY. Pull it down and take a listen, then tell me what you think.

And her lawyer is going to make her first offer tomorrow.

To: The_Real_Dennis
From: Oldgent34
Time: 06/25/09 11:31:34
Subject: Whatever you thought you heard in that file…

…you did not hear a voice. You definitely did not hear a voice telling you to bring her back. And I didn't, either.

Unless, of course, you made that whole thing up, in which case, fuck you. I know you're going through a rough time, but that's low, man. Seriously low.

To: Oldgent34
From: The_Real_Dennis

Time: 06/27/09 03:12:58
Subject: You heard it too?
But it said something different to me.

To: The_Real_Dennis
From: Oldgent34
Time: 06/29/09 10:01:27
Subject: Dude

If you want me to come out there, say the word. This is getting entirely too fucked up. Whatever you thought you heard, you /thought/ you heard. You got it? It's just a house. Yeah, it makes noises at night, but every house makes noises at night. Yeah, you can't sleep because your life is pretty fucked up, but you have to deal with what's really going on, not this make-believe bullcrap.

Go see a doctor. Take some sleeping pills or something. Spend a night in a hotel and get your shit together, because the longer you go without a decent night's sleep, the more weird shit you're going to think you hear. And I say again, you are *not* actually hearing it.

And remember, I've got your back, bro.

To: Oldgent34
From: The_Real_Dennis
Time: 07/01/09 00:29:14
Subject: Maybe third time?

Sleeping pills sound like a decent idea. If this keeps up, I'll try them. You're right. I'm a wreck. If I don't get some sleep soon, I don't know what I'll do. I swear, the noises are getting worse, and the voices…you don't have to listen hard to hear them any more. They want me out of the house, Barry. They want me out and they want her in and that's all there is to it.

That's the really sick part, too. My lawyer called the offer from hers "the most generous he'd ever seen." Split the liquid assets, she keeps the stuff she entered the marriage with, she gets a couple of the stocks — and I get the house. Because, apparently, it's unfair to make me move out because she found someone else, and because she feels bad because she's the one who was fucking around. Her lawyer must have thought she was crazy for making the offer. Mine thinks I'm crazy for not jumping on it.

But I don't want the house.

No. That's not right.

The house doesn't want me.

To: The_Real_Dennis
From: Oldgent34

Time: 07/03/09 13:54:00
Subject: Fuck the house

It's a house. Fine. You don't want it? Fix it up and sell it after the divorce is final and she can't go after any of the cash. But in the meantime, it's just a fucking house. It doesn't want anything. It can't want anything, no matter how loud the pipes bang at night. You know why? BECAUSE IT'S A FUCKING HOUSE.

I'm your friend and I love you like a brother, man, but you've gotta stop being such a pussy.

To: Oldgent34
From: The_Real_Dennis
Time: 07/05/09 00:05:18
Subject: Easy 4 U 2 say

I told my lawyer to take the offer. I'll see if I can gut this out. Sooner or later, the house has to realize she's not coming back, right? I mean, yeah, she did all of the decoration, and she was the one who wanted the house in the first place, but it's not like I've ever punched a hole in a wall or screwed up some wiring or anything. It's not like I've ever done anything to the house. Hell, I'm not even the one who traveled all the time and left it. I was the one who stayed home and took care of the place. If the house should like anyone, it should like me. Not her, me.

Screw Chrissie. It's my house. It always has been. And if I can knock some sense into this place, it always will be.

To: The_Real_Dennis
From: Oldgent34
Time: 07/06/09 10:50:14
Subject: You're scaring me, man

Are you sure you don't want me to come down there? I can do the remote office thing, you know. Just until everything gets settled. Cause it sounds like you should *not* be alone right now.

To: Oldgent34
From: The_Real_Dennis
Time: 07/08/09 23:52:44
Subject: It's fine

I'll be all right. Tonight I'm gonna take your advice and knock my ass out. Let the place make all the noise it wants. I'm gonna sleep right through it. And I'll keep doing that until it realizes that my two-timing bitch of an ex-wife — cause that's how I should be thinking of her, right? My ex wife? Cause she's not my wife any more and wouldn't be, even if I changed my name to Armand or some shit like that — is gone and she ain't coming back. Not now, not ever.

Scuse me. It's midnight. Gonna go to bed. Thanks for listening. You're a pal, bro.

To: The_Real_Dennis
From: Oldgent34
Time: 07/08/09 23:57:38
Subject: ???
Are you faced? Damnit, you know better than to write email when you're drunk.

To: The_Real_Dennis
From: Oldgent34
Time: 07/09/09 11:45:12
Subject: ?!?!
Dude! Are you there? Talk to me, man.

To: The_Real_Dennis
From: Oldgent34
Time: 07/10/09 14:00:23
Subject: !!!
Dennis, please tell me you didn't get your drink on before you took those sleeping pills the other night. Just email me or call or send an IM or something to let me know you're all right, OK? I've called four times and you haven't picked up and this shit just ain't funny.

Talk to me, will you?

To: The_Real_Dennis
From: Oldgent34
Time: 07/12/09 15:07:22
Subjcct: ...
Dennis?

To: Oldgent34
From: CMatisse
Time: 07/14/09 21:07:45
Subject: Bad News
Hi.

I hope this is the right email. I found it in Dennis' address book. If the person reading this isn't Barry Harmon, I'm sorry. It's a hell of an email to send a complete stranger.

This is Chrissie Matisse. In case you don't remember, I was Dennis' wife. We filed for divorce recently, but I guess you knew that. Dennis talked about you a lot. I'm sure he would have told you what was going on, and, whatever you think of me, you have to understand that I never wanted anything like this. Dennis was a good man, and I was really hoping that we'd be able to stay friends after everything. I was really hoping there was going to be an "after".

Which, I suppose, is just me avoiding saying what you've probably already figured out. The police found Dennis the other morning. Apparently he'd taken some sleeping pills, and he'd been drinking, and...they say it was peaceful and he died in his sleep and that it didn't look like he meant to do it. Accidental death is what they told me. I'm sorry you have to learn about it this way, but that's how we do these things these days, I guess.

Anyway, the funeral is going to be here on the 22nd. I'd very much like it if you could attend. I know how important you were to Dennis and how much your friendship meant to him, and it would mean a lot if you were here. There are some things of Dennis' at the house that I think he would have wanted you to have, too, so maybe you could come by and pick those up as well. And I know all of this is really short notice, so if you need a place to stay you can stay here, at the house. There's lots of extra room.

Oh, God. I just realized how that sounded. I'm sorry. It's just all been a mess, what with the divorce and Dennis and everything, and having to unload the house, and I don't think I've gotten a decent night's sleep since I've gotten back. I can't sleep a wink in this place, not any more. It's so quiet without Dennis here, it's like a tomb. But I'm going to need to be here for a while, at least. Just until everything gets sorted out. It shouldn't be too long.

Anyway, please let me know if you'll be attending the funeral. It really would mean a lot if you came. And feel free to email back at any time. Trust me. I'll be up.

Sincerely,
Chrissie Matisse

Good Advice

"You got beaten up a lot as a kid, didn't you?'

That's what Jerry Brower asked me, and the entire Central Carolina Writers' Workshop burst into nervous laughter.

I looked up from the short sketch I'd been reading from and turned to face my questioner. Jerry Brower sat at the end of the table, down past a gauntlet of laughing faces. He, at least, wasn't laughing, and for that I was silently, desperately grateful. I nodded to him, slowly.

He nodded back. The laughter stopped. "I can tell. There's a real undercurrent of that in your writing, but you've chosen to deal with it through a sort of wry humor, which I really like. It's transformed, but it's not forgotten. It's hard to do humor well, but it works better when there's a little pain behind it. You write what you know, and it's clear that you know this. It's nicely done." His eyes held mine a moment longer, and then I looked away, certain I was already blushing. He'd said nice things about my writing, and I didn't hear him when he called on the next student to read her little autobiographical piece.

Brower wasn't what I'd expected when I'd signed up for the workshop. The figure in his dust jacket photo was brooding and mysterious, eyes flashing with some secret knowledge that he'd impart only to the truest of his true readers. The man in person was about five foot nine, with a neat black beard and a receding hairline, but no glint of anything mystical in his eyes. He wore thick glasses and earth tones, and had a habit of nervously looking left and right every time there was a loud noise. And with this bunch of would-be writers, there were loud noises often. Laptops popped open and shut, sheafs of papers slapped onto tables from great heights, books thumped to the floor to await the noble magister's autograph — it was a constant barrage of sound, and I started cringing for him with each *fwap* or *thud*. He noticed this, I think. I'm not sure. I was too nervous to pay much attention.

He had a soft voice, soft and almost musical, and he was informal and friendly from the get-go. This, too, ran contrary to my expectations. His writing had been so forceful, so potent that I'd imagined him the same way. My guess was that he'd come in wielding a red pen like a samurai sword, going all Toshiro Mifune on our manuscripts and our literary pretensions. I'd imagined a voice like thunder, spitting profanities and ruthless eviscerations of the work put in front of him.

Once or twice, I even imagined him liking my stuff. Once or twice, though, and that was all.

But no, he was funny and gentle and informative, and at the end of the first day everyone was buzzing about how great he was. We were bunked out in some of the outlying dorms on campus, one to a room if you could afford it or sharing with a stranger if you couldn't. I'd come alone, and alone I stayed, the only one in the entire workshop. I'd considered getting a roommate, but my imagination kept on sticking me with some hyperactive romance novelist wannabe who'd spend the entire conference telling me about his pomeranian. For the peace of mind it gave me, it was worth it to me to suck up the extra cost and stay alone.

Over the course of the long walk from the classrooms to the cinderblock palace where we were housed, the group broke up, stringing itself into knots and clumps of eager writers. Two here, three there, a clot of five in the middle; I brought up the rear, by myself. It wasn't that I didn't like the other attendees, now that I'd met them. They were all perfectly nice people and pretty much hit the same range as the folks at every other writers' workshop I'd attended. There was the elderly housewife who'd finally decided to try to write, the eager young student with more enthusiasm than grammar or experience, the serious artiste who was going to be crushed at the first real criticism — you get the idea. They were all nice and polite and friendly, and some of them were attractive and one or two might even have had some talent, though I doubted it. Every curve's got two ends to it, after all. But my reason for being there had nothing to do with bonding or networking or having a transformative sharing experience, God forbid.

More than any of them, I wanted to learn from Jerry Brower. And when I thought about it, part of me resented the fact that he was spending just as much time on them as he was on me.

They fed us in the small dining hall attached to our dorm, and much to my surprise Brower joined the students for his meal. The food was unremarkable, the sort of cafeteria slop that's more identifiable by shape and color than by taste, but he grabbed himself a tray and sat down to eat with us. Most of the others spent the entire meal pestering the poor man with questions — had he read this, would he sign that, what did he think of this author's latest work? He took it all with good grace in between bites, answering every question politely and gently deflecting the ones that crossed the lines of good taste.

For my part, I didn't take part in the conversation. I'd brought my PDA with me, and I'd set it and its traveling keyboard up so I could write during the meal. Besides, I was still basking in the glow of Brower's comment during the session, and didn't want to spoil the memory with something so prosaic as "Could you pass the salt?"

Instead, he asked me for it. I looked up. "Excuse me?"

He smiled. "The salt. Could you shoot it down here, or if you need to season your PDA, I understand. Those things rarely make good eating *au naturel*."

The entire table — we'd taken to all gathering around one, for no reason I could imagine — burst into laughter, some of it genuine, and I felt myself flushing. *They* were laughing at *me*? In front of Jerry Brower? I couldn't imagine anything more humiliating. I wanted to run. I wanted to flip the table over and see who'd laugh then. I wanted to smash in one of those laughing faces so the rest would just shut up.

I didn't do any of those things, of course. It wouldn't have been polite. "Of course," I said, and handed it over as quickly as I could. "Sorry to have been an inconvenience," I mumbled, and put my head down in an effort to show how emphatically I was ignoring everyone else. Brower, however, wouldn't let it be.

"Seriously," he said, and this time his voice came from much closer. I raised my head, and discovered that he'd taken the seat next to mine. "You should get involved in the conversation. You learn a lot from people at these things, sometimes more than in the classroom. These people," and he waved to include the rest of the group, "are your peers, and will someday be your professional peers if you keep writing. Don't shut them out. Writers who do nothing but writing very quickly run out of things to write about."

I opened my mouth to apologize, but he put a hand up to stop me. "Devotion to your craft is a good thing, Michael. No need to apologize for that. But part of your craft, and this is one of the toughest things to learn, is that you need to have a life outside of writing." He glanced around the room. "Even if it is just talking to other writers. Mind you, this situation is hardly typical."

"Oh?" I managed not to squeak. "Why?"

He grinned, bringing everyone in on the joke. "Normally, the only way to get this many writers together is in a bar." Again, everyone laughed. This time I joined them.

* * *

Somehow, Jerry and I were the last two left at the end of dinner. Everyone else had drifted off in ones and twos. A couple of people had, as the kids say, hooked up and went off looking for privacy; others wandered back to work on their assignments for tomorrow, or to call their families and reassure them that no, no one had asked them to smoke pot or get naked before writing. And so it came down to Jerry and me, and my occasional attempts to get the crumbs out of my keyboard.

He watched the last of my classmates straggle out the door, then turned to me with an apologetic half-smile. "I'm really sorry if I embarrassed you there, Michael. That really wasn't my intention."

Shaking my head, I smiled. "Nothing to worry about. You're right, I needed to be more a part of things."

He nodded. "Mind you, that was more for their benefit than for yours."

I blinked. "Beg pardon?"

"Well," he began, his voice dropping to a conspiratorial whisper. "I'm not sure how much benefit talking with them is going to do you in the long term, but talking to you might be a big help for them."

The glass of soda in my hand found its way to my mouth. I took a swallow to buy a few seconds, then put it down on the table and stared at Brower. "I'm not sure I understand what you're saying."

He shrugged. "I think you do. You're good, Michael. By far the best at this conference. I've read your samples and I've read theirs, and there's no comparison. There's one person at this workshop who's close to publication ready, and you're it. Everyone else, well, they can learn from talking with you in ways they can't learn from me. I'm the teacher. They're trying to impress me, and that means that they'll listen for as long as I'm watching. You, you're one of them, and you can sneak ideas about good writing under the wire and into their heads."

"I'm not that good," I heard myself protesting, but my head was buzzing. *Jerry Brower liked my writing! He liked it a lot! Sweet Jesus on flapjacks, he likes me.* I could die happy now, be buried with pages of my unfinished manuscripts scattered over my grave like confetti. Jerry Brower liked my stuff.

Frowning, he blinked those sad eyes at me. "One of the hardest things you're going to have to learn how to do, Michael — you don't mind if I call you Michael, yes? — is recognizing how good you are. Until you do that, you'll be holding yourself back. So don't worry about being humble. Accept that you have talent, and the talent will drive you."

"I'm just...I didn't think," I caught myself stammering, hated myself for it for a long white-hot moment, and then forced myself to move on. "I guess I'm just surprised. I didn't think my work was that much better than, say, Joelle's, or Bruce's."

His smile was back. "Now you're catching on. Hear that? You didn't think your work was that much better. But you thought it was better, right? That's good. That's the sort of confidence you'll need when you're trying to sell your stuff, because believe me, it's all swimming upstream once you start trying to sell. Hang onto that. You'll need it. And before you ask again, yes, I really do think you're that good. Now say thank you, or I'll be terribly insulted that you don't trust my judgment."

I swallowed, hard. "Thank you," I mumbled, and found that I couldn't make eye contact, not for the life of me.

"That's better," Brower said, and stood. "I've got to head back to my room — would you believe they've got me in the same cinderblock hell as you guys? — but I'll tell you what. Tomorrow after class, why don't you hand me whatever it is you're working on at home, and I'll give it a critique and get it back to you. Sound good?"

"Sounds...great. Amazing. That's really kind of you." The words tumbled out, one after the other as my mind raced. He wanted to see my writing. Oh God, what if it wasn't good enough? What if it was, and he showed it to someone else? What if — there were a million what ifs.

And as I pondered them, he quietly bid me good night and walked out, leaving me alone in the cafeteria.

Only when I was sure that he was gone did I finally give a loud whoop of pure delight, then sweep up my PDA in my arms and run, literally run, all the way back to my room. After all, there were only hours to prepare. Jerry Brower was going to be reading me!

* * *

"Hmm," Jerry said. And a little later, "Interesting."

We sat in the lounge at the end of the dorm hallway, a square room with two vending machines and the same number of sofas. He sat on one, reading the first few chapters of my in-progress novel, "Hanging Tree." I sat on the other, trying not to say anything that might interfere with his concentration. Occasionally other students would bustle in and out, and I'd shoot them dirty looks which utterly failed to impress anyone.

After an agonizing eternity of ten to fifteen minutes, Jerry put the manuscript down on the blocky table in front of him. "Well, Michael," he said, "Thank you for letting me take a look at that."

I thought about ways I could say "What did you think?" and yet still be cool, suave and debonair. There weren't any, so I settled for the straightforward approach. "What did you think?"

He looked down at the pile of paper, rather than at me, and my heart sank. His fingers drummed the tabletop, and I cringed. Finally, he looked up at me. "It shows a lot of promise," he said.

The world lurched out from under me. "A lot of promise" is what you tell a kid who's trying to hang a finger-painting on your fridge. It's what you tell the girl you really don't want to date the morning after you've slept with her. It's what to say to the interview candidate whose resume you're about to recycle. In other words, it's not a good thing.

Stomach sinking with dread, I managed to force a single word past my lips. "But?"

He smiled. "You're way ahead of me. But, there are some things you need to polish before you send this particular piece out. You haven't been in a lot of real fights, have you? It shows in your writing — your action sequences aren't believable. You don't hang out in bars enough, either. Go. Spend some time in one. Take notes. You don't need to become an expert in everything you write about, but you should have good experience of it. This," and he tapped the pile of pages, "shows a lot of promise. You have a good turn of phrase, your plot moves along well, and your characters are sketched out pretty nicely. But you don't know their world well enough to make it believable. Does that help?"

Molten lead pooled in my throat. I couldn't speak. I felt a tightness at the corners of my mouth, blurring at the edges of my eyes. Damnit, I would not cry. Not in front of Jerry Brower. Not while he was watching me.

I took a deep breath. Jerry's eyes were on me, kind and grey and understanding, and I couldn't look away. "I thought..." My voice trailed off. I sucked in more air and tried again. "I thought you said you liked my work. Yesterday. At dinner. I mean..." I trailed off lamely and forced myself to stare at the pile of pages on the table. I knew how pathetic I sounded, and hated myself for it.

"Well," Jerry said, and smiled, and tapped the manuscript. "I did. And I meant it. But there's a big difference between a class exercise, or even a short story, and a novel. You've got all of the talent necessary, sure. Now you just need to hone your craft, and part of the way you do that is by going out and experiencing what you're writing about. I mean, you wouldn't write about stamp collecting without doing some research on it, right? Just to make sure you got all the phrasings and terminology right. Well, your characters are supposed to live. They go to work and drink and screw around and do all sorts of things. So go out and research them, as well as numismatics or oncology or whatever other topics you write on. Like I said in class, you can only write what you know."

Miserably, I nodded. "I think I see," I told him, and gnawed my lower lip. "Maybe there's an example you could point out from Hanging Tree?"

He was all smiles. "Sure, no problem." Flip, flip went the pages onto the table as he went burrowing through them to find what he was looking for. I edged closer as he did so.

"Ah. Here. Chapter four." He held up the offending page.

I peered at it to show I was paying attention, but I already knew what it said. I knew every word in that manuscript by heart. "That's where the hangman's ghost first attacks someone walking past the tree." I tried to hold back, but couldn't; it was one of my favorite scenes. "The ghost is perched up in the tree, looking down, and he sees the policeman approaching, the policeman who *never looks up...*"

"Exactly." Jerry held up a warning hand to stop me. "It's a good moment, full of tension, but it really could be great. The way you have it written now, the ghost jumps down on the cop, punches him a few times, and then it gets kind of messy. Like I said earlier, you've always been on the receiving end of the rough stuff, right? People picked fights with you instead of you attacking them, yes?"

I nodded, not trusting myself to speak.

"Well, here's where it shows in your writing. The attack just wouldn't work, not the way you've written it. The way your ghost — and let me add he's a pretty solid ghost — leaps down, he'd probably glance off the victim and keep going, maybe break both his ankles. He wouldn't put up much of a fight."

Gently, I took the pages out of his hand. He let go easily. "So what are you saying here? That I shouldn't write about this sort of thing because I've never done it? There's not a lot I can write about then."

He shook his head. "No, no. I'm saying learn about it so you can write it. Watch some action movies and take notes. Try a martial arts class. Watch boxing on television. You don't need to be jumping out of trees to know how to write something like that, but you do need to know how people move and fight and how bodies work in conditions like that."

Abruptly, he looked at his watch. "It's getting late, Michael. I need to get some sleep if I'm going to be any good in class tomorrow at all. Thank you very much for letting me see your work. I'd like to see what you do with it after you give it another pass. I think there's real promise here, some very good potential and some excellent use of language. You're going to be published someday. All you need is a little more polish, and a little more experience."

Someday, I heard him say. *Potential.*

He stood and offered me his hand. Numb, I took it. "My pleasure," I said mechanically. "Thank you for taking the time to look at it."

"Not at all." He shook my hand once, then released it. "I'll see you in the morning. It's our last day here, so I want to make sure we hit the ground running." And with that, he opened the door to the stairwell and headed downstairs.

The door slammed back shut before I could say goodnight, and I found myself alone in the lounge. My hands still clutched the pile of papers, and I found myself suddenly, irrationally hating my work. And in the depths of my hatred, I found something else. I found insight.

Jerry had been right, of course. I could see that now. I'd been stupid to think that my work was up to snuff to begin with. I needed to get out more, to really inform my writing with first-hand experience. Only then would my work really sing. Until then, it was all guesswork, not good enough. I needed to stop guessing and start knowing.

And I'd start tonight.

Jerry only had a couple of landings' worth of head start, after all, and chapter four needed work.

My fingers loosened, almost involuntarily, their grip on the manuscript. The pages wafted to the floor, tumbling down in every order except the one they'd been written in.

It didn't matter. I left them behind and opened the door to the stairwell.

From down below, Jerry's footsteps echoed up to me. I could still catch him. I *would* still catch him.

Write what you know.

Missing Pages

Grandpa Crawford once told me that I worried too much about doing what was right, but Grandpa Crawford's dead. At least, he was when he told me that. He was right, though. Grandpa Crawford is always right.

I guess I should start at the beginning. My name's Joseph. My full name is Joseph Ambrose Whitley, but everyone calls me Joe. Mom and Dad only call me Joseph when they're mad at me, which is kind of funny. Dad told me once that I was named after my great-grandpa, but Mom told him to shush. Mom told Dad to shush a lot back then.

We moved to Kingston last summer. Dad got a new job with a company there, so me and Mom and my brother Tommy all had to move to Rhode Island with him. Dad said the new job was a good one, and they'd be paying him lots of money, so we bought a big house with a big yard in front and lots of trees in back. Tommy liked the front yard better, because he's bigger than me and good at sports. I liked the backyard, because it's dark and cool, and I can sit under all the trees and read. Tommy doesn't read much, and he thinks I'm weird 'cause I do. He also says that Mom likes him better, but I don't think so. Mom reads a lot, too.

We all moved into this house just before school started. There were a couple of other kids in the neighborhood, but they were all Tommy's age. Tommy's good at making friends, so they started playing with him. There were three of them who played with him a lot. The biggest one was William, and then there were two others named Jason and David.

So anyway, Tommy started playing with William and David and Jason. Sometimes they'd let me play too, but not often. They were bigger than I was, and besides I made the sides uneven when they played football or stickball. They made me steady hitter for a while, but that didn't work because I'm not very good at hitting. But at least they'd let me play, when Mom made them anyway.

Dad wasn't home too much at first, and then he stopped coming home at all. He was starting his new job, and they made him fly all over to do it. He promised us that it wouldn't stay that way forever, but I didn't think so. Mom didn't either. I asked her once when Dad was going to be home more and she said "The twelfth of never." I asked her when that was, and she didn't say anything else. She just sort of laughed. Then I asked her where Dad was and she said that he was all the other way on the other side of the world, on an island in Indonesia. I wonder why we had to move to Rhode Island for Dad to go there.

When school started, Tommy made more friends. I didn't make as many as he did, because I'm short and I get good grades all the time. At least the kids at my new school didn't beat me up the way the kids at my old one did. Once they did it right in front of the teacher, and he didn't do anything. He told my Mom that he thought we were playing, but he was lying.

Tommy's friends came over to play a lot. Sometimes Tommy would go over to their houses instead, but most of the time everyone played at our house. Once in a while Mom would even let Tommy have friends sleep over. They'd stay up real late and tell ghost stories and try to scare each other.

One time, Jason thought it would be really funny if they scared me, so they went to my room and woke me up. They put blankets over their heads and pretended to be ghosts, and tried to get me to cry. I didn't though. I knew it was them. Real ghosts would be scarier, and wouldn't say "Woo woo."

So since they couldn't make me cry, they told me to come with them. We went back to Tommy's room. He'd stolen some candy and some graham crackers and some pop from downstairs, and Dad's old pocket light was in the middle of the floor like a campfire. We all sat down and they started telling stories again. They kept trying to scare me. David told a story about a monster who lived in trash cans waiting for little kids to run away, so he could catch them and eat them. I wasn't scared, but I think William was.

After a while, it was my turn to tell a story. I told them that I didn't know any, but they told me that I was chicken, and that they'd tell Mom I'd stolen the candy if I didn't try. So I told them the only one that I knew. It was a story that I must have dreamed or read somewhere, because I don't think I could have made it up, but I knew it anyway. So I just started talking, and the story came out.

It was a story about an old house and the family that lived in it. The house was three stories tall and had three basements, so that you could only see half of it when you walked by. There were trees out front, but they never had any leaves, so it looked like skeletons waving their hands at the sky when the wind blew. The house was painted gray, with red shutters, and the roof was black. The windows of the house were never open, and the door had a big knocker like a face on it, but no one ever came up to knock. They were scared of the people who lived inside.

A whole family lived in there. There was a grandpa, who was old and had a long white beard. He spent all his time in the basement reading from old books and mixing chemicals. Sometimes they'd explode and sometimes they'd smell bad and sometimes they'd do other things, like make the wind blow or the trees all bend toward the house. They locked the door to the basement when the grandpa was working.

No one had seen his son for years. He was supposed to be off working somewhere, like our Dad was, but no one knew when he was coming home. Sometimes letters would arrive from places like Singapore, saying that he'd be home soon. Other times packages would arrive, and they'd be little gold statues. They had a whole collection of these over the fireplace, and the son's wife was very careful to arrange them in just a certain way. They'd had a housekeeper who'd knocked a couple over when she was dusting, and the son's wife was very upset. The housekeeper never came back after that, and she told people that the statues had tried to move themselves when she put them in the wrong place. No one believed her, though, and she got hit by a streetcar when she was crossing the street one day. It was the same streetcar that she used to take to go clean the family's house.

The son's wife always wore gloves. She never took them off, even to wash, because she was afraid of her hands. Once, when she was just married, she went down to the basement to look at her husband's father's books. When she was sure no one was looking, she took one down off the shelf and started reading. The writing was very small, so she put her finger on the page to make out what the letters read. She shouldn't have done that, though, 'cause when she did, her fingers sank into the book. It wouldn't let go, so she tried to use her other hand to pull herself out. But something from the book reached out from the page and grabbed her. She started screaming, and her husband heard her and ran downstairs. He pulled her hands out of the book, which was a good thing because she was in it nearly up to her elbows. Her arms and hands were all marked like they were burned or dipped in really hot water, and she couldn't stop screaming. Her husband put the book back on the shelf and took her upstairs, and ever since that she wore gloves to hide what the book had done to her. After that, she never went downstairs again, and she spent the last years of her life afraid to go anywhere but the attic. She thought that downstairs, the book was waiting for her.

There were three boys in the house. One was named Timothy, and one was named Jared, and the last was named Daniel. There had been another boy, named James, but no one talked about him. He'd gone down to his grandfather's basement one day, and then he'd gone down to the second basement and the third, and he never came back up. But there was a new tree in the front yard the next day, and people said when the moon hit it just right, you could see James' face in the bark. They said he was yelling for his mother.

They made me stop there, because David started crying since he was scared. Mom came upstairs and found the candy, and Tommy tried to blame me for it. I was sent back to my room while Mom yelled at my brother, then she came in and told me never to do anything like that again. Then she went back to bed, but when I went in to tell her I was sorry, I saw she still had her light on.

The next day, Mom got a telephone call. It was Jason's mother, and she was upset. She was talking so loud that I could hear her, and so fast that Mom couldn't say anything. Jason's mom said that I'd scared the dickens out of her son with my story, and that Mom was irresponsible for letting me do that. She also wanted to know why on earth Mom had told me the story of the old Crawford House, because that was the story I'd told and it was no story for a child. Mom told Jason's mom that she didn't know anything about a Crawford House and that she'd thank her to mind her own business. Then she hung up.

Jason didn't play at our house for a long time after that.

Just before Halloween, though, he came over after school one day. He and William and David and Tommy were all excited. They asked me if I wanted to see a real haunted house. I asked them where they'd find one. They said it was right around the corner. Their class had gotten a storyteller in, and he'd told them all about the old Crawford House around the corner. It was supposed to have real ghosts, and trees that would lean down and tap you on the shoulder, and all sorts of scary stuff.

I asked if one of the ghosts was the lady in the attic. David looked scared and said yes. So I said I'd go with them.

Tommy and Mom and I live in a house on Wickford Street. I'd say Dad lives there too, but he's never home. All that's there are the weird things he brought back for us when he visited. Once he gave Tommy and me little statues made out of seashells and metal. They looked like men with big fish eyes. Mom didn't like those much. Neither did I.

Anyway, that's where we live. Shelton Street is the next street down, and then comes Abbey. Abbey Street is a dead end, and the very last house on the end is the Crawford House — the haunted house. I'd never seen it. When we moved in, we drove past Abbey Street in the dark, and all the stores in town were in the other direction. I wasn't allowed to cross streets on my own, so I'd never been there. But with Tommy and his friends taking me, I could go.

It took us ten minutes to get there, and then another five to walk down the block. No other houses were near the one at the end. There were lots of trees in front, and it didn't look like the grass had been cut in a long time. The house was three stories tall, and it had a black slate roof. Someone had tried to paint it a nice shade of green, but the paint was peeling and you could see the gray underneath.

There was a fence and a gate and a sign on it that read "Keep Out," but it was unlocked so we just walked through and up to the house. There was a front porch with a swing on it, so we went up the porch steps. David and Jason sat in the swing, but it made a snapping sound when they did so they jumped up. Tommy laughed at them, 'cause they looked so afraid.

The front door had a big knocker on it like an old man's face with a long beard. The beard was the part that moved, so I grabbed it and knocked. Tommy yelled at me, but I told him it was polite to let the ghosts know we were coming in. We wouldn't like it if they came into our house without knocking. William started to tell me that it was stupid to be polite to the ghosts, but then the door opened.

Everyone looked at everyone else and said "Did you do that?" but we were all standing on the porch, so none of us could have. There was no one standing at the door, either. It just opened on its own.

Tommy was the first one inside. He was smart enough to turn on his pocket light, so we could see where we were going. Everything inside was covered with white cloths, and they were covered with dust. There was dust on the floor, too. When we walked it sounded like thud-thud-thud, because there were no carpets, and little clouds popped up every time we took a step. William coughed a lot with each cloud.

There was a big staircase that led up to the second floor, and a door that led down to the basement. All the doors on the upstairs hallway were closed, at least the ones I could see from the bottom of the stairs. There was a painting on the wall in the first room we walked into. It was a picture of a man wearing some sort of uniform and a big hat. Tommy said he looked kind of like Dad, but I didn't think so. The picture made it look like he was looking at the basement door, though.

Tommy wanted to go downstairs, but his friends wanted to go upstairs. They argued for a minute or two, then started stomping up the staircase. I think they were trying to make the biggest noise they could to show they weren't afraid. I didn't go with them, though. I just stood at the foot of the stairs. I knew they'd never make it to the top.

They were halfway up when I noticed her. She was very pretty, and her hair was tied back the way Mom used to tie hers. She wore a dress that was all brown with a white apron over it, and she had a sad look on her face. There were white gloves on both of her hands, the sort of long gloves that went all the way up to her elbows. She looked down at Tommy and his friends, and shook her head. Then she looked right at me, and her eyes got real big. She knew I could see her, and that surprised her. She didn't like us being there, though. I could tell that. Still, she didn't look like she was going to do anything to us, so I stopped being afraid for a minute. I even thought I should wave hello.

That's when the basement door started slamming, open and shut, over and over. David screamed the first time it happened, and the other two looked at him. Then it did it again and again, faster and faster, until it sounded like the door was going to fall off. Then it stopped, and for a second everything was quiet. David shut up and looked real scared, and the other two looked nervous. Then the floor started creaking, like something heavy was walking across it towards the stairs. The dust clouds it made were really big.

We ran away, then. At least we tried to. I don't know why, but I waited until the others had gotten down the stairs and past me before I started running. I shouldn't have. Jason slammed the door when he ran out, but when I got to it, it was locked. I tried to open it. I didn't turn around, because I knew if I did I'd see the thing that came up from the basement. I could hear someone screaming, very quietly, and then I realized it was the lady at the top of the stairs. She was saying "Father don't," but it was so faint that you almost didn't hear it. I tried the door again, but it was still locked, and that's when I felt the hand on my shoulder.

"Stop," someone said.

I stopped.

"Turn around," he said. It was a man's voice. He sounded like he was used to giving people orders. So I said, "You didn't say the magic word."

He laughed, but it wasn't a nice laugh. "Please, then. Turn around. Now." Suddenly, he stopped laughing. I turned around.

He was old, but not old and sick like my grandpa had been before he died. He just looked like he'd been around for a long time. He wore funny clothes, and when he moved too fast I could sort of see through him. That's how I knew he was a ghost. No one today wears clothes like that.

He looked at me the same way Grandpa used to, up and down like he was trying to figure out how much I'd grown since my last visit. He did this a couple of times, and then he said, "You're welcome here. They're not. Tell them that, then come back someday soon. There's things you and I should discuss."

The woman at the top of the stairs said "Father!" but not very loud. He turned and looked at her. "I let them leave, didn't I? They come back, it's on their heads. This one's the right one." She didn't say anything after that, but she looked sad.

Then he looked at me again, and he kneeled down so we were kind of face to face. "Where's your father, boy? A boy should have a father."

I told him that my dad was working far away and that he'd be home sometime, at least that's what Mom had said. He made tsk-tsk noises and said that wasn't good enough. Then he asked where Dad was working, and I said Indonesia. Mom had always told me not to talk to strangers, but she never said anything about not talking to ghosts, so I figured this was OK.

"Do you want him back?" he said. I nodded, and said that I did, and that it would make Mom happy, too. He smiled, and patted me on the head. It was cold where he touched me.

"Come back and visit again, boy. Come down to the basement. If you do, I'll show you something that just might bring your father back."

I nodded, and then I kneeled down and wrote my initials in the dust on the floor, just to show that I'd been there.

The old man laughed.

Then the door opened, and I ran.

* * *

The other boys were waiting for me in the street in front of the house. They asked me what I'd seen, and I said nothing. I told them we shouldn't come back, though, because it might make the ghosts mad. Tommy looked at me funny and asked about the door. I told him it had just gotten stuck. He shrugged, and we all walked home to get yelled at.

I didn't ask why none of them had come back to get me.

* * *

It was three more days before I went back to the house. Tommy and his friends were playing football and they didn't want me to play, so I could go alone. The door was open when I got there, and so was the door to the basement. There was no woman upstairs, though, and the steps were all covered in dust. I looked up there for a minute, then went downstairs instead.

It was dark on the basement stairs, but there was some kind of dim light at the bottom of the first staircase. I could hear someone saying something in a kind of slow voice, like the one Dad used to use when he was trying to sing. Dad didn't sing very well. Whoever was trying to sing this wasn't much better, and I couldn't understand the words he was saying. I tried to ignore it, and I looked around when I got to the bottom of the stairs.

The room was really big, and it was full of old things. There were bicycles, and rusty swords, and big iron candlesticks. There was lots of furniture, too, all covered in sheets that used to be white but weren't any more. There were no spiders or bugs, though it sounded like there were rats off in the corners. I don't like rats.

There was another staircase, too, and that one had a kind of dim light coming out of it. The voice was louder there, so I thought I should probably follow it. I guess I should have been afraid, but I wasn't. I wanted to hear what the man (I knew it was a man because his voice was really deep) was trying to say. I felt like I could almost understand it, but not quite. I knew I'd have to get closer to understand it, so I went down the second set of stairs.

These were brick, not wood. My feet didn't make any sound on them, but the singing was getting louder as I went down. It was getting colder, too, and when I looked around the room my breath made little clouds of steam.

There was nothing in the second room. It was big, too, and it had big holes in the walls where it looked like stuff had been ripped out of them. The floor was stone, and someone had spilled all sorts of stuff on it because it was stained really badly. It looked like someone had written things in a couple of spots on the floor, but someone else had tried to scrub it away. In some places, they'd hit the floor with a hammer or something, because it was all broken up. I guess they really didn't like what someone had put there.

I knew there would be another staircase. It was in the middle of the room, and it had a big stone trap door that was open. I knew that if I turned the trap door over, I'd see it had a big iron ring in it, but I knew it would be heavy, too. These steps were stone, and the light at the bottom of the stairs looked normal, like it came from candles or something. The singing was so loud I couldn't hear anything else, but I decided to keep going anyway. The old man had told me to come visit him, after all. Besides, this was something I could do that Tommy couldn't.

So I went down the stairs, and when I got to the bottom, I stopped. The singing stopped, too, and all I could hear was my heart. Everything there was messy and old. There were books on shelves and tables with glass on them, but everything was covered in cobwebs and really dirty. It didn't look like anyone had been here for a very long time.

Then the old man turned around and saw me, and everything changed. It all looked new. The books weren't dusty and the tables were clean, and all the glass bottles were sparkly and full of weird colored stuff. The air smelled funny, like someone had been burning something they shouldn't have, but all I could see was lots of candles.

The old man thanked me for coming, and said that he'd been hoping I'd be back today. I asked him if he'd been the one singing and he corrected me. He said he'd been chanting, and that the difference was important. I asked him what that meant, and he said it was like praying. I told him Mom and Dad didn't believe in praying, and he laughed. He said it all depended on what you prayed to.

I asked him why he was praying, and he asked me to keep a secret. I nodded, so he said that he hadn't been praying, not really. He'd been casting a spell. I asked him what kind of spell, and he said, "A spell for you."

I told him I didn't believe in magic, and that his spell hadn't done anything. He told me that I was wrong.

"It's from a book by a man named Albertus Magnus," he said. "That means Albert the Great, but it could mean Big Albert, if you took it that way. Albert was a very wise man, and he wrote a lot of very interesting things down in this book. I'll even tell you a secret: It lets you see ghosts."

I told him that I already saw ghosts, because if I didn't, how would I be talking to him. He smiled at me like I'd given the right answer at school. "That's true," he said. "That's why I want to talk to you. But you can only see the ghosts of people. I cast that spell so you could see the ghosts of things, things. Welcome, my dear boy, to history."

He showed me all around his laboratory, cause that's what it was, now — a ghost of a place. I saw the books, rows and rows of them, even though they hadn't been there when I'd first gone through the trap door. He pulled a few off the shelf and handed them to me, and even though they looked all new and stuff, they felt old. One big one had a really soft cover, and it made me feel weird to touch it. I opened it, and inside there were pictures of circles and triangles and stars, and lots of things that were supposed to be magic spells. I couldn't read the part of the book that wasn't spells, though.

"Latin," said the old man, and closed the book. He put it on the shelf again, and then he showed me the rest of his room. There was a stuffed crocodile, and test tubes and beakers, and little jars of powder that made the candles burn red or green or blue when you dropped some on them. I had a really good time, and the old man seemed glad.

He asked me to keep coming back. I said I guessed I could, but I felt bad coming over and not bringing the other boys. He said that it would be a very bad thing if the other boys came with me, and that this was just for me. If I came back, he'd show me more magic, and maybe even teach me some, too. Then when I got really good, I might learn a spell that would make Dad want to come home.

I asked him if he could really do that. He said he could, and he could show me Dad if I brought him something Dad had given to me. I told him I'd be back as soon as I could. He just smiled, then the whole basement went dark.

It took a long time for me to get home.

* * *

After that, I started coming back a couple of times a week. I'd always go down to the third basement, and the old man would show me things. The first time I came back, I brought him a toy fire truck that Dad had given me, but the old man said it wasn't enough. It hadn't been Dad's first, or he hadn't really cared about it. I needed to bring something stronger. But he still showed me more magic, and told me he'd start teaching me how to do it myself soon.

My fourth trip back, I brought him one of the statues Dad had sent me, one of those gold ones with big fish eyes. The old man smiled when he saw it, and then he said it was perfect. He put it on a table and sprinkled some kind of gray powder around it in a circle. When he finished, he chanted again. I still couldn't understand what he was saying, but it was like I knew *why* he was saying it, all of a sudden. He was calling on something that lived deep under the water, something that lived near where Dad was. He was asking it to show me Dad. So it did.

I saw Dad, but Dad didn't see me. I even saw what he was doing.

I don't think he should have been doing that. Not with the woman I saw with him. Not with her.

I told the old man I didn't want to see that any more, and he waved his hand. Suddenly the picture in the air went away. I went to grab the statue, but the old man caught my hand in his and told me that would be very dangerous. "This belongs to something else now," he said. "It would get very angry if you took them back."

I said that I didn't care, and that I wanted it back because Dad had given it to me. He looked sad. "Your father shouldn't have given it to you. He should have given you time instead. Let me show you something." He walked over to the bookshelf and pulled off the same book I'd looked in the first time I'd come down here. He flipped through the pages until he found one he wanted. Then he turned the book toward me and pointed one finger at a spot on the page. His fingernail was black.

"This," he said, "is a spell for making someone who's gone far away come home. I can teach it to you, and you can make your father return. He should be with you. He should be with your mother. You should have a family. You *do* want your father to come home, don't you, boy?"

"My name is Joseph, not boy," I said.

He said, "I know," and smiled. I think he knew why I was called Joseph, too, and he shouldn't have.

He asked me if I wanted him to teach me the spell. I thought about that for a minute. "Why do you want to teach me?" I asked him. He said it was because I reminded him of his grandson, and his grandson's father hadn't been home much either. He said he didn't like seeing it happen again.

I was getting allowance from Mom, so I told the ghost I would pay him for the magic lessons. He said that I shouldn't, but that I should keep bringing the statues that Dad had sent me. That would make things easier, he said. They really weren't the sort of things Mom should be keeping around the house, anyway.

It seemed like a good idea. Mom hated the statues and wanted Dad back. So if I could get them out of the house and use them to get Dad home, she'd be happy.

I told him I'd be back with the statues. "One at a time," he told me. "It's best if we don't rush."

* * *

So I kept coming back, and I kept bringing the statues with me. Mom asked where they had gone once or twice, but she didn't really seem to care. I think she was just happy they were gone. I didn't play much with Tommy and his friends any more, but they didn't seem to mind. It made their games even. Instead, I just kept going back to the house. Once I asked him how strong the spell was. He told me that Albertus Magnus had been a very powerful magician, and that the spell could call back anything from anywhere. "Not just people like Dad?" I asked. He smiled and told me it could call back much, much more. I didn't know what he meant by that. I decided not to ask.

The old man said I was a very good student, and he would teach me as much magic as I could learn. It turned out to be a lot, and not just that one spell. Some of what he taught me was in that chanting he'd used to cast the spell on me, and

I started to learn what it meant. I still had trouble reading some of the big words and big names, though, so he told me not to try to learn those spells yet. He told me that if I made a mistake saying them, it would be very dangerous.

Once, when I came in, I saw the woman in the upstairs hallway. I smiled at her, but she never came down. She looked like she was afraid to.

* * *

It was Tommy's fault that things went wrong. It wasn't mine. Tommy lied to me. He told me he was playing stickball with Jason and David, but he wasn't. He followed me to the house, and even though he was chicken to come inside, he listened. He told me he'd tell Mom what I was doing if I didn't bring him along next time.

I told him that I couldn't, and that the old man had said he couldn't come. He said that he was going to tell Mom, then, and I'd get grounded. I said that he couldn't do that because I was learning magic so I could bring Dad home.

He hit me. He hit me and he knocked me down and he kept hitting me. My nose started bleeding and one of my teeth got loose but he didn't stop. He told me I was a liar and that he was going to tell Mom, and that if I ever told him a lie like that again he'd really beat me up, 'cause Dad wasn't coming home and me lying just made it worse.

I kind of felt sorry for him. He missed Dad a lot more than I did.

Finally, he got off me. I was crying, and he was crying too. He gave me a tissue and told me to hold my head back, which was his way of saying he was sorry. I did, and the nosebleed stopped. He kept sniffling, though, like he had a cold. So I told him that I would bring him next time, and he could see that I was trying to bring Dad home. The old man wouldn't mind that. Tommy asked when. I told him tomorrow.

He ended up bringing his friends along. I told him not to, but he told me that it was all of them or none of them, and then he'd tell Mom. So I took them all down into the basement. The house was very dark. There was light, and the old man wasn't there. I guess he was angry. But the books were still down there, and the statues were on the table in a little circle.

At least, they were for me. The other boys couldn't see them, not the way I could. All they saw was dust and cobwebs and dark.

I went over to the bookshelf and got down the book he'd been teaching me from. Jason had a pocket light, so he held it up for me while I opened the book to the right page — the page with the spell for seeing Dad — and started reading it. The old man hadn't taught me this one, but I'd heard him read it once, and I thought I could read it, too.

Maybe I should have waited until I'd heard it a couple more times. I think I made a mistake while I was chanting. I think I said something I shouldn't have.

I asked for help from the thing that the old man used to talk to. I knew I got that right. But I think I got its name wrong, because all of a sudden I could feel it looking right at me. It felt old and cold and scary, and most of all it felt hungry. Then I realized it was looking at all of us. That's when David started screaming, and the pocket light went out. There was a crashing noise, and one more scream that finished very suddenly, and then everything was quiet.

They found us down there a little while later. It was a whole bunch of parents — Mom and David's parents and Jason's mom and William's parents. Jason had left a note for his mom saying where we were going, so when she found it, she got on the phone and then came looking for us. They called an ambulance for David. I didn't get a good look at him when they carried him out. I think that was a good thing.

Jason's mom was yelling at my mom about how it was all my fault. She started going through the old man's things and saying that they were all of the devil, and that they all should be burned. David's father said that they should go to a museum, but Jason's mom kept yelling. She said they should all be burned right up so no one else came down here, and finally the other parents said OK just to shut her up, I think. So she took out a lighter and picked up one of the white cloths, then set it on fire. I don't think she saw the books. I don't think anyone else did.

David's father told her that this was arson, but she didn't let him finish. "It was an accident, and everyone here is going to remember it as an accident, so help me God," she said, and marched right on up the stairs. Everyone else followed. We went last.

Mom was holding my hand and Tommy's as we walked up the stairs, and she looked so sad. I told her that I'd just been trying to get Dad home, and she looked at me and started crying.

She cried all the way home, then she started yelling at me, then she told me how glad she was I was safe. Then she grounded Tommy for a week and me for two, and told me never to do anything like that again.

I could see the smoke from the burning house through my window. It took the fire trucks a very long time to come.

* * *

I wasn't grounded any more two weeks later, but I didn't go back. Everyone was watching me and expecting me to, and everyone was whispering about what had happened to David. He never came back to school, you know, and then his family moved away without telling anyone where they were going.

But mostly they watched me, so I waited. Eventually the grownups got bored of keeping an eye me. Even Jason's mom stopped staring at me the way she had, mostly. I waited a little longer after that before I went back, though. After all, I didn't want to get followed again.

When I got there, the house was gone. There was just some burned wood and stone, but that was all. The basement was all burned up, too. So I let myself down into the hole in the ground and went looking for the stairs down. They were still there. I followed them, and the stairs after that, until I was in the lowest basement again.

The old man was waiting for me. "That was very foolish," he said. "I told you they couldn't come back."

"I know," I told him. "But Tommy was going to tell Mom."

He frowned. "I'm training you in the black arts, boy. You should be able to handle a tattle-tale." He shook his head. "You should have done better. I'm disappointed. Now look around. What do you see?"

I looked. The room was all burned up. The floor was covered with ash, like in a fireplace. The glass on the tables had melted, and some of the tables had collapsed. The only thing that wasn't burned was the ring of little gold statues. Somehow Jason's mom had missed them, and the fire had missed them, too. The old man pointed. "Can you still see ghosts, boy? What do you see here?"

I nodded at him. "I can still see," I said. "I can still see everything." And suddenly, I could.

"Can you?" He stood there, waiting. So I walked over to where the bookshelf had stood and picked up the ghost of a book, a big book with a soft leather cover and pages I'd seen before.

"Oh yes," I said, and started reading out loud.

There is No Bird

There is certainly not a golden bird, caged just above my heart.

That would be silly. He's on the other side. A little higher than the heart, I think — that's where I feel the fluttering. When I cough, or lose my breath, or just hold very, very still when he thinks I'm not paying attention.

The fault is mine. I caught him. I put him there. One lung down, the other failing, and so I did what any sensible man would do — caught a mythological creature, bound it to my breast with half-understood magics, and lived in fear of its leaving every moment thereafter.

Because the bird will leave someday. That I know. He will burst through the bars of his prison and shatter them. Shatter me. Leave me behind, broken and gasping and empty, and forget me as he flies away. He is immortal, after all. Were I to keep him for a hundred years, it would be as nothing to him. But he will be free.

This will happen. I have seen it in a dream, heard it in the song he sings late at night when sane men have long since gone to sleep. He is warning me, I think. It is a kindness, or a warning, or a torment. His ways are inscrutable, as, perhaps they should be. He is, after all, eternal. He is, after all, not human.

He hasn't left me yet. I don't know why. Pity, perhaps. Or fear.

Silence.

Flutter.

I wait.

Shadows in Green

A smart Yankee boy should always know his place, and that place sure as hell isn't the South Carolina woods in the middle of the night. That's what I told myself afterwards, but afterwards isn't any good. It never is, not when it comes to things like that.

The whole mess started on what was euphemistically called a company retreat. I worked for a small publishing company in those days, a place called Damocles House that used words like "non-traditional" and "edgy" to cover up the fact that the people running the joint didn't have any damn idea of what they were doing. They'd heard just enough buzzwords to be dangerous, and that's how the entire company wound up hip-deep in the Carolina woods.

It was supposed to be a team-building exercise, which is marketing-speak for "everybody gets hammered together and bonds over puking in the same toilet bowl." The schedule called for personality tests and workshops in the morning, wacky sports competitions in the afternoon, and evenings full of beer, vodka and violent illness while the few single women we employed got dive-bombed by opportunistic suitors. The last wasn't on the *official* schedule, but frankly, it was the only set of activities anyone was liable to pay attention to.

Management's first mistake, of course, was coming up with the whole thing. Their second was the choice of location. They had rented out one of those southern "resort" complexes, all white-sided cabins in the middle of nowhere, that you find along the Carolina-Georgia border. There's a huge manmade lake there and not much else, except for a couple stores that sell fireworks and moon pies. As a result, the entire area is littered with that sort of joint, places with names like "Pine Grove Acres" where car dealers from Marietta can take their wives and kids off for a weekend in the "country." It's all very nice and sedate and whitebread, and that's why the muckety-mucks had rented out the entire place for us. It wasn't that there were that many of us; at our biggest, we never had more than a hundred people. No, it was that they were afraid one of the artists would hit on the wife of some minister from Cobb County and all hell would break loose.

We'd gone up on a hot and sunny Friday morning, the entire company caravaning along because the site's printed directions would have sent anyone who followed them a hundred miles deep into Alabama. A long line of cars, equal parts SUVs and Saturns, snaked its way up I-85. The conga line was slowed only by frequent breaks for stops for bathroom breaks, and lightning-fast runs into roadside liquor stores for "supplies". I drove, mainly because I didn't trust most of my coworkers' cars to get us there in one piece. Raises had been small that year, in part to pay for the misbegotten retreat, and as such most of the creative staff was operating on the "keep a roll of duct tape and a can of oil in the trunk" theory of auto maintenance.

The car was full for the trip up. I'd foolishly volunteered to play pack mule, so my noble little sedan had the burden of transporting three of my coworkers and their small mountain of stuff to the wilds of South Carolina. The entire trip up I drove with one eye on the rearview, half-expecting to see the trunk explode open and evacuate a potpourri of sleeping bags, black t-shirts and small, carefully sealed baggies full of grade-A Tallahassee-grown weed.

The latter belonged to one of the occupants of the back seat, an accountant named Harris Brahms. The office's serious stoner, he was in his mid-30s but liked to chase college women, and had a haircut that made him look like a roadie for Grand Funk Railroad. Harris came from a long line of law enforcement officers, and his stated goal was to someday go to work for the DEA. I'd made the mistake of asking him what job he thought he was qualified for with them, and he just smiled. "Easy, man," he'd said. "Tester."

Sitting next to him was Felix Gotti, who insisted on being called "The Cat." Felix was six foot two and balding, a horndog of the first water. He'd stumbled into a job as a line editor a few years back and clung to it with the ferocity of a man hanging onto a branch over a sleeping grizzly. He was from Georgia and spoke with a deep twang, something which was made much more amusing by his penchant for wearing colors that came right out of a post-volcanic sunset. If it wasn't orange, it wasn't stylish enough for Felix, and that was that. No one had yet figured out what was so particularly catlike about the man, but no one had been brave enough to ask him about it. Felix and Harris had diametrically opposed tastes in music, if not pharmaceuticals, and that was one of the reasons I'd stuck them in the back seat together.

And sitting in the front seat, as always, was Ellie. One of the copy editors, she looked like someone had ordered a feisty pixie from Central Casting. She was maybe five feet tall on a good day, a brunette with a pageboy haircut and a strong Laura Ashley tropism. Her face was dusted with freckles, her eyelashes were impossibly long, and her mouth made a man really want to be an oboe reed on the off chance she decided to take up playing woodwinds.

And needless to say, I had it for her, bad.

The trip took all of two hours, though the unpacking took longer. By the time everyone had settled into their bungalows — the four of us were tucked into one, with me sleeping on the couch to ensure Ellie a private bedroom — the day was pretty much shot. There was a half-hearted attempt at getting everyone together for an organizational meeting to discuss the next day's agenda, but attendance was pitiful. Hector, the company's CFO, tried to explain how the next few days were important for getting to know our coworkers, learning each others' personalities, and finding new ways to work together, but at the end of his spiel, the only question anyone had was "When's dinner?" Outside the main meeting room, you could hear the whooping and the shouting; the party had already started.

By sundown, things had gotten out of hand. People were hanging out of windows waving half-empty bottles, screaming and laughing like it was going out of style. A half-dozen stereos had been cranked, each with a different CD, turning the central area between the bungalows into the audio equivalent of the Somme. Somewhere nearby, glass was breaking as empties fired at a trash can missed their mark.

I sat on the front step of our little cabin, nursed a Sam Adams, and shook my head. I didn't actually like drinking Sam, mind you, but it was from Boston, and as a recent transplant from New England I felt that I had to keep up appearances. "What a mess," I said to no one in particular, and took another drink.

"Agreed," Ellie replied from over my shoulder. "Got room for two on that step, Ben?"

"Sure," I said as enthusiastically as I dared, and wiggled over to the side a bit. She dropped down next to me, a can of Sprite in her hand, and tucked her legs up under her. "Some party," she commented, without enthusiasm.

I nodded, took a swig of beer, and turned to face her. "Not exactly my speed, I confess. I don't mind the occasional drink, but this..." My voice trailed off and I waved in the general direction of the idiocy. Forty feet away, two of the assistant editors were swinging broomsticks at each other in a miserable impersonation of a swordfight. I averted my eyes from the incipient carnage, and managed to wince only a little when I heard one of them yelp in pain.

"Yeah, this is just kind of stupid." Her voice was surprisingly fierce. "I'm not sure how it's supposed to make me work better with these guys because I've seen them fall over drunk into a rain barrel."

I chuckled. "That's the point, you see? The next time Noel or one of the other guys from content management comes down and bitches you out, just think about what they looked like out here, hanging from some tree by their underpants and trying to remember their own names. I guarantee you the conversation will be much more amusing after that. She laughed, and I grinned back at her.

"You're going to get me in trouble," she accused, but there was no heat to her words.

That's the idea, I nearly said, but bit back the words and instead put on my best innocent face. It didn't work, but it did send her into a whole new spasm of laughter.

"So," she said when her giggles finally subsided, "what else is there to do here?"

"Not much," I admitted. "You can get drunk with layout, get drunk with editing, get drunk with the finance department..."

"Or we could explore," she said firmly, and bounced to her feet.

"Explore?" I looked up at her quizzically. "Explore what?"

"Harris found something. It's neat." And with that, she vanished back into the cottage. I thought about not following her for all of six-tenths of a second, then got up and went inside.

Harris and The Cat were sitting around the living room coffee table when I meandered back, Cat and Ellie on the couch and Harris squatting on the floor. "What's up?" I asked the gathered assemblage.

"Harris had a great idea," Ellie announced breathlessly. "Why don't you tell him about it?"

"Sure thing." He blinked owlishly, then looked up at me. "Basically, the one thing all four of us have in common is that we don't really dig the party scene they've got going right now, right? I mean, you don't look like you're having fun, Ellie's got her face scrunched up like she just swallowed a lemon every time she looks out the window, and Felix and I both prefer a more...relaxing sort of chemical recreation."

"Damn drunks are too damn loud," Felix chimed in, scowling.

I nodded in cautious agreement. Sad as it seemed, drinking was the social equalizer inside the company. If management hadn't seen you half-wasted and licking a fence post, you weren't their kind of people and they flat-out didn't trust you as a result. This meant that even if you weren't necessarily the biggest partier out there, you kept your mouth shut about your entertainment preferences lest you get labeled as having "the wrong attitude." Having the wrong attitude got people fired, demoted, or put on shitwork projects, and I wasn't particularly interested in any of those outcomes.

Harris, to his credit, didn't seem to notice my internal dissertation, and plowed right on. "Cool. So unless we want to hang around all night listening to those tools have fun, we need to find something else to do."

"But we're in the middle of nowhere, dumbass," The Cat interjected, his accent getting thicker as he got more animated. "There ain't a damn thing else to do around here, unless we want to get lost and then get sodomized by some hillbillies on a fishing trip." He held up his hands and mimed playing the banjo. Ellie hit him on the arm, hard. He winced and held up his hands in a gesture of surrender, and she flashed me a tiny victory grin. For that alone, I was ready to marry her.

"We don't need to go anywhere," Harris replied, unperturbed. "I was poking around the main office after I finished unpacking, and they have all these informational packets and maps and things. It turns out this whole place is built on an old plantation, and there's a lake around here somewhere, too."

"So what are you proposing?" I asked, warily. "A midnight swim? Or an amateur archaeology expedition?"

"Sort of," he admitted, and grinned. "Look, being around here is going to suck. It's going to suck a lot. So why don't we just all go for a walk and explore the place a little bit? You know, see if we can find the ruins of the house, find the lake in case we want to blow off the programming tomorrow and go for a swim, and just generally get away from the idiots." He turned to me, as if sensing my reluctance. "Don't be such a city boy, Ben. Don't be such a *Yankee*. Contrary to what you might believe, the woods are not full of gators, snakes and rednecks just waiting for their chance at your wallet and firm white ass. Hell, it's safer here than walking around oh-so-civilized Atlanta." As if to accentuate his words, a string of firecrackers went off outside. Screams and giggles followed, muted slightly by distance.

Cat shuddered. Ellie looked over at me. "What do you think?" she asked.

I chewed on my lower lip for a minute. Going off exploring with Ellie sounded just fine to me; going off exploring with Ellie and the boys considerably less so. "Well, it beats waiting for the fireworks to come in the front window," I muttered, mostly to myself.

"What?" Cat asked.

"Nothing." I set my beer down on the table. "Screw it. Let's go."

* * *

In actuality, it took us about an hour to get everyone vertical, fed and ready to roll. This was enough time for me to grab both another Sam and time to talk to Ellie. The former became necessary as I listened to Harris and Cat snipe back and forth at each other over where exactly we'd be exploring; the latter was just a happy accident.

"You sure you want to do this?" I asked her.

She nodded. "What else could we do tonight?"

A few answers ran through my head, but I stopped them before they got to my mouth. "Well, I was thinking that if you wanted to just go somewhere and talk, that would be fine, too. Less chance of stepping on a snake, for one thing."

She grinned, prettily, and I blushed. "That's very sweet," she said, and patted my cheek. "Maybe tomorrow night, OK?"

"OK," I said, even as she was walking off.

OK indeed, I thought, and watched her walk, in every sense of the term.

It was dark by the time we left the bungalow, the sort of dark you don't get back in the city. As we trooped out of the front door, armed with bug spray, one lonely flashlight and a vague idea of where we were going, I gaped up at how big the sky seemed. The lights on and in the bungalows seemed very small somehow — there was just a huge expanse of open sky, filled with stars and a fat, lazy moon peeking through the trees. Back home in Connecticut, you were lucky to get a couple dozen stars, even on the nights when the Hartford city lights didn't turn the sky dull purple. But here, the sky was something else, something huge.

"That's one hell of a view," I said, and pointed straight up with the flashlight. Harris nodded, while The Cat just whistled.

Ellie took my arm proprietarily and pulled me forward. "It'll get better when we get away from the buildings and the lights and the noise. Come on!"

We went, her enthusiasm tugging us all along in her wake. Moving up the paved driveway we walked, we took a turn onto the gravel road that had so thoroughly assaulted my sedan's undercarriage on the way in. Right would have taken us back toward the highway; we turned left, and went deeper into what we imagined would be our little magical mystery tour. Our footsteps crunched in lumpy syncopation as we stomped along, and within a couple of minutes, a bend in the road left the resort — and its lights — behind.

Ellie halted. "Now, look up," she said. Obediently, we stopped and did.

It was breathtaking. The slash of sky visible between the trees that lined the road was liberally spangled with stars, brighter and fiercer than any I'd ever seen before. For the first time in my life, I could see the pale band of the Milky Way. It was astonishing. Unencumbered by street lamps and fast food marquees, the stars glowed aggressively down on us.

Harris whistled. The Cat nodded a few times and said something that was probably "Dang." Ellie stood there, face upturned so the stars could bathe it in their light, her expression a mask of rapturous glee.

And me? My attention was already slipping to something else.

Because on either side of that ribbon of sky were the trees, and they were not to be ignored.

That's not quite true, now that I think back on it. The trees themselves you could ignore, but the shapes they made in the night, those you couldn't tear your eyes away from. If you did, something would move in the corner of your sight and convince you the whole forest was just as interested in you as you were in it. There was reasonable evidence that trees were in there *somewhere*, looming over us from either side. *Something* had to be under that curtain of greenery, after all, something that grew straight and tall and threw out branches in every direction to hold it up. But the trees themselves were invisible; trunk, branch and leaf. Every inch of forest was covered in leaves so thick they looked like snake scales, overlapping and hissing against each other in the evening quiet.

Ellie followed my eyes and nodded. "Kudzu," she said, and that was enough.

I nodded, and added a thoughtful "Hmm." I'd heard of kudzu, of course — some southern plant or other that grew fast and wrapped itself around whatever was handy — but I never imagined it like this. It smothered the trees from root to crown, giving them a new skin of hungry leaves. It was impossible to tell where one left off and the next began, so thick was the greenery between the trunks. And the branches — the branches were worst of all. Heavy with their parasitic load, they leaned out toward the road, dripping long lengths of vine.

Look at them just right, and the trees were no longer trees; they were hooded, misshapen figures lurching toward the road, the play of their branches' shadows evidence that they were reaching out for us. I found myself scanning the rows of smothered pine and sycamore for dark eyes looking out at us, waiting to hear the tell-tale creak of a splayed-root foot pulling free from the earth and lurching toward the road that dared cut its way through their domain.

"Spooky, isn't it?" Ellie said, and leaned in close. I pulled her in a little closer, and it didn't seem like she minded.

"You can say that again. What is this stuff again?"

"Kudzu," The Cat interjected, parking himself on Ellie's other side. "Amazing stuff, ain't it? Came over from Japan 'bout a hundred years ago, and now it's everywhere. Grows 18 inches a day. Y'all can actually see it getting bigger as you watch. It's damn near impossible to kill, too. You pretty much have to burn it out, or anything it starts growing on is screwed."

"What happens to the trees once it starts growing?" I asked, and pointed to one particularly fearsome-looking specimen. It had no fewer than four branches extended over the road, each enrobed in vines and dipping dangerously low over our heads. Never before had I seen a tree that looked so ready to *pounce*.

"Shit, man, that's easy." Harris walked up, shaking his head. "It dies."

I looked around our little circle, and was unsurprised that we'd closed ranks against the night. I saw Ellie turning from left to right and realized she'd noticed the same thing, so I gave her a smile and looked up at the sky again.

Blinked.

Took a deep breath.

And told myself that it was just my imagination, and that the little strip of sky visible over the road had *not* gotten narrower in the last five minutes.

"..thing left."

"What?" I tore my eyes away from that thin slice of sky and focused on The Cat. He was nodding slowly, his hands moving animatedly as he expounded on the wonders of kudzu. He looked at me, annoyed I hadn't listened the first time but pleased he got to serve as an authority again. "Like I said, man, this here stuff is unbelievable. It grows up on a tree and the tree can't get any light. It just dies under there."

I waved my arms, pointing to everything in the vicinity. "So you're saying that all of those trees are dying?"

He grinned like a blissed-out Cheshire Cat. "Yup. Or dead. Just smooth grey wood and gnarly branches, like long fingers under there, and all of it starting to rot."

I shuddered. "Thanks so goddamned much for the image, man. Do we want to stay here? One of these things might be rotting enough to fall over on us."

"I think they make sure the ones near the road will stand up," Ellie offered, but she was the first to start off down the narrow strip of gravel and into the further dark. Harris and I looked at each other and then followed, leaving The Cat to bring up the rear.

After a good fifteen minutes' walking time, we found the first evidence of the old plantation: the remnants of a small house's foundation, stone mortared to stone in a square ten feet on a side. "Smokehouse, maybe?" I offered doubtfully as the flashlight beam played over it, a bare five feet from the side of the road.

"Maybe," Ellie said, unconvinced. "I wonder where the main house is." "Back in there," I replied, gesturing toward the deeper woods. As I was still holding the flashlight, this caused the beam to dance crazily over the leaves. The kudzu had started making inroads here, too, and while the trees weren't entirely encased in the stuff, it looked to be only a matter of time.

Felix leaned in toward the woods, then shook his head. "No way. We are not going back in there at this hour of the night. All we need is to have someone fall down an old well or pop an ankle in a gopher hole because y'all couldn't wait until morning to go play in the dirt. The rocks will be there in the morning, guys, I promise."

"But it won't be as much fun in the morning," Ellie protested, only half jokingly.

I caught her eye and winked. "And besides, we have programming that we *have* to do in the morning. Now's our only free time."

"Free time, my ass," Felix grumbled. "You can go. I'm not wandering around in the woods in the pitch dark. Probably redneck cannibal zombies waiting back in there with their pet cottonmouths." Harris stood beside him, nodding agreement that was silent apart from the occasional "Yeah, man." Both looked grim.

I frowned, and started to feel my resolve slip a little bit. Going off into the woods at this hour wasn't exactly my idea of a brilliant notion either, but Ellie wanted to and Harris didn't, which meant that backing Ellie was a moral and hormonal necessity. Besides, I had the flashlight, and we were still within shouting distance of all our drunken coworkers in case there actually were some kind of emergency. Faced with such unassailable logic and moral conviction, common sense packed up its bags and left, leaving me standing there racking my brain for something witty to say.

To buy time, I played the flashlight's beam back and forth in the gap between the lowest tree branches and the ground. The light stabbed out into the woods and I waggled it a bit, hoping for a direction to emerge from the darkness.

At the edge of vision, one did. Or maybe it had been there all along, and I'd just missed it the first time I'd looked that way. Something that looked like stone and metal gleamed there in the light, just at the edge of vision. I squinted, trying to get a better look, and took a step toward it off the road.

"What are you looking at?" Ellie asked, hope in her voice.

"I'm not sure." I took another step off the gravel and raised the angle of the beam. More stone reared its head into the light. "I think I may have found the main house, though. There. Do you see it?"

She turned, triumphant, and jabbed Harris in the chest. "See? It's right there. We won't even be out of sight of the road. Come on." She grabbed his hand with both of hers and tugged.

He didn't move, instead shaking his hand free. "No way," he said stubbornly, and tucked his thumbs into his armpits. "I'm not going in there, not at night, anyhow."

"Fine." Ellie deliberately turned her back on him. "I'll be going alone, then, unless someone," — she gave me a pointed look — "wants to escort me with the flashlight and keep me safe?"

"I'd be honored," I said, and felt my face melt into a shit-eating grin. Harris saw it too, and his expression went as sour as year-old yogurt. "Why don't you and Felix stay here and wait, Harris, in case we get into any trouble. That sound good to you?"

"Yeah, whatever." He sounded equal parts disinterested and pissed off, but The Cat had already plopped down on the road crosslegged and pulled out a lighter. Looking down with disgust, he waved us into the woods. "Just don't take too long, OK? I still don't think it's safe out there."

"Five minutes," Ellie promised, and then dragged me under the trees.

It was quiet off the road, and dark. The sound of Harris' bitching faded within a few footsteps, and then it was the sound of our feet on the dried branches and dead leaves. A quick look up told me that no starlight or moonlight was making it through the canopy of leaves. It left us to wander by flashlight in what seemed more and more with every step like a sort of cave, one with stalactites of leafy vines and stalagmites of rotting tree stumps thrusting up from the mulch.

"Listen," I said, and stopped. Ellie did the same, then turned to me, puzzled.

"What is it?" she asked, her voice managing to echo off the trees.

I waved at her with my off hand. "Don't say anything. Just listen. What do you hear?"

She looked around for a moment, trying to understand my concern. "I don't hear anything."

"That's what I mean." I looked around nervously, then brought the flashlight around to illuminate her face. "Shouldn't there be insects or frogs or something making noise out here?"

"Well, there should be, yes." She looked briefly confused, then turned toward our destination. "The camp owners probably bugsprayed them out of existence," she said over her shoulder. She didn't sound terribly convinced, but she didn't stop, either, and pressed on into the dark. Holding the flashlight more tightly and looking down every time I stepped on something that crunched, I followed.

It wasn't the foundations of a house we'd seen. I realized that when we got close. Instead, it was a low, wrought-iron fence half-gone to rust, and inside it, a double row of stones. "Jesus," I said when we were close enough to see what we were approaching, but Ellie's response was "Cool!" and she ran forward to check the little graveyard out.

There were eight upright stones set four and four, I saw when I joined her at the fence. Four more flat grave markers rested off a bit, in the corner of the plot. The stones were old, that much was certain — weather had eroded the names enough that they were unreadable by flashlight. The graveyard itself was perhaps twelve feet by twenty, mostly overgrown with weeds and brambles, and bounded by that rusty, waist-high fence. The tops of the fence poles, I noticed with relief, were rounded, which meant that Ellie wasn't liable to give herself tetanus by leaning over them the way she was. There was a gate, which looked to have rusted shut, and something vaguely reminiscent of a path between the stones, but there was no other sign that this graveyard had been tended any time in the last ten years.

"Look," said Ellie, and pointed. "The little stones. They're all off in the corner. Must have been children who died."

I nodded. "I guess this was the family burial ground, though it's not very big. They must have lost the land pretty quickly."

"Probably after the Civil War," she agreed, and wandered off into what presumably was thought about the long-ago events that had transpired in that very place.

I stood there as she poked about for long minutes, looking at the gravestones one after the other. "We should go," I finally ventured, when it was clear that she'd seen about all there was to see.

"I guess so," Ellie replied absently. "I just wish I could see the names on the tombstones, so we could look the family up and see what happened to them."

I scanned the flashlight beam over the largest of the grave markers. It was red granite, unusual down here, and showed nothing more than the fact that carving had once adorned its face. "We're not going to see anything tonight. Maybe we should come back tomorrow, like Harris said."

"What, and miss the Myers-Briggs test?" For a moment I thought she was serious, and she laughed delightedly when she saw my expression. "Of course we'll come back tomorrow. I don't want to do any teambuilding exercises. I don't particularly want any of our coworkers on my team." "Not any of them?"

"Well," and she smiled. "Maybe one. Let's go."

We got back to the road in short order and without incident. The entire way back, Ellie spun elaborate fantasies about what we'd seen and what might have happened here. She was ready to burst at the seams with things she wanted to tell our erstwhile partners in crime, whom she was convinced were bitterly regretting their decision to stay behind.

But when we shlepped through that last curtain of leaves, we got a nasty surprise. Harris and The Cat were gone.

"Fuckers!" I said, which I thought was quite reasonable under the circumstances.

"They probably just got bored," Ellie said in a soothing tone, though she wasn't able to keep the annoyance entirely out of her voice either. "I'm sure it's no big deal. Let's just go back to the resort and find out what happened."

I nodded, muttered something about the goddamned stoner freaks under my breath, and started trudging back up the hill toward the bungalows. Ellie walked with me, close by my side, and our footsteps synched up within a couple of paces. Somewhere off in the distance, a single cicada started its song, waited for its friends to join in, and then thought better of the whole idea.

Good call, little bug, I thought, and marched homeward in silence.

* * *

"What the fuck happened to you two?" I asked Harris and The Cat over breakfast the next morning, somehow keeping my voice just under a roar.

They exchanged guilty glances. Ellie and I exchanged quizzical ones as she took a bite of her English muffin, and then Harris said, "You tell them."

"Aww, crap." The Cat put his fork down in the middle of his scrambled eggs. "Y'all are not going to believe this, guys, but I swear it's true. We didn't want to go back, but after you went in there, things got...well, they just got plain weird." "Weird," I echoed tonelessly.

"Weird," he repeated, and nodded with all the vigor he could muster at 8:30 AM. "Seriously weird-like. First of all, we should be pissed at you. Y'all said you were going in for five minutes, but you were gone for over an hour, with us sitting there getting more and more worried, and — "

"Wait a minute," I interrupted. "No way were we gone for an hour. That was a five-minute walk each way, and we spent maybe five minutes total in the graveyard."

"It was an *hour*, man," Felix insisted.

"You were stoned, Felix," I said through gritted teeth. "You think it takes half an hour to make minute rice when you've been smoking."

"No way. I was looking at my watch."

"In the dark?" I snorted.

He held it up for me to see. "It's got one of those light-up faces, asshole. And it was at least an hour, I swear. And when you stepped off the road, you guys just vanished into the woods."

"Now that's ridiculous." Ellie jumped in, full of righteous disapproval. "We were just off the road the whole time, and you should have seen the flashlight beam, even through the leaves."

"Should have, yeah." Now it was Harris' turn. "But you went in there and it was like the leaves just walled themselves up behind you. We couldn't see a thing. Couldn't hear you, either, though we tried yelling."

Ellie and I exchanged a worried look. "We didn't hear you at all," I said, more softly. "Are you sure you shouted?"

"Positive." Harris took his fork and jabbed in my direction with it. "Nice and loud, even. But that's not why we left, even if we did think you two were being pricks."

"Or screwing around," The Cat added. Ellie wadded up her napkin and threw it at him. She missed.

"We were not screwing around," she said firmly. "We walked in, looked at the graveyard, and walked out. It did not take us an hour, we didn't hear you calling, and I think you're both just lying."

They looked at each other again, clearly uncomfortable. When angry, Ellie was formidable in the way only small pretty women could be, and no man within her sphere of influence ever wanted to risk her wrath.

"There was one other thing," Harris reluctantly offered. "That's what really made us go. We would have waited otherwise, I swear."

"We were going to stay, honest," The Cat chimed in.

"Uh-huh," I said. "Do tell."

Harris swallowed nervously and fidgeted with his fork. "It was the trees."

"The trees?"

He swallowed, hard. "It looked like — and I know neither of you are going to believe this, but I swear it's the truth — it looked like they were moving."

"That's called wind, Harris," Ellie said icily.

"Not like that!" He took a deep breath and shuddered. Next to him, Felix wouldn't meet my eyes. "So help me God, they looked like they were leaning down towards us, and the branches were curving and moving against the wind, and then they started even edging closer to the side of the road — "

"Enough." I held up my hand in what I hoped was a commanding gesture. "You two have got to be kidding me. You ran off and left us in the woods because you thought the trees were chasing you? What the hell were you smoking last night, anyway?"

"You don't hallucinate on weed," Harris said sullenly. "And I know what I saw. What we saw. You saw it too, didn't you, Felix?"

Felix stared intently into his own lap. "I think so," he said softly. "It was really dark."

"Great." I smiled cheerlessly. "Well, now that that's cleared up, why don't we move on. Ellie wanted to go back there during the daytime so we could get a look at the graveyard we found back in the woods."

"You found a graveyard?" Harris perked up a bit. "That's cool."

I nodded. "It is cool, and I promise you the trees will stand absolutely still during the daytime." I waggled my fingers at him menacingly. "They only come out at night, you know."

"Screw you," he said, but it was without heat. "So, what, you want to go back there?"

"After breakfast," Ellie nodded.

"Fuck breakfast," said Felix, and gave the scorched strips of bacon on his plate the hairy eyeball. "This stuff will kill you, man." As one, we rose and dumped our trays at the trash barrel, then headed for the door. Ellie bounced outside first, The Cat following.

Before we got outside, I grabbed Harris by the elbow and hauled him out of Ellie's earshot. He faced me, mouth set in a thin line. "Yes?" he asked, and fluttered his eyelashes.

"Look, I know it's none of my business," I said, "but do me a favor? No goofy bush today until we get back, OK?"

"You know not what you ask," he replied theatrically, then grinned. "No worries, bro. Don't need it during the day. But tonight, you just might want some."

"I don't think so," I said, and let him go.

* * *

The hike to the old plantation site took longer during the day, something that surprised me. Most of the walk was done without conversation, though Harris occasionally moaned about the fact that we hadn't found the lake. Only Ellie felt like talking, and she kept up a constant stream of commentary on plants, birds, and anything else we walked past.

"You know," she said to me softly at one point, "I can understand now what they saw last night when they were..." she mimed toking, and went on. "The trees really do look like figures under the kudzu." I nodded. In the daylight, the vegetative amoeba was less eerie, but more impressive. I could see now how thick the growth was, and how fast it scaled new trees. Dozens of yards of woods at a time were covered in broad, flat leaves, a landscape in living green. Even trees that I could have sworn were clear the night before were now part of the vast emerald carpet.

"They still left without us," I replied in something that wasn't quite a grumble.

"Well, yes, but that left us more time together. To talk," she added hurriedly, and then skipped off to point out to Felix some variant or other of the yellow-bellied sap-sucker.

I grinned, and kept grinning all the way back to the spot where we'd dared enter the woods.

It wasn't hard to find. For one thing, the walk was ninety percent downhill, which made it a pleasant, fast stroll. For another, the detritus from The Cat's late-night adventure in pharmaceuticals was still sitting on the gravel road. The greenery seemed a little thicker than it had in the dark, but I chalked that up to imagination and poor eyesight.

"This is it," I announced unnecessarily, and ground to a halt. "Who's for a little grave robbing?"

"Not robbing," Ellie correct me primly. "We're just going to observe, and to pay our respects."

"Well, yes, that's what I meant..." I began, but she'd already marched off into the greenery, and we had no choice but to follow.

The graveyard, at least, seemed less impressive by day, and here and there shafts of sunlight managed to poke through to the forest floor. "Neat," said Harris, and I was inclined to agree. By night, the spot had a mystery and a power to it. By day it was ramshackle and quaint, still interesting but distinctly unmagical. "Neat" seemed to be about the best way to describe it, and I said so.

"You men. No sense of wonder," said Ellie, distinctly annoyed, and hoisted herself over the fence.

"Ellie, don't!" I called out. "This is private property. You shouldn't trespass."

She looked at me and laughed. "We're in the middle of the woods, silly. Who's going to see me? Besides, we're just here for a minute. I'll see what the stones say, and then we can leave and go back to," her voice shifted to a stentorian monotone, "building cross-departmental relationships by drinking heavily."

"Fine, whatever," I said, and turned away, irritated at myself. In truth, I really didn't want her going in there, but for reasons having nothing to do with trespassing. *How the hell am I supposed to impress her*, I asked myself, *if she keeps on taking all the chances*? And making the lame comment about property rights had, no doubt, made me look like even more of an idiot in her eyes. I kicked the fence angrily and spat down onto the dead leaves.

"Hey," Felix sidled up to me and gave me a disapproving look. "Don't kick the fence, dude. That's vandalism."

"Whatever." I shrugged and looked down at the fencepost I'd banged my foot against. It now leaned at a definite angle, and a surge of embarrassment shot through me. "Maybe the trees will come out and straighten the fence tonight," I said, a bit more harshly than was strictly necessary, and stared after Ellie as she picked her way among the brambles.

"If you'd seen what we'd seen, you wouldn't be making fun." The Cat's tone was dead serious, and I looked at him, surprised. Normally he couldn't keep a joke going for longer than your average commercial, but this time he seemed absolutely sincere. "You should probably tell Ellie to hold off on poking around in the woods tonight," he added, a trifle hesitantly. "She'll listen to you."

I laughed, softly. "She won't listen to me, even if I felt like telling her something like that, which I don't. You know how it is, man. You just get caught up in whatever she's doing, and go along for the ride." I gestured broadly, taking in the trees, the forest floor, and whatever else was in our vicinity. "Honestly, this is probably safer than hanging around our co-workers. At least the kudzu won't try to grope her, or throw up on her shoes."

He didn't laugh, instead poking me in the ribs with his elbow. "She will listen to you, man. She always does when it counts, whether you notice or not. And this counts. It really does." He paused and took a deep breath. "I've got a bad feeling, a real bad feeling about this place. If you care about her, keep her out of the woods at night."

I turned to face him. "She's a grown woman," I said softly. "She can make her own decisions."

"You can help her decide not to do something bone-stupid," he replied. "That means it's on you if you don't." And then he turned and walked away, heading for the road.

"Weird," I muttered, and turned back to watch Ellie. She was still in the graveyard, her jeans carefully dusted clean of rust and paint and whatever else she'd gotten on them while fencehopping. Now she squatted on her haunches in front of the biggest of the stones, her fingers tracing lines on its surface and her face screwed up in concentration.

I thought she looked adorable.

"What does it say?" I asked.

"It's hard to tell," she called back. From her tone of voice, she sounded like she was shouting, but it was almost hard to hear her. I looked around for evidence of wind that might drown her out, but there was none. Even the tops of the trees were perfectly still. The air was calm, and again, nothing living moved or betrayed its existence besides us.

"I think these are names," she said, and I leaned over the fence to hear her better. "It's the names of the family members. You can read the little flat stones —

those are babies. No names. They died before they were christened. It's really sad."

"And the big ones?" I asked.

"The grownups, I guess." Her hand moved over the face of the tombstone, flat now against the dull red rock. "It's strange. The edges of the gravestones are sharp, like they're new, but the faces are all weathered and the writing's impossible to read. All I can really see are the dates. It's mostly 1820s to 1860s."

"So you were right," Harris interjected from across the graveyard. I shot him a look of annoyance, while Ellie grinned at him in delight. Needless to say, he kept his eyes on her.

"I was right!" she said, and bounced to her feet. "You know what I need?"

I sighed. "What?"

"Paper," she said firmly. "It's what you're supposed to do with tombstones. You put paper over them and do a rubbing," She rubbed her chin with her thumb. "I'll bet no one's ever done these before."

"Very few people wander into the South Carolina woods with an art studio in their back pocket," I responded, but she was already off, estimating the number of sheets she'd need, where she'd get the crayons to do the rubbings with, and so forth.

I looked down at my watch. It read 11:45, and I frowned. Surely we hadn't been there that long, and yet there the evidence was in blinking digital. "We should head back if we want lunch," I said, a little more softly. "If you want to get your tracing paper or whatever and get back here before it gets dark, the sooner we go, the better."

"Spoilsport," Ellie said, and stuck her tongue out at me. But then she smiled and hopped over the fence. "You're right, and I'm hungry." She hooked one arm through mine and the other through Harris' and grinned. "I feel like Dorothy," she said. "Let's go off to see the wizard."

"Marketing is doing the cooking," I warned. "It's not likely to be very magical."

"All the more reason to have fun now," she replied, and off we went.

* * *

Something decidedly unmagical was waiting for us back at the bungalows, namely the looming figure of Hector. He was scowling when we trundled our way down the driveway, and kept scowling when we skidded to a halt in front of him.

"You missed the morning's programming," he said accusingly, waving a finger in my face for emphasis.

"Yes. We did." I said, as contrite as I could manage. "We went out for a walk after breakfast and...lost track of time."

"Yeah, yeah." He looked back over his shoulder at the main building. "Felix told me all about it when he got back an hour ago."

"An hour?" I was genuinely surprised. "I thought he was only five minutes ahead of us."

"Maybe on your planet," Hector said, and rubbed his eyes. "Look, there's been a change of plans. Due to discussions between us and the facility owners, we're going to leave first thing in the morning." My "What happened?" was simultaneous with Ellie's "That's not fair" and Harris' knowing chuckle.

"Someone broke something, right?" he asked, and grinned wickedly.

"Something like that." Hector looked uncomfortable, and I got a sudden inkling that whatever had happened was extremely embarrassing for Hector personally. "There was what we will politely refer to as an *incident*, and they've asked us to leave. The details are unimportant. All you have to know is that we'll be going right after breakfast tomorrow." He paused and looked around, then continued in a lower voice, "I shouldn't tell you this, but they wanted us out immediately, but then we could have gotten most of our money back. Greedy bastards."

"That's just rude," Ellie opined, and stuck her hands on her hips like a '40s recruiting poster. "They can't do that, can they?"

"They can and they did, and we're not going to argue." Hector's tone was firm, and weary. "This weekend has not exactly been what you'd call a smashing success. Drinking, yes. Screwing, yes. Broken appliances in the bungalows, yes indeedy. Workshopping, not so much. And that's before we get into staff members taking off into the woods in the middle of the night to do God-knows-what in the local graveyards. So, here's what's going to happen. You three," and he pointed to each of us in turn, "are going to do the dishes from lunch, because not only did you skip out on morning programming, but you had a really stupid excuse for doing so. This afternoon, you get to go to the workshops and sit front and center, and if I don't see you there, I'll be telling your managers that you disobeyed a direct request from upper management. If that happens, it will be reflected in your performance and salary reviews. Tonight, you can do whatever the hell you want, but this afternoon your asses are mine. Or at least our workshop coordinator's. Am I understood?"

I could physically feel Ellie slumping next to me, and she dragged my heart down with her as she went. "Understood," I mumbled, and then put an arm around Ellie's shoulders. I turned to her. "Let's go get some lunch, OK? It'll make you feel better."

"In theory," Hector said, and walked off.

* * *

Night fell hard, and as it did, all hell broke loose. Word had gotten around the compound, reliable or not, that we were being forced to leave because an editor named John Blauser had smashed a lamp over someone's head in the complex's front office. Blauser denied the story vehemently, but it was too late; people had decided to stand up for his honor by being drunken louts. By 7:45, a hue and cry had gone up for us to get our money's worth out of being blacklisted, and the staff set to celebrating their last night out in the woods with a will. I counted at least two chairs in the bonfire down past the second row of bungalows, and one more that came flying through a second story window. Bottles were everywhere — full, empty, and in transit — and to the untrained ear, the sound of merriment would have been suspiciously similar to that of a riot.

"Let's go," Ellie said softly as we stood by the bonfire, our communal bag of marshmallows emphatically ignored by the other revelers.

I looked over at her. "Yeah, sure. Whatever. This is depressing the shit out of me."

"Me, too," and she headed for the main complex. "I almost wish we'd just gone back home this afternoon."

"Part of me does, too. This little bacchanal isn't going to help our company's reputation any. But we had to do those fucking workshops, and I don't feel like tackling these roads in the dark. Best to ignore the heathens," I said with an airy wave that took in our officemates, "and endure until morning."

"You're really not attractive when you swear," she said sweetly, and kept walking. "It's not you, and you sound silly doing it."

"Do I, now?" I walked a little faster, trying to catch up. "And what does make me attractive, if I may ask?"

"Being you," she said, and let it hang there for a moment. "I think that's attractive enough. Though I'm not sure about when you drink too much beer."

"The beer," I said firmly, "is an affectation, a feeble attempt to fit in with the rest of the company. I'll tell you a secret — I don't even really like the taste of it."

"I know," she said, and snickered, albeit nicely. "You make this really funny face every time you drink one."

I felt myself flushing bright red, and was thankful the bonfire light gave me camouflage. "I do? Damn. I'll have to stop that."

"Stop making the face?"

"Stop drinking beer." I stopped, and reached out for her hand. She let me, and turned to face me. Her face was very serious as she looked up at mine.

"Did you really mean that?" I asked. "That you find me attractive, I mean?"

A tiny smile quirked the corner of her mouth. "Do you always use pickup lines this smooth?"

"No, this is a special occasion." I blinked furiously, and thought very hard about what to say next. "What I mean to say is, well, I find you very attractive, too, and if you like me, maybe we could go someplace and just talk for a while. Get to know each other better." I caught myself before I said "and jump each others' bones," but I don't really think I needed to.

She smiled for real now, a very pretty smile. "That might be nice," she said softly. "But first, there's something I want to do with you."

"Yes?" Various visions floated through my head, most of them rated PG-13 and higher. "Name it."

She took a deep breath. "Let's go back to the graveyard tonight so I can do those rubbings. It will be so cool, and we can put them up in the office when we get back."

"I don't know," I said softly. "It sounded like Hector wasn't really up on the idea of us heading out there again, and besides, it might actually be dangerous."

"Oh, foo." Her face collapsed into a very pretty mask of disappointment. "I don't think it would be dangerous. I think it would be neat. And it's something that just you and I can do — something we can do together and share." The half-smile returned, and with it I knew I was doomed. "Besides," she added. "Wouldn't that make a great first date to tell people about?"

I thought about what I could possibly say to rebut that argument and realized that there were no arrows in my quiver. Say anything, and I risked losing her. Say nothing, and we'd take a short walk into woods that were noticeably free of any hostile critters, and get far enough away from the rest of the company that a little frisky business might be an option. I thought about Felix's warning for a moment, then dismissed it. Trees do not lean forward to eat pedestrians, even stoned ones, even in South Carolina.

I exhaled sharply. She stared up on me.

"Right. Let's go."

"Really?" Her face erupted into a smile and I felt ten feet tall. "You really want to go?"

"*Really* want to go is pushing it a bit," I confessed, "But I want to do it. Let's go get that paper you were talking about and do this thing before it gets too late."

"OK." She was positively chirping. "I got it and the crayons this afternoon, during the thing we did with the construction paper and the greeting cards we had to make for each other. Do you remember that?"

I did, and I shuddered at the memory. One of the interns had given me something that looked like an origami swan after a trip through a blender, and I was convinced she'd be peeking into my cube at least once a week from now on to make sure it occupied a place of honor. "Well, at least some good will come out of that exercise in timewasting."

"Yup. Lots of good." Very hesitantly, she pulled my face down to hers and kissed me. It was soft and it was quick, and the taste of her lips on mine was sweeter than I'd imagined it would be.

"Let's go," she whispered when we came up for air. "Let's hurry."

And then we were at the bungalow, and I held open the door with a smile that, I am quite certain, told Harris everything he needed to know.

He and Felix were inside, smoking gently and playing Uno. They both looked up at our entrance. Harris was pissed off, Felix disappointed.

"Just stopping in for a minute, guys," I said as Ellie vanished toward her room. "We're going out."

"Uh-huh," Harris said. "Where are you going?"

I shrugged. "She wants to do those rubbings. I can't stop her, so I might as well go along to make sure she doesn't get attacked by the local werewolves."

"Riiiiight." He turned back to his hand and studied it with calculated indifference. The Cat glowered at me and threw his cards down.

"I told you to stop her, man," he hissed, shaking his head. "Now you gotta protect her for real. Don't let anything get her out there, OK? Because it's your fault if they do."

"There is nothing out there to get her," I said through gritted teeth. "There aren't even any mosquitoes. She, and I, will be fine. We will go to the graveyard, she will do her rubbings, and we will come back here to join you gentlemen in your fine card game. This, I swear. Now will you please stop acting like a boy scout from a troop in Transylvania and leave me and her alone for a little while?"

"Her funeral, man," Felix grumbled, and turned away. Before I could call him on it, Ellie popped into the common area, a box of crayons under one arm and a poster tube under the other.

"I'm ready," she announced, and snuggled up close to me. She was smiling so hard, she practically glowed. All coherent thought left my head and took a sharp turn south.

Harris turned a delicate shade of pink. The Cat just glowered down at his cards, squeezing them so hard they creased.

I walked into the bungalow's tiny excuse for a kitchen and grabbed the flashlight from where it rested, upright on the table. "Let's go," I said to her. "Let's go right now."

* * *

The walk to the graveyard was fast this time, far faster than it had any right to be. I carried the poster tube full of paper, and Ellie took care of the crayons. The entire way down was one long discussion over what color she should use. I favored copper, but she didn't want to use up all of the metallics "because they're people's favorites." I pointed out that if she didn't use them, someone else would, and besides, even with the lousy quarter the company had just had they could afford to spot us a few new boxes of crayons. She didn't reply to that directly, but gave a thoughtful hum and walked — no, skipped, really — on.

Only twice did I look away from her as we made our way into the night. Once, I looked down to make sure that my shoes were in fact tied, because the last thing I wanted to do was trip in front of Ellie and make myself look like a fool. The other time, I looked up, and reassured myself that the sky and stars were still there.

They were.

Feeling much more secure about my place in the grand scheme of things, I put my eyes back on Ellie and followed her on into the night.

The stretch of road that ran past the grave site was ridiculously easy to find. The half-curtain of kudzu that had been there in the morning was entirely gone, leaving a gaping, not entirely inviting gap in the greenery.

"We must have knocked it down on the way out," Ellie said, a trifle hesitantly, and I nodded slightly. To cover my discomfort, I looked around for any fronds or leaves on the ground, but there weren't any. Apparently the voracious kudzu had already re-integrated its fallen manifestations, or some animal had come along and eaten it.

The thought that it had deliberately gotten out of our way didn't linger in my mind for more than a minute and a half, I swear. Honest.

"Shall we?" she asked, and I bowed.

"Allow me to go first. It might be dangerous."

She giggled. "And you have the flashlight."

"That I do," I said ruefully. "So much for trying to impress you."

"You don't have to impress me, silly. Now let's go."

Her tone brooked no argument, so I didn't argue. I just ducked under the lowest-hanging of the tree branches and stepped into the woods, and listened, like Orpheus, for the sound of her following.

The forest was different tonight. I could sense that immediately. Where the night before, everything had been silent as a newborn's nursery, tonight the trees were alive with sound. There were no animal noises, though — none of the cicada and cricket songs that I had heard back among the bungalows, no nightbird calls or frogsong or bat chirps tickling the upper edge of hearing. It just sounded leafy, for lack of a better term; wood creaking and branches snapping and leaves rustling against each other in the breeze.

There hadn't been a breeze when we'd walked down, I remembered. Just hot, sticky southern air.

It means nothing, I told myself. *Branches move all the time. You're letting Felix get to you. There's got to be a breeze higher up, away from the road.* And to prove the point to myself, I pointed the flashlight straight up for a moment, and illuminated the underside of the leaves on high.

They were, I saw as a cold feeling settled into my stomach, perfectly still.

"Ellie?" I ventured, hesitantly.

"Don't tell me you're getting scared!" she taunted from behind me, and then hurried past. I cursed, under my breath so she wouldn't hear, and went after her. She heard my footsteps in the leaves, laughed, and ran faster. I tripped over a hidden tree root but held onto the flashlight, cursed again, got to my feet, and kept running. *Keep the flashlight on her*, something told me. *Keep her in the light.* And so I did, even when that meant running my shins into tree stumps and my legs into thorns. I ran as fast as I dared, keeping her just in sight, and wondered how fucking far it was to the graveyard because it hadn't been one tenth this long in the morning. Vines I hadn't seen scored my face, patches in the dry ground suddenly became muddy and treacherous, and every step seemed to be uphill. Ellie, for her part, ran on as I fell further and further behind her.

And then suddenly, she was there at the fence, and I pulled up, puffing, ten seconds after she did.

"Slowpoke," she said, and pointed to the gate. "See?"

The gate was open. The graveyard itself was utterly bereft of weeds, and there was a note on yellow paper, taped to one of the fenceposts.

"What does it say?" I asked, and immediately felt like an idiot.

"I don't know," she replied. "I'll read it and find out."

She picked it up, and I took the flashlight and held it over her shoulder so she could read. The note was folded over a few times with great precision, but when she'd finished opening it up there were only a few words there, hand-written in a rough blocky print.

"Sorry the place is such a mess," it said. "If I'd known folks were going to be visiting family, I would have cleaned it up. Stay as long as you want." There was no signature.

"Well, that's very nice," Ellie said, and tucked the note in her pocket. "And you were so worried about trespassing."

"I don't know," I said. "Something about that note just doesn't feel right."

"You're being paranoid," she said firmly.

"Probably," I admitted. "But could I see the note anyway? Just in case?"

"Fine." She dug into her pocket and handed it over, wordless irritation emanating from her in all directions.

I cringed, but took the note. It seemed straightforward enough, but something still nagged at me. I stared at the yellow paper, trying to decipher hidden meaning in the words, when suddenly it hit me.

The paper itself was the problem. It felt rough underneath my fingers, and under the flashlight it seemed weathered and old. Whoever had cleaned out the graveyard had left their note on a scrap that seemed like it had been stuck in a bush for years, and that, I thought, was odd.

"Well?"

I started to open my mouth to explain what I'd discovered, but decided against it. What could I say? "Hey, the paper the note is on is old?" It hardly seemed enough to dissuade her. Instead, I just gestured with the flashlight to the open gate, and tucked the note away. She took the hint and walked into the graveyard. I followed, and when she silently extended her hand for the poster tube, I handed it over.

That's when I got the evening's second shock, third if you counted Ellie kissing me. The soil inside hadn't been weeded, I now saw. Instead, it had been ravaged. Someone had come through and yanked out every bit of plant life. Every bramble, every weed, every blade of grass — gone. Nothing had been merely trimmed and let off with a warning. It had all been pulled out by the roots, leaving nothing but soil dark with rotted leaf mulch and gaping holes where weeds and creepers used to be.

Ellie walked on. She didn't seem to have noticed any of this. I got the sense that she didn't want to.

Still, the disquiet wouldn't leave me alone. As Ellie looked at stones, I stared down at the soil until she finally caught me doing it.

"Would you cut that out?" she asked. "It's distracting. We're not here for the dirt, you know."

"Sorry," I apologized. "I was just wondering who left the note. I mean, no one lives here, so they couldn't have seen us. No one knew that this was where we'd been until Felix — excuse me, The Cat — shot his mouth off today. It's just weird, that's all."

"You worry too much," she said, as she held up crayon after crayon in the flashlight beam. "Someone probably saw us go in, saw the junk the guys left on the road, or came to visit the graveyard and saw our footprints." She pulled something reddish out and matched it to a parchment-colored piece of paper. "There, I think. That's it."

I gave a half-hearted nod. "If you say so. I just don't know who lives out here. We never heard any cars go past on the road while we were in here."

"Maybe they drove slowly. You know how weird the sound out here is. Now hush, and give me more light." She put the paper to the stone and began working. I stood there, occasionally adjusting the angle of the light as she requested it, and watched her work. Part of me wondered if our trespassing had been what had really gotten the company kicked out of the resort. If that were the case, though , they wouldn't have weeded and left a note. I pondered that for a minute, and then the rest of me told me to shut up and watch Ellie, because she was damned cute and if I held the light at just the right angle I could see a little further down her shirt than an entirely honorable man ought to.

"Done," she finally said, holding the rubbing up to the light. I peered in at it, but even as I looked she rolled it up and moved on to the next stone. I checked the flashlight, which still seemed to be going strong, and patted my pocket for the emergency backup: a lighter. It wasn't my first choice for a method of lighting our way in the woods, but things seemed reasonably green fireproof and besides, for all I knew we were a hundred miles from the nearest convenience store with a Duracell display. The last thing I wanted was to run out of light out here. It would be a long, long walk back in the dark.

Thinking about it made me nervous, so I decided to see if Ellie could be hurried a little bit. "How's it going?" I asked.

"Fine," she replied distractedly. "You could do one, too, if you wanted to."

"I wouldn't be able to hold the flashlight then," I replied sensibly.

"I'll hold it and you can do one when I'm done with this stone," she said, and her tone informed me that yes, I was going to be doing exactly as she had described.

"All right," I responded. "But only if I can use the copper crayon."

"Okay," she said, and then put her head down and went back to work.

An hour, or maybe five minutes later, she announced "Done!"

"Does that mean we can go back now?" I asked.

"No, silly. It means it's your turn. If you don't do one, we can hardly say we did this together."

"I feel I've shed a certain light on the proceedings," I half-protested.

"Very funny." She stood, handed me a piece of paper, and extended her empty hand. "Give me the flashlight."

"Fine, fine," I said. With one hand I took the paper, and with the other I gave her the flashlight. The beam was giving the faintest hints of dimming, or so my nervous hindbrain informed me, so I hurriedly grabbed a crayon that looked right out of the box and looked at my choice of work spaces. "Got any suggestions?"

"That one," she said, and pointed with the light to one at the end of a row. It was small and squat, but even from here looked to have been fairly intricately carved at one point. "Do that one."

"Works for me," I said, and set myself down by it to go to work.

The procedure for doing that sort of rubbing is pretty simple. You take the paper, tape it up so it holds still, then rub the side of the crayon along it so the carving underneath manifests itself in beeswax and coloring. We didn't have any tape, so instead I got to hold the paper up with one hand, thankful there was no wind, and scribble with the other.

And even as I did that, I heard the wind up there among the leaves, and did my damndest to ignore it. Behind me, Ellie held the flashlight, making suggestions as I went along, and I tried hard not to think about The Cat's warning.

By the time I was done, the flashlight had dimmed visibly, and, judging by the degree of recurring droopiness in the beam's position, Ellie's wrists had gotten tired. "I think we're done here," I said gently. "Let's go and look at these things in the light, to see what we've got." Carefully, I rolled up my rubbing and stuck it in the poster tube, then turned back to Ellie to show her I was ready to go.

She stood there, both hands clutching the dying light and pointing it straight up. I could see that she was shivering, even in the muggy heat of the forest, and her eyes were held tightly shut. "Could you tell me," she started in a high, shrill voice, and then stopped. She took a deep breath, swallowed, and tried again. "Could you tell me what you see behind me? Please?" She took another deep breath that was almost a sob, and whispered, "I thought I heard something."

"Something?" I said, and looked up.

"Something," she affirmed, and now she was crying for real, the flashlight shaking in her grip. "*Something called my name.*"

She stood at the edge of the graveyard, maybe a foot and a half from the fence. Her feet were carefully positioned on the neutral ground between two graves, so close together that she teetered as if she stood on a balance beam. Behind her, there should only have been the fence, and then a space of brush and undergrowth leading to the road. That's what had been there yesterday, that's what had been there that morning, that's what had been there when we'd been invited in among the tombstones.

But now the trees were there. Cloaked in green, reaching forward for her, wind-whispering something that might have been her name even as the branches creaked down and the boughs stretched out.

"Ellie," I said very calmly, "Why don't you take a step toward me? There's nothing to worry about. Just come on over here and give me the flashlight, OK?"

"OK," she said, and took a step. Behind her, a sheet of vines dropped to the ground with a hiss. Where the leaves hit the ground, they crept forward, toward Ellie.

She took another step, and another, and I walked towards her with the poster tube held up like I imagined a broadsword was supposed to be.

"What's behind me?" she asked, almost too softly to be heard.

"Nothing that's not supposed to be," I told her, and hated myself for the lie. "Nothing called your name."

And this wasn't a lie, because I could hear the trees now, hear the nonexistent wind moving the kudzu leaf tongues, and I knew what they were saying. They might have called Ellie once, but they weren't calling her name any more.

They were calling mine.

"We're going to go back now, Ellie," I said very loudly as I took the flashlight from her hands. "We're going to leave the crayons here as a present for the nice man who cleaned up the graveyard, and we're going to go back. I'll hold the flashlight and the rubbings. All you have to do is hold onto me. Do you think you can do that?"

She nodded, tears streaking her face. Her eyes were still closed, and her hands reached out and flattened themselves against my chest. "I think that's a very good idea," she said, and pulled herself close.

"That's good, stay close to me," I heard myself saying, all the while trying to figure out how the hell I was going to get us out of this. The carpet of vines had inched forward into the graveyard proper, snaking between the fence posts in places and yanking them out of the soil in others. All through the forest, I could hear the sounds they were making as the things that had once been trees pulled themselves closer to where we stood. There was no time, I knew that now. The longer we delayed, the tighter the green cordon would be pulled around us, and all I had was a dying flashlight and a three-foot length of cardboard.

And Ellie, whom I'd promised Felix I would keep safe.

"All right, Ellie," I said, keeping my voice as calm as I could. "I need you to do something else for me, right now."

"What?"

"I need you to open your eyes and not scream, all right?"

She managed most of it, the scream coming out as a sort of choking sound. I didn't blame her. I wanted to scream myself, but I knew that if I did, I would pretty much just get caught up in the screaming, at least until I got caught up in something worse and leafier.

I wrapped my left arm around her and pulled Ellie with me toward the gate. By some miracle, it was still unblocked, though the place where Ellie had been standing a minute before was already underneath the leaves. They were growing fast, snaking around the tombstones and probing in all directions. A half-dozen tendrils were already growing toward us, moving fast. Behind them, the things that had once been trees leaned in closer. Their voices were louder now. They didn't care who heard them.

We got through the gate and I pulled Ellie to the left. "We're going to have to run now," I said, but she was way ahead of me, sprinting back toward the way we'd come. I felt her slip out from under my arm and started pounding after her, the flashlight's beam fading to a dull yellow and barely keeping her in view. I could half-see, half-hear the terrain in front of us; I didn't dare look behind. Branches wrapped in leafy armor came crashing down, impaling the earth and narrowly missing Ellie. Curtains of vines threw themselves in front of her, reaching out to entangle, and she hurled herself past them.

I didn't have time for that, knew she'd slip out of the light if I dared dodge and weave, and so I trusted to brute strength and just charged straight through. Where I pushed through the vines, they grasped at me, tearing and clinging. Where they touched me, I could feel them probing and pushing, trying to get under the skin. They wanted me, I suddenly understood, to run me through and fill me up and turn me into another one of those figures in the wood.

That would be the beginning, at least. Because the vines here didn't want to stay in the woods, didn't want to just strangle trees and cover shrubs any more. They wanted something more challenging, something more *alive*. They wanted me to walk out in the morning with vines trailing out of my feet and curling out of my eyes, and to pass that contagion on to everyone else.

I thought about what might have tended the graves so very carefully, and wondered if right now that green figure was shambling after me, vines spilling out of his mouth and leaves covering his eyes.

I thought about it catching up to Ellie, and I ran faster.

That's when a tree stump came up out of the ground and hit me.

It had been there before. I'm sure I saw it on the way in. But then it had been a little thing, maybe six inches above the leaves. Now it was something more, wrapped in kudzu and punching its way upward even as I stepped over it. It slammed into my balls and I went over, howling. The flashlight flew out of my fingers, smashed into a tree, and went out. I hit the ground with my shoulder, rolled, and tried to stagger to my feet. The poster tube, of course, I'd managed to hang on to, and I leaned on it now like a cane. "Ellie!" I called. "Ellie!"

"I'm here!" she replied, faintly, far too faintly. "I can see the road!"

"Keep going!" I told her, even as I heard the vines slithering around my feet. "Don't worry about me! Go!"

The sound of her footsteps stopped. "Are you sure?"

"Yes!" My voice broke, and I prayed she wouldn't ask me again. I wasn't sure how I'd answer if she did.

She didn't respond, which I took as a good sign. Faintly, I heard her footsteps, and then they were gone.

That left me alone, in the dark, and all I had to do was concentrate on getting myself out of there. The flashlight was gone, and I was sure I'd heard the bulb shatter when it hit. There was no sense looking for it, not when the tree-things were lurching and roaring closer in the dark.

I started walking, half-bent over in pain, toward the direction from which I'd last heard Ellie's voice. I leaned on the poster tube as much as I dared, staggering on while I went through my pockets looking for the lighter. It took a couple of tries to find it, more time than I liked. With shaking fingers I pulled it out and tried to flick it.

No dice.

Panicking, I dropped the tube with the rubbings and grabbed the lighter with both hands, trying desperately to keep my grip from shaking.

In the near dark, tree limbs groaned with the effort of reaching out for me.

"Come on," I implored the lighter, and flicked it with trembling fingers. I caught a whiff of lighter fluid, but no spark.

Something moved underneath the leaves by my feet, slithering whip-fast and closer.

"Come on!" I flicked it again, praying under my breath.

It flared to life, a tiny beacon in the middle of a very dark place. "Thank you God, " I breathed, and looked around.

The vines had me. A solid wall of greenery hemmed me in. Every direction was blocked off. Even if I had known where to run, I wouldn't have gotten far before the kudzu would have caught me like a fly. I was trapped.

I held up the lighter. Trapped, yes, but with fire.

"Back off," I said, and spun in a slow circle. "You heard me, back off, or I'll burn you all down!" An empty threat, I knew, but it was the only card I had to play. I stared into the flame of the lighter, willing it to get bigger. It didn't listen.

There was a dry rattle of leaves, and a single vine snaked its way toward me from a low-hanging branch. Somehow I grabbed it, though it twisted like a snake, and held the lighter to it.

It didn't burn, but it smoked, and that was enough. It jerked itself out of my grasp in a manner of seconds.

A heartbeat after that, the trees were moving, creating a space for me. Branches jerked themselves away with a groan. Vines hissed on dry leaves as they drew back into the dark. The road beckoned, shockingly close.

"Oh yeah," I said, backing away quickly lest the forest change its mind. "I've got this, and there's more where it came from. Don't forget it, or I'll be back with aerosol cans and friends." I was hysterical now, laughing and crying and taunting the trees, and sure that there was one last trick they'd play on me before I reached the road.

I was wrong. There was none, no last ditch attempt to snag me around the ankles or by the throat. I just passed through that last curtain of leaves and suddenly, there was freedom right in front of me. Three steps, and I was in the road. I collapsed onto the gravel, bleeding from a dozen different places, and the lighter went out. I let it stay out and slowly picked myself up. Of Ellie, there was no sign.

"Must have kept running, like I told her," I told myself, and started limping back toward the resort. "She must have."

At the time, I even believed it.

* * *

Ellie's door was closed when I got back to the bungalow, and I didn't feel inclined to barge on in. Any thoughts of romance were long gone, replaced by bone weariness and pain. Bloody and dirty, I just collapsed on the couch. There was enough time to kick one shoe off before sleep claimed me, and I welcomed it when it did.

Harris woke me up what felt like five minutes later.

"Where is she, man? *Where is she?*"

I blinked and stared blearily up at him. "What?"

"Ellie!" His voice was frantic with worry. "Where is she?"

"She came home before I did. I told her to run, she ran, and...what?" I sat bolt upright. "She's not back?"

"No, she's not." He stood, arms crossed on his chest. Behind him, Felix was pulling on shoes. "You came in around five. She never did."

"But she left the woods before I did!" I exclaimed. "When the trees came for us, I got her out. I swear, I got her out!"

Felix shot me a look of pure disgust. "Sure you did," he said, and then to Harris, "Let's go."

"Wait." I swung my legs off the couch. "I'm coming with you."

"No, you're not," Harris replied. "You've done enough, thanks."

"Please," I said. "I have to. I need to find out that she's all right."

They looked at each other. "Fine," Harris said, finally. "Fuckup," said Felix at the same time.

We went in silence, neither of them willing to look at me. I limped along as best I could, but a few hours' sleep had made me realize how badly I'd been pummeled the night before. Every muscle was stiff, a hundred cuts burned where the kudzu had slashed me, and my balls ached so badly that I was afraid to contemplate the shape they were in.

Ahead of me, Harris and The Cat stopped. I limped up to where they stood, stared, and blinked back tears.

This was the place. I could see bloodstains, my bloodstains in the road. I could see the old evidence of Harris and The Cat sitting in the gravel and lighting up. I could see footprints new and old, and I could see a roughly me-sized hole in the curtain of kudzu that hid the undergrowth from the road.

But I couldn't find any evidence that Ellie had made it out last night.

"She said she could see the road," I said softly. "She said she was going to make it. I told her to leave me behind."

Felix turned and looked at me. He didn't say anything. He didn't have to.

Deep down, I knew. It wasn't the fire that had gotten me out. It was the fact that they already had Ellie.

"Are we going in?" I asked, afraid of the answer.

"No," said Harris. "The cops might be, though, so we're not going to mess anything up in there. Besides, you and I both know what sort of things happen here. There's not going to be anything to see. We won't find her."

As he spoke, the hole in the greenery started knitting itself back up. Felix saw this, shook his head, turned to go. He and Harris saw the kudzu, and they knew they wouldn't see anything more.

But I did. I saw something else, something the green wanted to show me.

I saw Ellie.

She was back there in the woods, leaves barely covering her soft white skin. She was naked now, naked except for the vines that had wrapped themselves around her waist and twined themselves in her hair. Her eyes were open, and I could tell she could see me just as I saw her. In her left hand was the poster tube, shot through now with leafy strands of kudzu. She held it up to me so I could see she had it, and as she did, the curtain widened again.

Harris and Felix didn't see any of it. They had already turned away.

I saw, though. I saw her lips move, impossibly far off in the forest, as she spoke to me.

I heard her, too, Ellie's voice whispered to me by a thousand leaves.

She said one word.

Together.

I felt myself blinking back tears. She smiled.

"Together soon enough," I told her, and walked away.

Jeremy's Castle

Jeremy played on the beach, building a sand castle by the water's edge. His mother lay on a beach towel thirty feet away, skin glistening with suntan lotion and eyes shaded from the glare.

"We're not staying much longer, Jeremy," she said, and turned her attention back to the novel she'd brought along in her tote. It was something light and romantic, perfect beach reading according to the bookstore clerk. Thus far, however, she felt inclined to disagree.

"Okay, Mom," Jeremy replied, and lugged another bucket of sand to his creation. It was tall now, almost as tall as he was and six feet across at the base. The crenellations were rough, the towers unsteady, but the lines were unmistakeable.

Forty minutes later, the book went back into the tote. Idiot characters and idiot plotting had conspired to do her patience in, and Jeremy's mother felt it was time to be getting home. She could see the sun low against the horizon, turning the clouds above the water a dangerous pink.

"Jeremy?" She looked down at the waterline and blinked in surprise at what she saw. "Oh my God."

Jeremy came around the side of the castle, bucket in his hand. "Do you want to see, Mom?"

"Yes, I do," she replied softly. "Jeremy, did you do all this?"

"I did." He nodded, smiling, and took his mother's hand. "Let me show you, okay?"

He led her around the base, pointing out those details he was most proud of. Seaweed draped the castle's walls, shells marked its windows and gates. Seagull feathers stood in for pennons, flying at the heights, and driftwood made a drawbridge over a moat that had two inches of water running in it, all the way around.

As she stood there, the cool sea washed around her ankles. She looked down and saw the water had kissed the sand guardpost that marked the castle's furthest outlier.

"Oh, honey," she said. "I wish I had a camera. I'd take a picture of this and send it to your father."

"It's all right, Mom," Jeremy replied. "It'll be here tomorrow, and you can take a picture then."

Her eyes searched her son's face. "I'm sorry," she said. "We're coming back tomorrow, but the castle won't be here. The waves will have washed it away."

Jeremy shrugged, and patted her hand. "No they won't, Mom. I asked them not to."

Without a word, she led him up to the towel and slipped a t-shirt over his thin shoulders. Her eyes drifted back to the sand castle, and she imagined the water devouring everything that Jeremy had built.

They left the beach then, Jeremy chattering about what he wanted to have for supper and a thousand other things.

And on the beach, the water came up to the edge of the moat, thought about it for a while, and then flowed around it instead.

The waves had kept their promise to Jeremy. Tomorrow, they'd ask him to keep his.

About the Author

Richard Dansky was named one of the top 20 videogame writers in the world by Gamasutra in 2009. The Central Clancy Writer for Red Storm/Ubisoft, he has credits on nearly 40 games, including Splinter Cell: Conviction, Rainbow Six: Raven Shield and Ghost Recon: Future Soldier. He is the author of the Booksense pick Firefly Rain, and contributes regularly to magazines including Publishers Weekly, Bull Spec, and Sleeping Hedgehog. Richard was also a major contributor to White Wolf's World of Darkness, and at one point was the world's greatest living authority on Denebian Slime Devils. He lives in North Carolina with his wife, their inevitable cats, and the ghost of a zombie frog.

www.ingramcontent.com/pod-product-compliance
Lightning Source LLC
Chambersburg PA
CBHW051821170626
46807CB00003B/969

* 9 7 8 0 9 8 9 1 3 0 9 0 5 *